DEATH IN WINTER

Ian McFadyen

The Book Guild Ltd

First published in Great Britain in 2016 by
The Book Guild Ltd
9 Priory Business Park
Wistow Road, Kibworth
Leicestershire, LE8 0RX
Freephone: 0800 999 2982
www.bookguild.co.uk
Email: info@bookguild.co.uk
Twitter: @bookguild

Typeset in Baskerville

Printed and bound in Great Britain by
CPI Group (UK) Ltd, Croydon, CR0 4YY

ISBN 978 1911320 272

British Library Cataloguing in Publication Data.
A catalogue record for this book is available from the British Library.

To Luke and Connor Sparks

Chapter 1

Friday, 21ˢᵗ December

Kirkwood railway station was jam-packed. Along every platform the heaving masses moved, some with purpose, others less so. Many in high spirits, singing and laughing as they clumsily blundered and jostled their way from their festive celebration just ended. There were lonesome looking individuals, too, single-handedly hurrying to catch a train which would transport them away, in all likelihood, to their friends, family or loved ones for Christmas.

As the station clock indicated the time was 10.25pm, five smartly-dressed women appeared in front of the barriers, laughing and talking loudly in an effort to be heard over the general din of the busy station.

"What a lovely evening," the oldest-looking lady remarked when the group came to a halt at the entrance to platform 4. "Have a Merry Christmas, everyone," she continued with a broad smile, before embracing each of the ladies one by one.

With her extravagant farewells concluded, she suddenly took to her heels and dashed down platform 4 to catch her train.

As they looked on, the four remaining ladies proceeded to giggle loudly and make jokes about the behaviour of their departed friend during the dinner they'd just shared at the Italian restaurant.

"It's a good job we know her well," one remarked, "if we weren't all friends you could quite easily fall out with Belinda, given the dreadful things she says at times."

"But she means well and, deep down, she has a really kind heart," remarked a lady in a black trouser suit with a patterned, green blouse.

"Anyway I need to be away, too," she continued before exchanging more hugs and pleasant Christmas wishes then scuttling off towards platform 8 at the farthest end of the station.

"Hayley never mentions her stepchildren," remarked one of the remaining women as the last three members of the party stood on the platform. "Have they fallen out?"

"I'm not sure, Max," one of the others replied with a faint shrug of her shoulder, "but neither James nor Suzanne appear to have any intention of coming home and, with them living in Vancouver and Brisbane, they couldn't have moved any further away."

Chapter 2

"You're kidding!" Robbie exclaimed. "Why does she have to come here for Christmas? She's a nightmare."

"She's your dad's aunty and she's nowhere else to go," replied Penny calmly, "she can't spend Christmas on her own."

"What about Aunty Rose?" Robbie enquired, the desperation palpable in his voice. "After all, she's her mum."

Penny shook her head. "You know why," she replied firmly. "Aunty Rose and Uncle Neil have decided to spend Christmas with Uncle Neil's brother in Canada and Great Aunty Audrey isn't up to travelling."

"I'm not surprised Aunty Rose is escaping," Robbie mumbled. "But I don't see why we have to endure Great Aunty Audrey for the whole of Christmas."

"Well, I'm sorry!" Penny replied with not a hint of remorse in her voice. "She's family, she's eighty-three and she's coming. So you'll just have to suck it up and get on with it."

Clearly unhappy about the announcement, Robbie sighed deeply before exiting the kitchen leaving Penny and his two sisters alone.

"He's got a point," Jemma remarked as soon as her brother was out of earshot. "Great Aunty Audrey can be very difficult when she wants to be, which, let's face it, is most of the time."

Penny nodded. "I know," she acknowledged. "But we had to invite her otherwise she'd have been all alone over Christmas."

3

Jemma nodded. "We know Mum," she replied. "I just hope she's not going to be a pain all the time."

"You and me both," Penny added, her resigned tone suggesting her daughter's wish stood no chance.

"Well I like her," Natalie piped-up. "I think she's really interesting, she's just a bit old."

Jemma and Penny exchanged a bewildered look.

"In that case," Jemma remarked. "You can be responsible for keeping her occupied."

Natalie, whose eyes had not left the screen of her tablet since the discussion started, seemed totally relaxed about the declaration of Great Aunty Audrey's arrival for Christmas and just shrugged her shoulders. "No problem," she replied calmly. "I'll show her how to play candy crush."

* * * *

When Carmichael arrived home it was almost midnight and his three children had retreated to their bedrooms for the night.

For the first time since they'd arrived in Moulton Bank, Carmichael had managed to wangle it so that he was off-duty for the whole week over Christmas and with that Friday being his last day on duty, he'd taken Cooper, Watson and Rachel Dalton out for a Chinese meal and a few drinks.

"That's me done until the 29th," he announced with glee, planting a kiss on Penny's forehead as soon as he'd joined her in the front room.

"Unless there's a crisis," replied Penny, who knew full well that Steve would almost certainly have told whichever member of the team was on duty to call him if something big came up.

"No," her husband insisted. "Only a terrorist attack, a high profile kidnapping or a murder will drag me away from my gorgeous wife and my three lovely children for the next eight days." As he spoke, Carmichael walked briskly to the drinks cabinet and started to pour himself a large Jack Daniels.

"You're forgetting Aunty Audrey," Penny added with a cruel, knowing smile.

Carmichael rolled his eyes upwards. "Well her too, I suppose," he replied with a hint of dread in his voice. "Did you tell the kids about her coming?"

"I did," Penny confirmed, "I broke it to them this evening."

"And what was their reaction?" Carmichael asked.

Penny considered her answer for a few seconds. "Well the good news is that Natalie seems happy," she replied.

Carmichael plonked himself down next to his wife. "But the other two aren't keen," he remarked before taking a sip from his glass.

"You could say that," said Penny.

"Well I can't blame them really," Carmichael replied. "I can't honestly say that I'm particularly looking forward to her company over Christmas either."

Penny snuggled up close to her husband. "We'll just have to manage," she remarked as positively as she could. "It's only for a few days. Then we can ship her off back to the care home."

Carmichael smiled. "But a few days with Aunty Audrey can seem like a lifetime," he remarked with gloomy resignation.

Chapter 3

Saturday, 22nd December

DC Rachel Dalton was never enthusiastic about being on duty at the weekend and given this was the last weekend before Christmas, she really could have done with finishing off her Christmas shopping. However, on the plus side, she was working with DS Cooper rather than DS Watson, so she was assured of at least being treated with a modicum of respect, something rarely evident when she had the misfortune to be on duty with Watson. Another positive was that Kirkwood police station on a Saturday was always a more relaxed place. With Chief Inspector Hewitt out of the way and to a lesser degree DCI Carmichael, the atmosphere was always less intense, allowing those on duty, if they were lucky, to catch up on their paperwork.

"One bacon roll and one regular black coffee," remarked Cooper as he returned from the canteen with his and Rachel's breakfasts on a small red plastic tray.

Rachel smiled up at him from behind her desk and removed her items off the tray. "I don't get this service when Marc's working with me," she said as a genuine compliment.

Cooper raised his eyebrows. "Me neither," he replied. "Not that Marc's ever here in time for breakfast when the boss is away."

Rachel giggled. "True," she added before taking a sip of coffee.

"So have we anything new this morning?" Cooper enquired before taking a large bite from his gigantic bacon and sausage barm cake.

Rachel shook her head. "Nothing so big as to warrant us calling Inspector Carmichael," she replied, a reference to the last instructions they'd received from their boss before he took his leave for Christmas. "We've a few acts of minor vandalism, which the uniform guys can investigate, a shopper claiming she was assaulted at the local supermarket in Moulton Bank by another woman during an altercation over their last bronze turkey and, apparently, some youngsters have been amusing themselves by throwing snowballs at cars from a bridge over the A59 near the ring road, but apart from that it looks like it's been pretty uneventful."

"All jobs for uniform," concurred Cooper, who had no desire whatsoever to become involved in any of the incidents.

Rachel smiled. "I've already passed them on," she reassured him.

Cooper picked up his mug of coffee and held it tightly in both hands. "It was bloody cold this morning," he remarked. "It took me ages to clear the ice off my car and, if it snows again this evening, as they are predicting, I'm betting that many of the country roads around here will become treacherous."

As he spoke, Rachel noticed details of a new incident appearing on her computer screen. "What's this," she remarked as she read the details. "Something has just come in about a woman reported missing after a night out in Kirkwood."

Cooper frowned. "What are the details?" he enquired.

"It's a lady called Hayley Bell," Rachel replied, her eyes focussed intently on her computer screen. "She was expected home at around 11.30pm but didn't arrive."

"11.30pm?" Cooper asked.

Rachel nodded. "Yes, she was out with some friends having a meal then a few drinks, but never arrived home."

Cooper shrugged his shoulders. "Maybe she had a few drinks too many and stayed with a friend or maybe she just copped off with someone," he suggested rather dismissively. "At this time of the year, I'd say that's the most likely scenario."

"Maybe," replied Rachel. "If she was a young woman, I'd agree, but she's in her late forties."

Cooper smiled. "Don't you think women in their late forties get drunk or have relationships?" he remarked mockingly.

Rachel laughed. "Yes, but this lady, by all accounts, is a happily married, respectable woman. She was also seen by her friends getting on her train at the station last night to go home."

Cooper's expression changed. "Who reported her missing?" he asked.

"Her husband," replied Rachel. "Apparently he called the station at about seven this morning, in a frantic state."

"I'm sure it's nothing, but to be on the safe side we do need to look into it," Cooper remarked. "Where does Mr Bell live?"

"The Laurels, Uplands Gardens, Much Martin," Rachel replied, reading the address off her computer screen.

"Very posh," Cooper replied. "I once knew a girl who lived in Uplands Gardens, and I'd imagine you wouldn't get much change out of a million quid for most of those houses."

Rachel grabbed her handbag and the two officers made their way out of the office to begin the thirty-minute drive to Much Martin.

"So tell me more about this old girlfriend," Rachel remarked as they disappeared down the corridor.

* * * *

It was almost 9am before Penny opened her eyes that morning. She and Steve had remained in the front room until 1am before she finally called time and headed off to bed. She had no recollection of when her husband had joined her, but the fact that he was still dead to the world suggested to Penny that he'd probably had at least one more Jack Daniels before calling it a night.

"Wake up," Penny instructed him, while at the same time shaking him furiously by the shoulders. "Audrey's train arrives at Manchester in less than two hours and you have to be there to get her off, remember."

It took a few more jolts, each one progressively more vigorous than the last, before Steve Carmichael finally stirred.

"I could charge you with assault," he remarked with a smirk on his face.

"Just try it, matey," Penny replied before planting a kiss on his lips. "Now shake yourself, otherwise you'll be late picking up Aunty Audrey."

Carmichael gazed at the bedside clock. "You're right," he replied. "Just two more hours of peace and serenity before the aunty from hell descends."

As Penny made her way towards the bathroom, she turned and smiled back in her husband's direction. "I only wish you were exaggerating," she remarked, "but we both know it's true."

* * * *

Cooper's clapped-out Volvo pulled up just outside The Laurels, Much Martin. As he'd correctly declared back at the office, the houses in Uplands Gardens were opulent and expensive-looking, not that it made much impact on Rachel, given she'd been brought up in a residence even more lavish than the ones in front of them.

"This all looks very Christmassy," Rachel remarked as the two officers clambered out of the car and onto the snow-covered pavements.

"Good job they've cleared their path," replied Cooper as they started to make their way up to the front door.

DC Dalton and DS Cooper were only three or four paces onto the long, block-paved driveway when the front door of the Laurels opened wide and a tall, elderly, well-dressed but gaunt-looking gentleman appeared.

"By the troubled look on his face, I'd guess that's Mr Bell," Cooper remarked in a quiet voice to avoid being overheard.

Rachel took a few seconds to take a good look at the person standing at the door before replying. "Poor old man," she whispered. "He looks sick with worry."

"I take it you're the police?" the man enquired, his diction crystal clear although his voice was understandably a little shaky. "Have you any news about Hayley?"

Cooper arrived at the front door first. "I'm DS Cooper and this is my colleague DC Dalton," he replied, while at the same time presenting his identity card to confirm who he was. "Are you Mr Bell?"

It took a few seconds for the old man to reply, he appeared to be preoccupied with Rachel, his small dark eyes examining her with forensic precision.

"Are you Mr Bell?" Cooper asked for a second time.

"Yes, I'm Duncan Bell," the old man replied.

"May we come inside, please?" added Cooper.

"Of course," he replied. "Do come through." As he spoke, Duncan Bell took a few steps back to allow the two police officers to enter into his lavish, white marble hallway dominated by a massive Christmas tree, its branches decked with expensive-looking blue and silver baubles.

"That's an impressive tree," Rachel remarked with a faint smile on her face.

At first, Rachel wasn't sure whether Bell had heard what she'd said. His total lack of response suggested the old man was either hard of hearing or had just chosen to ignore the compliment. However, after a few seconds Bell did reply. "I like stunning belongings," he remarked, in a way that made both officers feel a little uneasy.

Closing the front door behind them, Bell then pointed to a large oak door across the gleaming white-tiled floor. "Please go through into the autumn room and make yourselves comfortable," he said.

"Autumn room?" remarked Cooper, his expression one of puzzlement.

"Yes," replied Bell casually. "I've themed the four main rooms on the ground floor on the four seasons. They're used all year round of course, I inhabit them according to my mood."

"And what is an autumn mood?" enquired Cooper who was starting to have serious doubts about the state of mind of their host.

"One of melancholy," replied Bell without any hesitation. "Summer ended and the winter cold ever nearing."

Rachel Dalton and Cooper exchanged a quick glance of mutual bewilderment. "I'm afraid we've no news regarding your wife," Rachel added, keen to bring the conversation back on track and make sure the old man received an answer to his original question.

"We're here to ask you some questions, if we may," Cooper added. "Of course if it will help you locate my wife," replied Bell. "If you'd care to go through, Belinda and Lesley are already there."

"Belinda and Lesley?" repeated Rachel, in the form of a question rather than a statement.

"Yes," replied Bell, who sounded bemused as to why Rachel needed to ask. "Belinda Bishop and Lesley Saxham," he confirmed, his diction accentuating each syllable of the ladies' names. "They were with Hayley last night in Kirkwood."

"That's helpful," said Cooper. "We were planning to talk to Mrs Bell's friends, so them being here will certainly save us some time."

* * * *

The Milton Keynes train pulled into platform 6 at Manchester Piccadilly at 10.40am, about 10 minutes late, which was fortunate as the slippery roads had made the journey a little longer than Carmichael had anticipated and he'd arrived with only a few minutes to spare before Audrey's train arrived.

The text message Carmichael had received from his cousin, Rose, advising him that her mum had been successfully deposited in the second car from the front, enabled him to easily locate his unwanted charge for the festive period.

"Hello Audrey!" Carmichael remarked in a jovial tone as he strolled down the carriage aisle.

Carmichael's Aunty Audrey had left Scotland over fifty years before, but her border accent was as strong as it had ever been. "Oh, hello dear," she replied loudly, "I'm so glad to see you. It's been a really awful journey. The train was so crowded and do you know I had to tell that young man to turn his music down. Thump, thump, thump, some people are so inconsiderate."

As she spoke, she nodded in the direction of a young man who was putting on his jacket, but fortunately oblivious to her comments because of the red earplugs in his ears.

Carmichael managed to retain his smile. "Well I'm here now," he replied. "Let me help you up."

"I can do that," Aunty Audrey replied sharply, "I'm a little slow, but I can manage. You just get my bag." As she spoke, Aunty Audrey's eyes raised slightly up at the large red suitcase which had been jammed in the overhead luggage rack. "Be careful, though, as it's heavy."

Aunty Audrey wasn't wrong, the case must have weighed getting on for 15 kgs, and it took Carmichael all his strength to lower it down to the floor.

"We'd better hurry up," Audrey added as she slowly ambled down the aisle towards the door. "The train will be pulling away if we're not careful."

"There's no need to worry," Carmichael assured her. "The train won't be pulling out for a good while yet."

"You'll have to help me down," Aunty Audrey remarked as she arrived at the exit and realised there was a short step down from the train carriage.

Carmichael temporarily abandoned the suitcase to help his aunty descend onto the platform and was pleased when another passenger, the same young, athletic-looking man who Audrey had apparently confronted about his music, lent a hand by carrying the case down from the train and placing it next to them on the platform.

"Thank you," Carmichael said to the man, who smiled back before briskly making his way towards the ticket barrier.

"Do you know where the lavatories are?" Aunty Audrey enquired, "I'm not going to last until we get to your house."

Carmichael exhaled slowly and deeply, "I don't know," he admitted. "But we'll find them."

* * * *

The autumn room was decorated and furnished in keeping with its name, with three hefty, carroty-red sofas dominating the stained oak and burnished amber setting.

To the right of the door, a large granite fireplace jutted out with a bright-orange log fire at its base, spitting and crackling as it devoured its kindling meal. Equally imposing was a floor-to-ceiling window which took up almost the entire wall opposite the entrance to the room.

It was Lesley Saxham the officers noticed first when they entered the room. She was sitting quietly, on her own, on one of the three sofas which had been arranged to form a horseshoe pattern in the large spectacular room. It took a few seconds for the two officers to spot Belinda Bishop, who had been impatiently prowling up and down by the window for the last twenty minutes.

Belinda and Lesley were both ladies in their early sixties. However, their appearances and, as Cooper and Dalton were soon to discover, their personalities were far from similar.

Belinda was a tall, slender lady with jet black hair cut in a fashion that suggested functionality rather than style. This contrasted starkly with the way she dressed, as her clothes were clearly acquired from some of the more high-class shops and boutiques in the area. Belinda was articulate, forthright and supremely confident in her manner and had the habit of speaking her mind a little more than was always good for her, not that she realised, or cared.

Lesley, on the other hand, had a more relaxed demeanour. Wearing thick black glasses and with a mass of frizzy grey hair sprouting from her head, held less than successfully by a red hair band, she was evidently much less preoccupied with her appearance than her friend. As the two officers would soon learn, Lesley was more than happy to allow others to take centre stage, but when called upon to express her opinion or comment upon an issue, she would invariably demonstrate not only her undoubted intelligence, but also a knack for communicating her views in a lucid, persuasive yet diplomatic manner.

Despite their obvious differences, Belinda and Lesley were very close friends and, with Hayley Bell and Francis Scott, were the mainstay of the small reading group that they'd set up twenty years earlier.

"You took your time," Belinda announced rudely as soon

as she spied Cooper and Dalton. "It's now twelve hours since anyone saw Hayley, this is really not good enough."

Whether Lesley Saxham or Duncan Bell, who had followed Cooper and Dalton into the room, shared Belinda Bishop's sentiments was unclear, as neither spoke, however the look on their faces suggested that, not for the first time, Belinda's abruptness was embarrassing them.

"My name's DS Cooper and this is DC Dalton," said Cooper, ignoring completely Belinda's opening remarks. "We'd like to ask all of you some questions, if we may?"

Belinda stopped pacing and, with her arms folded, glared back at Cooper. Paying no heed to Belinda, Lesley smiled back at Cooper and gestured to Duncan Bell to join her on the sofa. "We will help you all we can, sergeant," she announced. "What would you like to know?"

****

It was 12.30pm by the time Carmichael's BMW pulled up on his drive.

"Here we go, Audrey," he remarked.

"You may have to help me up those steps, they look as though they may be slippy," Audrey replied as she noticed the four small steps leading up to Carmichael's front door.

Carmichael forced a smile and quickly clambered out of the car.

As he did so the front door opened and Penny and Natalie came out to greet their new arrivals. "Hi darling," she said quietly. "How's it been?"

Carmichael rolled his eyes skywards. "God knows how we're going to last five days with her," he replied. "It's been less than two hours and I could have happily strangled her at least a dozen times already. She's just so…" Before he had a chance to finish his sentence, out of the corner of his eye,

Carmichael spotted Audrey attempting rather unsuccessfully to climb out of the car.

Penny noticed too. "Let me help you," she shouted over.

Carmichael was happy to let his wife extract Aunty Audrey from his BMW and busied himself by walking to the back of the car and removing Audrey's huge, red case from the boot.

After a couple of minutes, Penny managed to manoeuvre Great Aunty Audrey into the house and through to the lounge.

"I can't sit on that sofa," Audrey announced abruptly. "It's far too low."

Penny glanced over at her husband before replying. "Well, maybe we could raise it up a few inches."

"It'll need to be at least six inches higher," Audrey continued. "Did Rose not tell you I can't sit down on low seats anymore?"

"She probably did," remarked Penny as tactfully as she could. "We obviously forgot."

Carmichael took a deep breath. "I'll see whether we've any wood in the garage," he remarked before leaving his poor wife and youngest daughter alone with Aunty Audrey.

* * * *

"What do you think?" Cooper asked Rachel as soon as they were back in his Volvo.

Rachel Dalton shuffled in her seat and looked back at him. "That house is something else," she replied. "I thought Lesley Saxham was very nice, but Duncan Bell and Belinda Bishop both seemed a bit strange."

Cooper laughed. "That's putting it mildly," he replied. "I'd say Duncan Bell is verging on the insane, but I guess we need to make allowances for him given his wife is missing. However, I didn't warm to that Belinda Bishop, she's a throwback from British rule in India."

Rachel grinned and nodded to signify she was broadly of the same opinion. "You're dead right," she remarked.

"What was clear to me was that they all seemed genuinely concerned," Cooper continued.

"And," interrupted Rachel, "from what they were saying there doesn't seem to be any reason why Mrs Bell would have gone off of her own accord."

"Other than to break free from her nutter of a husband," Cooper replied with a smile. "But, seriously, I agree with you and I'm now starting to hear alarm bells ringing."

Rachel nodded. "So what do we do from here?" she asked.

"We call Carmichael," replied Cooper. "I know he's off-duty but he needs to know."

Chapter 4

Carmichael was in his garage, sawing six-inch blocks of wood from an off-cut of four-by-four he'd found, when his mobile rang.

"Sorry to disturb you, sir," Cooper remarked. "But we've got a misper and I thought you needed to be informed."

As soon as Carmichael heard the colloquial term for a missing person, he stopped what he was doing and turned his full attention to the call. "Give me the details, Paul."

Cooper glanced over at Rachel Dalton before starting to outline what had happened. "It's a lady called Hayley Bell," he stated. "She's forty-eight years old and was last seen yesterday evening when she went to board the 10.37pm train from Kirkwood to Much Martin. However, she never arrived home and her husband reported her missing at seven this morning."

"Have you interviewed the husband?" Carmichael enquired.

"We've just done that, sir," Cooper replied. "He's called Duncan and he genuinely seems very worried. He maintains there's absolutely no reason for Hayley to abscond. He also says there's been no arguments and is clearly fearing the worst."

"What sort of person is he?" Carmichael asked.

Cooper considered the question for a few seconds. "Pretty eccentric really," he replied. "He's a fair bit older than his wife. I'd say he's in his early seventies and certainly a bit odd."

"What do you mean odd?" Carmichael asked.

Cooper thought for a while before answering. "It's hard to put your finger on it," he replied a little awkwardly. "But you should see his house. The hallway is all done in white marble and he apparently has four rooms each of which is themed on the four seasons."

"The pop group!" remarked Carmichael, who genuinely started to picture in his head a house themed on Frankie Valli's 1960s backing band.

"No," Cooper replied. "Spring, summer, autumn and winter. We only went into the autumn room, but it was pretty bizarre."

Carmichael wasn't keen to continue that particular line of conversation any further. "Who was Mrs Bell with last night?" he asked.

"She spent the evening at an Italian restaurant on Broad Street," Cooper replied. "She was having a Christmas meal with five other ladies who are all part of a reading group with Mrs Bell. Apparently one of them left early, but Hayley and the other four women all walked to the train station together and boarded their various trains home."

"Have you interviewed the other women yet?" Carmichael asked.

"We've talked with two of them." Cooper replied, "One of the ladies, a woman called Lesley Saxham, maintains they all last saw Mrs Bell at about ten thirty when she walked down platform three to board her train."

"What about CCTV footage from the station and from Much Martin station?" Carmichael enquired.

"We've not checked that yet," Cooper replied. "Rachel and I were just about to get on to it."

Carmichael thought for a few seconds. "You need to get help on this one, Paul," he said, his instructions firm and clear. "It's critical that we get statements from the other three women who were with her last night and we need to take a good look at any CCTV footage at Kirkwood train station and any other station where she may have got off. It's vital we get this all done in a matter of hours, so you will need some support."

"Understood," Cooper replied. "We'll speak to the duty sergeant and ask him to provide us with a few PCs to help."

Carmichael looked at his watch. It was just after 1pm. "If she was last seen at 10.30pm, it's still less than fifteen hours since she went missing, so there's a chance she'll turn up. However, we can't drag our feet on this one. Let's get together at the station at five this evening and review where we are then. If there's been no real progress we may need to call upon the media for their support."

"Should we organise a full search of Hayley Bell's house?" Cooper asked, knowing full well that this was normal practice in missing person cases.

Carmichael again paused for a few seconds. "We should really," he remarked. "Get Rachel to sort that out while you co-ordinate the other statements and get hold of any CCTV footage. Tell Rachel to draft in help from the station."

"Will do, sir," Cooper replied. "Is there anything else?"

"No," said Carmichael. "Let me know if you don't get the support you need, otherwise I'll see you at five."

As soon as the phone went dead Cooper turned to face Rachel Dalton, "It's a good job we called him," he remarked. "He wants us to get the other women interviewed, view any footage from the CCTV cameras at the train station…"

"And, if I'm not mistaken," Rachel added, "he wants me to sort out a search of Mrs Bell's house."

Cooper nodded. "Sorry, Rachel," he added with genuine sympathy. "You've drawn the short straw on that one."

"It's okay," replied Rachel. "I should take it as a compliment, I suppose. But I suspect Mr Bell may get the wrong impression and I'm even more certain Belinda Bishop will have something to say about it, too, if she's still there."

Cooper smiled. "You'll definitely need to get some support before you go back in. Do you want to call the station now before I abandon you?"

Rachel grinned and opened the car door. "No, you get off," she replied as she eased herself out of the passenger seat. "I'll call the station then wait around the corner until the cavalry arrive."

* * * *

As soon as the call was over, Carmichael put his mobile down on his workbench and picked up his tenon saw.

"At least I'll get a few hours' respite from Aunty Audrey," he muttered to himself as he started to lop off the next six-inch block from the lump of wood and work out how he was going to break the news to Penny.

Chapter 5

There was no doubt that Carmichael felt some remorse as he drove through the frozen country lanes on his way to Kirkwood police station. After all, Aunty Audrey was his blood-relative, not Penny's. However, his overriding emotion was one of relief to have been handed a legitimate reason to escape the constant moaning and harping of such an awkward, rude and frustrating old woman. The fact that it would be left to Penny and his three children to shoulder the brunt of her outbursts and perpetual complaining did resonate with his conscience, but he reconciled his guilt by reminding himself that whether Audrey had been there or not, he would have had to leave the house for the next three or four hours to ensure the investigation into the missing woman was being conducted thoroughly.

"I'll be back by 8pm," he'd assured Penny when he'd abandoned her on their doorstep. Although Penny hadn't said anything, her eyes betrayed her feelings and left Carmichael in no doubt that his wife fully expected him to break his promise.

Despite the snow and ice, the roads were relatively clear of traffic and, as a result, Carmichael's journey was swift and he found himself ensconced in the incident room at Kirkwood Police Station well before the allotted time of 5pm.

To his surprise, he was joined fairly soon by DS Watson who, like Carmichael, was supposed to be off-duty.

"Hello, Marc," Carmichael announced as he noticed the casually-dressed DS saunter into the room. "I wasn't expecting to see you this afternoon."

Watson forced a smile and shrugged his shoulders. "Cooper called me earlier to tell me what had happened so I figured I should be here, too, given that I'm officially back on-duty on Monday."

"That's much appreciated, Marc," Carmichael replied. "Dependent upon what Cooper and Dalton tell us, I fear we may all find our leave disrupted over Christmas."

"To be honest," Watson added. "I won't be too unhappy to get out of the house a bit over the festive period. Susan's still out buying her brother's kids' presents. They're all due to stay with us for Christmas Day and Boxing Day and his two boys are little sods. So as long as I get time to eat my Christmas dinner, I'll not be too upset if there's a bit of overtime up for grabs on either of those two days."

Carmichael grinned broadly. In a perverse way, knowing Watson was also going to have a troublesome Christmas lessened his frustration about spending Christmas with Aunty Audrey, not that Carmichael was prepared to share his plight with one of his team.

"I'll bear that in mind, should we need you," Carmichael replied just as Cooper and Rachel Dalton entered the incident room.

Carmichael gazed up at the clock on the wall. It read 4.55pm. As he did so, out of the corner of his eye, he saw Rachel Dalton widen her eyes and stare in Watson's direction, as if to demonstrate her surprise at seeing him, too.

"Thanks everyone," Carmichael announced in a loud voice. "I appreciate you all being here, and on time. Given that neither Marc nor I have been involved as yet, can you two please provide an update on the incident and a summary of where you are so far?" As he spoke, Carmichael looked at Cooper and Dalton.

23

"Of course," replied Cooper who took this as his cue, being the senior of the two, to take the lead.

"The missing woman is Mrs Hayley Bell, a respectable lady, aged forty-eight, who spent yesterday evening at Antonio's, the Italian restaurant on Broad Street. There were five other ladies with her who are all members of a local reading group. Hayley was last seen at 10.32pm walking down platform three at Kirkwood train station, before getting onto the 10.37pm train to Much Martin."

As he spoke, he began to play the CCTV footage from Kirkwood station, which quite clearly showed a middle-aged woman in dark-coloured trousers and a smart black jacket, walk briskly down the platform and clamber into the second of four carriages which made up the 10.37pm train.

"I assume you've watched the footage until the train departs?" Carmichael enquired. "And that she doesn't get off before it leaves the platform?"

Cooper shook his head. "There is no way she got off again."

"So what about Much Martin station?" Carmichael asked. "Do they have CCTV there?"

Cooper nodded. "Yes," he replied. "She definitely didn't get off at Much Martin. I've looked at the footage and, of the ten people that did get off, she certainly wasn't one of them. Apart from two teenage girls, the rest all looked like men. And all ten are clearly visible getting on the train at Kirkwood."

"Are those the girls there?" Watson enquired, as the footage from Kirkwood train station showed two teenagers dashing to catch the train.

"Yes," Cooper replied. "That's them."

The four officers watched as the two girls just managed to clamber onto the train before the doors closed and the train started to pull out of the station.

"It looks like they got into the same carriage as Hayley Bell," Rachel observed, this being the first time she'd seen the footage, too.

"Yes, they did," Cooper confirmed. "As did three men, one of whom got on before Hayley, and the others afterwards."

"So what about the other stations along the line?" Carmichael asked.

Cooper shook his head. "Apart from the last stop in Southport, none of the other stations on the line have CCTV cameras," he remarked. "There are three other stops, two before Much Martin and one after, but all three are very small stations and, I suspect, hardly used."

"I take it the footage from Southport doesn't show Hayley getting off the train," Carmichael remarked.

"It doesn't," Cooper confirmed.

"Which means she must have got off at one of the three smaller stations," Carmichael added, just to make sure everyone was in agreement.

"Yes," Cooper confirmed. "That's certainly what I think."

Carmichael thought for a moment. "So what are the three other stations on the line?" he asked.

"Alcar and Barton Bridge are the two before Much Martin and Linbold is the one in-between Much Martin and Southport," Cooper replied.

"Has anyone spoken to the driver yet?" Carmichael asked.

Cooper nodded his head again. "PC Dyer has taken a statement from him." he replied. "He told Dyer the service was on time with nothing unusual," Cooper remarked. "According to Dyer, the driver can't remember anyone either getting on or off the train at Alcar or Linbold, but he did seem to think people got on and off at Barton Bridge, however he wasn't able to confirm how many."

Carmichael shrugged his shoulders. "And I assume there's no CCTV on the train," he added.

Cooper shook his head. "None, I'm afraid," he replied.

Carmichael took a few moments to think about what he'd just heard. "Good job," he said. "I know we've not been able to identify where she got off, but it sounds like we are looking at Barton Bridge, so it's a start. And we have at least identified five people who were in the same carriage as her."

Cooper looked relieved that his boss was content with the progress he'd made. "I'll see if any of the other cameras at the train station show us a clearer picture of the teenage girls so we can trace them," he remarked.

Carmichael nodded. "Also check the ticket offices at Much Martin and Kirkwood. I'm guessing they'd have bought their tickets at one of the two stations, so that may help us track them down."

"Assuming they bought tickets," Watson sarcastically suggested.

Rachel Dalton shook her head in disbelief. "Not all young people are dishonest, Marc," she remarked caustically. "In my opinion it's more likely they bought their tickets online rather than they evaded paying."

"Either way, we need to trace them," Carmichael remarked, in an effort to bring the discussion back on track.

"So, what else do we know?" Carmichael asked, looking directly at Rachel Dalton.

"We've now interviewed four of the five women who Hayley had dinner with last night," Rachel announced. "We've yet to speak to one, a lady called Francis Scott, as she left to drive down to Devon early this morning. I've left a voice message on her mobile, but she's not got back to me."

"What about the four you've spoken to, what are they saying?" Carmichael asked.

"We interviewed two of them this morning," Rachel replied. "Belinda Bishop and Lesley Saxham. From what they told me, Belinda had boarded her train before Hayley, but Lesley was one of the three ladies still on the platform when Hayley got on the train at Kirkwood station. According to Lesley Saxham, her train left about ten minutes after Hayley's."

"So, out of the group, this Lesley Saxham was one of the last ones to see Hayley last night?"

Rachel nodded. "That's correct sir," she confirmed. "The other women are called Maxine Lowe and Hannah Ringrose."

"What did they have to say?" Carmichael added.

"I've not had a chance to speak to them face to face, yet," Rachel replied, "but I've spoken to them both on the phone and they're with a couple of uniformed officers giving their statements. To be honest, they were both shocked at Hayley's disappearance and neither of them was able to add anything to what we already know. "

"So none of the four ladies have any idea what might have happened to Hayley?" Carmichael added.

Rachel shook her head. "Assuming they're not hiding something, none of them," she remarked, rather hesitantly. "Their response when I asked them was almost like they were reading from the same song sheet. They all maintain that Hayley seemed to be having a nice time at the meal and not one of them could come up with any reason for her to leave suddenly."

"What about the husband?" Carmichael enquired.

Rachel looked across at Cooper before answering. "As Paul said earlier, Duncan Bell's a bit odd. Even though he's getting on a bit, there was something about him that…"

"That what?" Carmichael asked as Rachel struggled to find the right words.

"I'm not sure exactly," Rachel replied. "I felt quite sorry for him as he seemed genuinely worried, but I have to say he gave me the creeps."

Carmichael frowned. "So do you think he's involved in his wife's disappearance in some way?" he enquired.

Rachel took a few seconds to think about her answer, and then gave a faint shrug of her shoulders. "He maintains he's no idea where she is and couldn't provide any reason as to why she'd have gone off by herself. And, to be honest, I did believe him. But, all the same, I felt uncomfortable in his presence. He was just a bit… well a bit creepy."

"He was strange," Cooper concurred, "but he was also very co-operative. It could all be an act, but, in my view, if anything sinister has happened to Hayley, I'd be surprised if he was involved. For one thing he looks a pretty feeble man."

"You don't have to be ultra-fit to commit murder," remarked Carmichael. "And anyway, how come it took him until this morning to report her missing? Why not last night when the last train had been and gone, and she wasn't on it?"

"We asked him that," Rachel replied. "Mr Bell's a bad snorer, apparently, so they sleep in different rooms. He maintains that he went to bed early and fell asleep. He's saying that he only realised she hadn't returned home at about 6.30am when he woke up and went to check her room."

"That's right," continued Cooper. "When he saw her bed hadn't been slept in, he tried Hayley on her mobile. When he got no response, he then called Lesley Saxham and Belinda Bishop to find out if they had any idea where Hayley was."

Carmichael looked directly at the sergeant. "Obviously, at this stage, we shouldn't make any rash assumptions," he remarked, his face looking stern and uneasy. "But, between the four of us, it's all starting to sound worrying. I really don't like the feel of this one."

"I agree," Watson remarked, his words appearing to be in keeping with what the other two officers were thinking, too.

"How's the search going at Hayley Bell's house?" Carmichael asked.

"The team are still there," Rachel added.

"What are the other rooms like?" Cooper enquired. "Are they as weird as the autumn room?"

Rachel nodded. "Oh yes," she replied with a knowing look. "Winter, apparently, has an Icelandic theme, is full of dark-blue colours and dominated by a large granite hearth."

"What's all this?" Watson enquired with a bemused frown.

Rachel shrugged her shoulders again. As we've said, Duncan Bell is a little on the unusual side," she remarked. "He's made four of his downstairs rooms seasonally themed."

Watson said nothing, but his expression confirmed that he also believed that sort of behaviour was bizarre.

"But, to answer your question, sir, we've found nothing incriminating at all and nothing to suggest why Hayley would run off." Rachel continued. "Her room, which seemed very normal, was exactly as you'd expect if someone had just gone out for an evening. The clothes she got changed out of were still on her bed, her passport was still in her drawer and it looked like most of her credit cards had been taken out of her bag and left on her dressing table."

"Is that what women do?" Cooper asked.

Rachel nodded. "If I'm going out in the evening and taking a small handbag or a clutch bag, like Hayley did, I'd only take a few essential items with me. I'd only ever take one credit card."

"Good point," Carmichael added, who had seen Penny do the same thing numerous times. "In the CCTV footage at the train station Hayley only had a small bag with her, suggesting that if she did plan to take off she would almost certainly need an accomplice."

"Maybe she met a secret boyfriend at Barton Bank station," Watson suggested. "If her husband is so much older than Hayley, and a weirdo, maybe she's been playing around and, if the boyfriend did meet her at Barton Bank station, he could have quite easily had more stuff of hers in his car."

"It's possible, I suppose," Carmichael remarked. "But we don't seem to have anything to support your theory."

"Not yet," Watson added. "But it's got to be more than just a possibility."

"Is that everything, Rachel?" Carmichael asked, not wanting to encourage further unsubstantiated speculation.

The young DC nodded. "Yes," she replied.

"Well, as I said before," continued Carmichael, "we need to keep an open mind here, but I think we're all agreed there's sufficient reason for us to suspect that some harm may have come to Hayley. I think we need to step up the search and get the press involved. I'll talk with Chief Inspector Hewitt and see how he wants us to play it, but, knowing him, I would suspect he'll want to be actively involved."

As he finished his sentence, Carmichael could see his three officers smirking at the thought of Hewitt once again jumping at the chance to appear on TV.

"We won't be able to get anything set up with the press until the morning," Carmichael added. "But, in the interim, we can't waste any time. I need you, Rachel, to find and talk to Francis Scott. Contact the local police in Devon if need be. Also get back over to Hayley Bell's house and find out if the team have discovered anything that will help us understand why she's gone missing."

"Right you are, sir," Rachel replied.

"I'd like you to get a trace put on Hayley Bell's mobile and start tracking down those two young women who were in Hayley's carriage last night," Carmichael instructed Cooper, who nodded his understanding of his tasks.

"What about me?" Watson asked. "I know I'm supposed to be off-duty, but I'm happy helping out."

Carmichael smiled. "Thanks, Marc," he replied. "Why don't you take a second look at the CCTV tapes from Kirkwood, Much Martin and Southport train stations. Make a detailed note of everyone who got on or got off the train at any of the stops and try and work out which carriage they were in. I'd also like a diagram of the train network and the train timetable for last night posted up here so we can see what we're talking about. Can you get someone to do that tonight please, Marc? "

Watson nodded. "Will do, sir," he replied.

"Actually we've got a few photos of all the women at the dinner last night," Rachel added. "Lesley Saxham had taken some shots on her mobile and has forwarded them to me. Do you want me to print them off and put them up, too?"

"That would be great," Carmichael replied. "If there's a good one of Hayley, we can use that to give the press. If not, you need to ask her husband for a good, recent photo."

"Will do," Rachel dutifully replied.

Carmichael puffed out his cheeks and stood up. "I'm not sure what else we can do tonight," he remarked looking at his watch. "Let's all get back together at seven thirty tomorrow morning. We can have a briefing session then to make sure Chief Inspector Hewitt and I are fully up-to-date before we talk to the press."

Carmichael's three officers quickly departed, leaving him alone to make his call to Chief Inspector Hewitt.

Chapter 6

Penny was certainly surprised when, at 7.25pm, the front door opened and her husband walked into the hallway.

She'd been married to Steve long enough to know almost immediately from the look on his face how the case was going. And his expression that evening made it abundantly clear that he was worried.

"What's happening?" Penny asked as he was taking off his jacket at the door.

"We've no leads at all," he replied before planting a kiss on Penny's cheek. "But my gut feel is that there's something disturbing about this missing person. I'm not sure why, but I just have that feeling."

"So what's the plan?" Penny asked, knowing he'd already have a pretty well-developed strategy.

"We're having a briefing session in the morning," Carmichael replied. "If we've not managed to locate the missing woman by then, we're going to get the press involved with Hewitt at the helm."

Penny put her arms around him. "He'll love that," she remarked with a discerning grin.

"Oh yes," Carmichael replied. "He'll be polishing his buttons and shining his shoes all night for another ten minutes of fame. But, to be fair, he's very good at the press side of things so I'm happy to play the supporting role on this one."

Penny tactfully decided not to mention her husband's awkward appearance on local TV from a previous case, knowing those scars had yet to fully heal.

"So how has your afternoon been?" Carmichael asked his wife. "Has our guest behaved herself?"

Penny's eyes widened. "Well apart from telling me I looked tired, asking Jemma if she'd put on weight, informing Robbie that a university degree wasn't worth anything anymore and proclaiming that dogs should not be allowed in the house because of the germs they carry, she's been delightful company."

Carmichael pulled his wife close to him. "But what about the blocks I put under the furniture in the lounge?"

"No complaints about them," Penny confirmed. "However, she's informed me that she'll need them under her bed, too, so I hope there's more wood in that garage of yours."

Carmichael rolled his eyes and sighed deeply.

"On the bright side though," Penny added, "you'll have company in there while doing your carpentry as that's where we've put the dog, at least until Aunty Audrey goes to bed."

"Poor Mr Swaffy," remarked Carmichael. "I bet he hates that."

"He does," replied Penny. "But he may well be the lucky one. I might decamp there myself if she carries on like this much longer."

* * * *

"So you've got a missing person, Steven," Aunty Audrey remarked as the family sat watching TV. "I remember your grandfather having a similar case back in Lockerbie when we were youngsters."

"Really," Carmichael replied, as insipidly as he could, his way of trying to head off one of Audrey's monologues. It didn't work.

33

"It was a woman called Margie McKevitt," Audrey continued. "She was a respectable woman, a god fearing sort and the wife of the local Bailie…"

"What's a Bailie, Dad?" Natalie enquired, seemingly the only one of the five Carmichaels in the room who appeared in any way interested in what Audrey was saying.

"It's a sort of magistrate," replied her father, his eyes still fixed on the TV.

"Anyway," continued Audrey, in a slightly louder voice. "She went missing and everyone searched for her. It went on for three or four days. We searched everywhere and, in the end, do you know what we found?"

Four Carmichaels remained silent and kept their focus clearly on the TV screen. Only Natalie replied. "What did they find, Great Aunty Audrey?" she said, very much to the frustration of her elder siblings. "Well," continued Audrey, oblivious to the lack of interest that pervaded with 80% of her potential audience. "It was her husband all along. She hadn't run off or been taken hostage like he'd maintained, no, he'd discovered that she'd been carrying on with the local farmer, a man called Wattie Wilson, and he'd caught them and strangled her."

"Really," remarked Natalie excitedly. "So what happened?"

"It was a really gruesome case," Audrey continued. "They discovered her remains in his cellar. He'd not just killed her, but…"

Realising that Audrey's story was about to go into far too much detail, Penny decided to interrupt.

"Natalie," she said loudly, getting up from her chair as she spoke. "Come and help me make some drinks. Would you like a hot drink Audrey?"

"Oh no, dear," replied Audrey. "I try not to have a drink after 8pm or I'll be up and down to the lavvy all night."

"I don't want anything," Robbie remarked with exasperation, before getting to his feet. "I'm going to play a few games in my room."

"I'll join you," added Jemma eagerly, something she'd never done before, but it was all she could think of to escape.

"Good idea," Penny remarked, nodding to her two eldest children as if to say 'flee while you get a chance.'

"Do you want a drink, Steve?" Penny asked in a way that suggested the answer could only be yes.

"Yes," her husband replied obediently. "I'll have a hot chocolate."

"Come on, Natalie," Penny ordered. "Let's sort out the drinks."

Natalie looked over at her Mum with consternation etched across her furrowed brow. "But you're only making two drinks at the most as Great Aunty Audrey doesn't want one and I don't either."

"Don't argue," Penny replied resolutely, "I need your help."

Although completely baffled by her mother's behaviour, Natalie gave up trying to justify remaining in the room and followed Penny into the hall.

"Anyway, as I was saying," continued Audrey as soon as she and Carmichael were alone. "Her wicked husband chopped up poor Margie McKevitt with an axe and a saw and tried to dispose of the pieces…"

"Audrey!" Carmichael interrupted in a calm but firm tone. "It's probably best if you don't share the details of grandad's cases with the children. Penny and I make it a rule to discuss cases only when they're out of the way."

"Really!" replied Audrey, the pitch of her voice indicating some surprise at Carmichael's disclosure. "In my view, they're old enough to understand the world's not all good," she added. "But it's your house and your rules."

"Thank you, Audrey," Carmichael replied, with a forced smile, in an attempt to avoid any unwanted animosity between them.

For the next five minutes nephew and aunty watched the TV in silence which, although Carmichael welcomed, did suggest to him that Aunty Audrey was smarting a little.

"Here you go," Penny remarked as she placed a mug of chocolate by Carmichael's chair.

"Some biscuits, too," Natalie added before plonking a small plate of digestives on the arm of her dad's chair.

"Well, I'll shoot off to bed," Audrey declared. "It's been a long day and I dare say I'll not sleep that well tonight. I never do when I'm not in my own bed."

"Do you want someone to help you up the stairs?" Penny asked with a friendly smile.

"No," replied Audrey. "It may take me a wee while but I'm quite capable of getting up there by myself."

"But you never finished your story about Margie McKevitt," Natalie announced, the disappointment clear in her voice.

"We'll maybe leave that for another day, child," Audrey replied before precariously hauling herself off the sofa. "Goodnight, everyone," the old woman added as she shuffled towards the door.

"Actually, I might go to bed, too," said Natalie, who kissed her Mum before following the octogenarian into the hallway, closing the door behind her.

"I fear the next five days may prove to be the longest of our lives," Carmichael proclaimed as his wife sat herself down on his lap. "I swear she's getting worse."

Penny laughed. "I wish I could say you're exaggerating, but I think you're right. The main thing is that we don't let her ruin Christmas."

Carmichael nodded. "That has to be our target," he concurred. "But it's going to be a pretty damn difficult one to achieve given she's here until the day after Boxing Day. In fact, my money's on me strangling her and chopping her into bits like poor old Margie McKevitt."

36

As he mentioned the name of the unfortunate victim of Audrey's tale, Carmichael broke out into his best Scottish accent, one of the only accents he could do with reasonable proficiency.

"Is that what happened to her?" Penny enquired, while wrapping her arms around her husband.

"Yep," Carmichael replied. "And I dare say she'll be telling Natalie all about it, too, regardless of our attempts to prevent her."

Penny shrugged her shoulders, "I guess she sees worse on the TV and, even if it's true, it was fifty-odd years ago."

"I guess so," he concurred, before taking a sip of his hot chocolate drink.

Chapter 7

Sunday, 23rd December

When Carmichael's alarm went off at 5.50am his bedroom was still pitch black. Bleary-eyed, he scrambled out of bed and peeked through a crack in the curtains. Although dawn had still to break, he could clearly see his BMW illuminated by the light of the lamp post a few yards away. To his delight, the car was not covered in frost, so he'd be spared the horrendous task of having to scrape the ice off his windscreen.

Penny hadn't made a sound, but she was evidently at least partly awake, for when he turned back from the window she had already rolled over and cocooned herself in the entire duvet.

Conscious of the time, Carmichael scuttled off down the hall to have a shower.

Penny had asked him on several occasions to sand a few millimetres off the bathroom door, as it did have the habit of sticking making it difficult to open at times. So when Carmichael found himself unable to enter, he instinctively imagined it was stuck. Turning the knob sharply in a clockwise direction, Carmichael leaned heavily against the door.

"Who's that?" came the familiar voice of Audrey from within.

"Oh sorry," replied Carmichael, who hadn't even considered there would be someone in the bathroom at such an hour on a Sunday. "I didn't realise there was anyone in there."

"I just thought I'd take a bath before everybody got up,"

replied Audrey. "It takes me so long these days, I thought I'd have one early so as not to inconvenience anyone."

"Right," replied Carmichael, who could feel his stress levels building. "Do you know how long you'll be?"

"I've only just this minute got in, Steven," replied Audrey, who sounded totally unaware of her nephew's desire to evict her promptly. "I usually like to soak for at least twenty minutes, it helps my creaky old joints. Is that OK?"

"Yes," Carmichael replied as reassuringly as he could. "I'll use the small one downstairs."

Carmichael stood outside the door for a few seconds contemplating how he'd be able to get himself reasonably presentable for work, given the toilet downstairs only had a small hand basin and his toothbrush and shaving kit were located behind the door with Aunty Audrey.

"Bugger," he muttered under his breath as he scurried off down the stairs.

Fifteen minutes later, having washed as best he could in the tiny sink, Carmichael rushed back upstairs and once more into the bedroom.

"Who has a bloody bath at 5.50am?" he grumbled to his wife, who remained submerged under the duvet.

"What?" Penny replied, her tone indicating some displeasure at being asked to enter into communications at such an unearthly hour.

"Audrey's taking a bloody bath!" Carmichael remarked. "So I couldn't have a shower. My razor is in there, so I can't shave and I can't even brush my teeth."

Penny's head poked up from under the duvet. "Poor you," she remarked, as if his predicament was insignificant. "Can't you wait until she's out?"

"No," replied Carmichael in an angry whisper. "I've got to be at the office by seven thirty for the briefing before we talk to the press."

Penny sat up in bed and put on the bedside lamp. "You've got loads of time," she replied bemusedly.

"No," Carmichael responded, his voice hushed but full of irritation. "I don't want to risk being late. Anyway she could be in there for ages."

Penny rolled her tired eyes with incredulity. "I can't help you with a razor but there's a spare toothbrush in my toiletry bag in the wardrobe and I'm sure there's some toothpaste there, too." As she spoke, Penny pointed in the direction of her wardrobe.

Carmichael, now half-dressed, rushed to the wardrobe and started to rummage around.

"You finish getting ready," Penny remarked, in a tone normally reserved for her children. "Let me find them."

To Penny's relief, she managed to locate the said items and, within a further ten minutes had successfully assisted her husband to leave the house on time, looking reasonably presentable, having been assured by her that he looked fine and that sporting a few hours' growth on his chin was not the worst offence he could commit.

As the door shut behind him, Penny heard the sound of water being released down the plug hole upstairs, which indicated that Audrey was close to completing her ablutions.

"I'm not sure what's worse," she mumbled to herself, "having to help Mr Grumpy get ready, or the prospect of spending a morning trying to keep calm with the aunty from hell."

Now fully awake, Penny walked through to the kitchen to make herself a cup of coffee. At least, she comforted herself, with Steve being called into the station he wouldn't be dragging her off to church, as was his wont most Sunday mornings.

* * * *

Carmichael was pleased to see the team all assembled in the incident room when he and Chief Inspector Hewitt arrived.

"Morning, everyone," he remarked as he marched to the front, with Hewitt a few paces behind in his smartly-pressed uniform and shiny black shoes. "Thanks again for getting in early this morning. I briefed Chief Inspector Hewitt last night after our meeting and the plan is for the Chief and I to talk to the press at nine o'clock, so we should have plenty of time to get up to speed."

Carmichael's eyes scoured the room. "DC Dalton, do you want to go first?" he remarked.

Rachel nodded. "As you can see, I've put up a series of photos of Hayley and the group she went out with on Friday evening."

As she spoke, her colleagues looked at the board where several enlarged photos had been posted, with names written neatly next to each picture. As they did so, Rachel held up a pile of paper. "I've also got photos of Hayley for the press."

"Well done," Carmichael remarked. "What about the initial search of Hayley's house. Did it yield anything?"

Rachel shook her head. "The team finished late last night, but they found nothing."

"What about Francis Scott. Have you spoken to her yet?" Carmichael asked.

"Yes, I have," Rachel replied. "She called me late last night. Apparently her mobile battery ran out when she was driving down to Devon, and she only received my message at about 9pm."

"What did she have to say?" Carmichael asked.

"She was devastated by Hayley's disappearance," Rachel continued. "But she had no idea why Hayley would make off. Her story is the same as the others. She says that Hayley seemed in good spirits on Friday night and Francis maintains that everything seemed normal."

"What about the husband?" Hewitt enquired. "What sort of man is he?"

Rachel considered the question for a few seconds before replying.

"Duncan Bell is seventy-six," she remarked. "He's co-operated fully with us and appears to be very worried. Like everyone else, he says he has no idea why his wife would abscond. He maintains she and he had a very happy marriage and there was nothing worrying her."

"In your opinion, could there be another person involved?" Hewitt continued. "A lover, perhaps?"

Rachel shook her head. "There's no evidence of that, sir," she replied.

"Is he going to join us with the press?" Hewitt asked, his gaze now firmly on Carmichael.

"I took the decision not to involve him at this stage," Carmichael replied. "I'd like to keep the press brief focussed on finding anyone who may have seen her after she got on the train last night."

Hewitt nodded. "Quite right," he remarked.

"How about you, DS Cooper?" Carmichael enquired. "What else have you found out since our last briefing?"

"I checked with the ticket offices at Kirkwood and Much Martin," Cooper replied. "The two young women appear to have bought return tickets at about 7.30pm on Friday from Much Martin. The man on duty at the ticket office says they paid cash, so we can't at this stage identify them."

"So, not online," Watson whispered in Rachel Dalton's ear.

"But they did buy a ticket," she replied, as quietly as she could.

"Would he recognise them again?" Carmichael asked.

"Although he had no names for us," Cooper replied, "he's certain one of the young women gets a train every weekday morning at between 8 and 8.30, so we should be able to find her tomorrow morning. I'm also going to have a look at the

CCTV footage from Much Martin to see if we can get a better picture of them boarding the train to Kirkwood."

"Well done," Carmichael acknowledged. "But we could do with finding them sooner than tomorrow morning, so see what sort of pictures you can get. If you get some clear ones hopefully the press can help us locate them."

"I'll see what I can do," Cooper replied.

Carmichael nodded as if to reassure Cooper further that he was happy with his efforts.

"What about the trace on Hayley Bell's mobile," Carmichael asked.

"I've just got the activity report from her provider," Cooper replied. "It doesn't show any activity at all since 6.23pm on Friday when Hayley made a thirty-second call to Francis Scott."

Carmichael considered what Cooper had just told them. "That was before the women met that night," he confirmed. "And I'd imagine that Hayley was just checking on the arrangements, however just to be sure, I need you to call Francis Scott again, Rachel, and ask her what the call was all about."

Rachel nodded. "Will do, sir," she replied obediently.

Carmichael turned his attention to DS Watson. "Did you take a second look at the CCTV tapes from Kirkwood, Much Martin and Southport train stations?"

"I did," Watson replied, his tone suggesting he was pleased with his efforts. "They're written up behind you on the board." As he spoke, he pointed at the notes he'd made on the board behind Chief Inspector Hewitt's head. "At Kirkwood fifteen people boarded the train, nine before Hayley then five after her. Apart from Hayley and the two young women mentioned before, all the rest looked like they were males, but, to be honest, the footage wasn't brilliant. Only the two women we've already mentioned got on together, all the rest got on alone."

"Did you make a note of which carriages they got into?" Carmichael asked.

"I did," Watson replied self-righteously. "I've made a note of that on the board, too. Apart from the two women, there were just three other people in the missing woman's carriage when the train left Kirkwood. They were all men, one who got on before Hayley and two after."

"We need to find those three men as a priority," Carmichael replied. "What about at Much Martin?"

"At Much Martin ten people got off the train including one of the men in Hayley's carriage and the two women we know about," replied Watson.

"And did anyone get on the train at Much Martin?" Carmichael enquired.

"Just three people," Watson replied. "They were all male and appeared to be together."

"Which carriage did they get into?" Carmichael asked.

"Not Hayley's," Watson replied. "They were two carriages down from her."

"Then what about at Southport?" Carmichael asked. "How many people got off the train?"

"There were just five people," Watson replied. "And all of them males, as far as I can see."

"So, just so I've got this right," remarked Cooper. "In total you saw fifteen men and, including Hayley, three women getting onto the train at the three stops. And, if my maths are correct, you also saw thirteen men and the two women get off the train. So that means that unless there were other people getting on the train at the three other stops, Hayley and two men got off the train at one or more of the other stops."

"That's correct," Watson replied with a degree of enthusiasm. "And I'm certain that the two men in Hayley's carriage got off at one or more of those stops, as they didn't get off at either Much Martin or Southport."

"So, if Hayley was abducted," remarked Hewitt. "These two men could well be prime suspects."

"Absolutely," replied Watson. "That's what I think, although there were at least two other people who must have got on at one of the stops without CCTV footage, as there were two people who got off at Southport who I didn't see board the train at either Much Martin or Kirkwood."

"We need still photos of those two people, as well, in that case," Carmichael remarked.

"The lab's on to that already," Watson replied, with smug satisfaction.

"Good work, sergeant," Hewitt replied, his face lighting up with delight. "In fact, well done, everyone. It's encouraging to see that you're making progress and it looks like we've got plenty of information to share with the press this morning." As he spoke, Hewitt started to make his way out of the room. "In addition to the photograph of the missing woman, I need the photos of the two women and all three men who we know were in her carriage, before 9am. I want to hand them all out to the press."

Then, as Hewitt reached the door, he stopped and looked in Carmichael's direction. "Can you meet me in my office about thirty minutes before we talk to the press, Inspector," he remarked. "It's important we have a plan of what we share with the public at this stage."

"Of course," Carmichael replied, just before the Chief Inspector disappeared out of the room, closing the door behind him.

As soon as Carmichael was alone with the team, he rolled his eyes upwards. "Well done, team," he remarked. "Hewitt's right, you've done a great job so far. However, let's not jump to conclusions too soon. It's really important we trace everyone who was on that train on Friday evening, not just the people in Hayley's carriage."

Carmichael looked up at the clock, it was still not yet 8am.

"I'll leave you all to get on with the investigation," he added as he made his exit. "Let's get together again at five o'clock to compare notes."

"Good luck with the press," Cooper remarked as Carmichael reached the door.

Carmichael half turned and smiled back at his three officers. "I doubt I'll have a major part," he replied. "I think Hewitt will want to be centre stage, don't you?"

Chapter 8

"Hi, Angela," Carmichael remarked as he breezed into Chief Inspector Hewitt's office. "Is he ready to see me?"

Hewitt's secretary smiled back. "He's on the phone to the Deputy Chief Constable," she replied. "I don't think he'll be long."

Carmichael was happy to wait. And, in fairness to Hewitt, it was still only 8.25am, so not yet the time his boss had asked him to go up to his office.

"Are you ready for Christmas?" Angela enquired.

"Penny is, but I'm nowhere near," Carmichael replied. "It's going to be a mad dash as usual for me. How about you?"

Angela had the serene look of someone who'd got everything under control.

"I'm almost there," she replied. "Just the last of the food shopping to do, which I was going to do this morning. That was before I got the call from Chief Inspector Hewitt last night."

Carmichael smiled. "Yes, this missing person has messed up a few people's plans for a quiet lead up to Christmas," he replied.

"Let's hope you get a good response from the public, then," Angela added.

Carmichael nodded and was about to reply when the door to Chief Inspector Hewitt's office burst open. "Come in, Inspector," Hewitt instructed. "Let's work out our media strategy."

Even before he'd finished his sentence, Hewitt had already turned his back on Carmichael and was returning to his desk, giving Carmichael the opportunity to roll his eyes skyward and indicate to Angela his opinion of Hewitt's need for a media strategy, a gesture which made Angela smile broadly.

"I'll bring you both some coffee," Hewitt's PA whispered, in an attempt to try and lessen Carmichael's woes.

"And a few digestives, please, Angela," boomed the voice of Hewitt, whose hearing was clearly still working perfectly, despite him being just a few years short of sixty.

* * * *

The media strategy meeting went exactly as Carmichael had expected, with Hewitt spending the majority of the thirty minutes they had together making sure he knew all the details, so that his performance would be as slick and polished as his appearance.

"I'll lead," he'd announced almost as soon as they'd both sat down. Carmichael had no problems with that, as he was still a little ruffled by the fact that he'd not been able to shave that morning.

"You can help out when we come to the Qs and As," Hewitt remarked as the two headed downstairs to meet the press.

Carmichael nodded. "That's fine," he replied as they entered the small room they always used for press briefings.

"Good morning, ladies and gentlemen," Hewitt announced, as if he was a host on a daytime TV show. "Many thanks for coming."

As Hewitt spoke, Carmichael looked around to see who they'd managed to drum up at such short notice.

Considering it was a Sunday morning, Carmichael was impressed by the number of press people gathered around the small desk. He didn't recognise everyone, but of the twenty or so there he could identify at least half of them, which included teams from the local BBC news channel and the regional independent TV company, both equipped with their microphones and video cameras. In addition, Carmichael spotted reporters from three or four of the regional newspapers, including his old friend Norfolk George, the editor and lead reporter of the *Observer*, the most widely read local paper in the area.

"We are looking for your help," continued Hewitt, his eyes fixed on the notes in front of him, but his voice booming out across the room. "We are trying to discover the whereabouts of a lady called Hayley Bell, who was last seen on Friday evening boarding the 10.37 train from Kirkwood to Southport."

At that point, Hewitt looked up from his notes and stopped speaking for a few seconds, his eyes panning around the room.

"Mrs Bell was expected to leave the train at Much Martin station when it arrived at about 11.10pm. However, the CCTV footage indicates clearly that she did not disembark from the train at Much Martin or at Southport, which is the only other station with CCTV cameras. Given that there are no obvious reasons for Mrs Bell to have changed her plans and with her family and friends having been unable to contact her for almost thirty-six hours, we are all starting to become concerned for her safety."

Again Hewitt stopped talking for a few seconds, his eyes once more scanning the room.

"From our initial investigations we know that the train was relatively quiet with no more than twenty people using the service between Kirkwood and Southport. We are keen to talk to anyone who was on the train on Friday evening and to anyone who may have seen a woman fitting Hayley's description in the vicinity of any of the stations en route between Kirkwood and Southport."

"Are you able to give us a description of the missing woman?" enquired one of the reporters.

Without hesitation, Hewitt turned his head ninety degrees to his left and nodded in Carmichael's direction. "Inspector Carmichael, who is leading the investigation, can help you," Hewitt replied.

Carmichael lifted up a photograph of Hayley Bell which Rachel had provided. "Mrs Bell is forty-eight years old," Carmichael announced. "She is 5 ft 6 ins tall, of medium build and was last seen wearing a black trouser suit with a patterned green blouse." As he spoke, Carmichael passed the large pile of photographs to the nearest reporter, who took one copy before passing the rest down the line. "As Chief Inspector Hewitt has already indicated," continued Carmichael, "we are anxious to speak to anyone who may have seen Hayley after 10.37 on Friday evening, or who may have any information regarding her whereabouts. We are particularly keen to talk to the five people who we know shared the same train carriage as Hayley on Friday."

As he finished his sentence, Carmichael started to pass around the photographs of the three men and two women Watson had identified as being in Hayley Bell's carriage.

"I realise these are not the clearest images," Carmichael added, "but hopefully your viewers and readers may be able to help identify these people."

Once Carmichael had finished, Chief Inspector Hewitt nodded at him before turning to face the gathered ranks of reporters. "Are there any questions?" he enquired.

"Harry Cole, from *BBC Radio Lancashire*," shouted a voice from the rear of the room. "Can you clarify the names of the stations where you believe the missing lady could have left the train?"

"Alcar and Barton Bridge are the two stops before Much Martin and Linbold is the one between Much Martin and Southport," Carmichael replied.

"Chloe Manson, *North West Today*," announced the young-looking reporter sat a matter of feet away from Carmichael, in the front row. "Do you have any leads regarding Hayley Bell's disappearance that you can share with us?"

Carmichael opened his mouth and was about to answer, when Hewitt piped up in his customary loud yet pretentious tone. "At the moment we are keeping an open mind," he remarked. "All potential avenues are being investigated."

The mechanical way Hewitt flippantly parried the young reporter's question seemed to signify to the collected media that the briefing was over, as no further questions were raised.

"We greatly appreciate your help," Carmichael added in an attempt to ensure the media left feeling at least they had a modicum of thanks from the police. "If you can please ask anyone who knows anything that may help us, however small or insignificant it may seem, to contact either myself or one of my colleagues here at Kirkwood police station."

As the press started to disperse, Hewitt leaned over and quietly muttered into Carmichael's ear that he had to dash for an appointment and without bothering to wait for a response from his Inspector, quickly rose and hurried out of the room.

Carmichael elected to remain in the room for a few minutes in case any of the reporters wanted to ask him anything before they left. He also wanted to grab a quick word with Norfolk George, the reporter whose knowledge of local people was almost encyclopaedic and whose ability to recall information, in Carmichael's opinion, was second to none.

Chapter 9

"How did it go?" Rachel Dalton enquired as soon as she spied her boss entering the incident room.

Carmichael shrugged his shoulders. "OK, I think," he replied without any great conviction. "Hopefully the photos you managed to provide will be clear enough for some eagle-eyed members of the public to identify the people in Hayley Bell's carriage. The sooner we speak to them the better."

Rachel nodded. "I hope so," she replied.

"Where are the other two?" Carmichael enquired, as if he'd have liked to make an announcement to the full team.

"Cooper's gone over to Much Martin to try and see if he can find anyone who can identify the two young women who were in Hayley's carriage," Rachel replied. "Watson's gone home."

Carmichael's face looked shocked at the news that Watson wasn't actively following up a lead. However, before he could make any comment, Rachel followed up with… "after all, he is off-duty," which seemed to jog Carmichael's memory. "And he said he's going to come back for the debrief at 5pm," she added in her colleague's defence.

"Have you spoken with Francis Scott again?" Carmichael asked.

Rachel nodded. "Yes," she replied. "Miss Scott confirmed precisely what you'd assumed, namely that Hayley had called her on Friday to simply confirm the arrangements."

Carmichael propped himself up against the desk next to Rachel Dalton, smiled smugly and folded his arms.

"Tell me again about Duncan Bell," he instructed.

Rachel Dalton had got to know Carmichael well enough to realise that he rarely asked a question unless there was a reason. She looked up at her boss and after a few seconds pause, replied. "He's hard to work out. He seems genuinely worried, or at least that was the impression he gave me, but he is creepy. I'm sure he's harmless, but he is one of those men who appear to undress you with their eyes."

Carmichael frowned. "I don't have that problem," he remarked flippantly, "but I think I know what you mean."

"But if you're asking me for a gut feeling whether he's involved in Hayley's disappearance," continued Rachel, "then I'd have to say no."

Carmichael considered Rachel's response before adding. "According to Norfolk George, who as you know is the fount of knowledge when it comes to the lives of people in the area, Duncan was an architect, a bit of a writer, poetry mainly, and he's on his third wife."

"Really," replied Rachel, her response void of any trace of excitement. "Is that relevant?"

"It may be," Carmichael added. "You see according to George, wife number one left him over forty years ago, before even George was a journalist, but wife number two, who was the mother of his two children, died in mysterious circumstances. George wasn't able to remember all the details, but he does seem to recall that her death was sudden and unexpected and that Duncan Bell received a sizeable payment from a life insurance policy he'd taken out on her no more than a year before she died."

"Really," Rachel replied for a second time, this time with eyebrows raised and much more curiosity in her voice.

"Yes," Carmichael continued. "And what's more, according

to Norfolk George, Hayley was the children's nanny and Duncan Bell married her within six months of his second wife's death."

"So where are the children now?" Rachel enquired.

Carmichael nodded. "They'll be grown up now and probably married with families of their own."

"I realise that," Rachel replied, "however, if my old nanny and stepmother went missing, I'd be worried. Don't you think it's strange they haven't come forward before now?"

Carmichael pondered Rachel's question for a few seconds before looking up at the clock, which indicated it was 10.10am. "Like Sergeant Watson, I'm also supposed to be off-duty and I need to get myself home for a few hours," Carmichael remarked. "But I think I'll pop in to talk to Duncan Bell on my way. I'll ask him about his children when I'm there."

"Do you want me to come with you, sir?" Rachel enquired, her tone suggesting she'd very much like to be party to the meeting.

Carmichael shook his head. "No," he replied firmly. "I can do that by myself. I need you to remain here and take personal charge of the calls we get from the general public following the press conference. I'd also like you to try and find out as much as you can about the circumstances of the death of Mrs Bell number two."

Rachel nodded. "Will do, sir," she replied dutifully.

"Also, if you've time," Carmichael continued, "can you arrange for a diagram of the layout of the train Hayley Bell was on? Enlarge it and put it up so we can start to make an exact plan of where everyone was sitting."

Rachel nodded. "I'll do my best," she replied, although she had no idea how successful she would be in accomplishing all the tasks Carmichael had allotted her by the briefing at 5pm.

* * * *

On the car journey to Much Martin, Carmichael tuned into the local radio station to hear if there would be any mention of Hayley Bell on the 10.30am news bulletin. To his delight, their plea for information was the main news feature and even more satisfying for Carmichael was the fact that the only part of the conference they transmitted, was him asking for the public to come forward with information.

"We are anxious to speak to anyone who may have seen Hayley after 10.37pm on Friday or who may have any information about her whereabouts," he heard himself saying in a clear, commanding voice. "We are particularly keen to talk to the five people who we know shared the same train carriage as Hayley on Friday."

As a rule, Carmichael didn't normally care to hear his own voice on the radio, but on this occasion, he took delight in knowing Hewitt had been edited out of the transmission, despite his best efforts to take centre stage.

As the piece ended and the newsreader moved on to an item about the likelihood of a shortage of sprouts in the run up to Christmas, Carmichael's car arrived outside The Laurels, Uplands Gardens, Much Martin.

Although it was mid-morning and the sun was now out, the air was still icy-cold and there was little sign of the hard, white, snow-covered earth starting to thaw.

As Carmichael walked briskly up the long, block-paved driveway, his breath creating small white clouds from his mouth and nostrils, he couldn't help noticing a slight movement of the blinds in one of the upstairs windows, as if someone was watching him as he made his way to the front door.

Using the hefty, brass knocker in the centre of the large, wooden front door, Carmichael rapped three times. Within a matter of seconds the door opened and the lofty, lean figure of Duncan Bell, dressed in a bright-orange jacket, lime-green shirt and a pair of dark-blue trousers, appeared in front of him.

"Good morning, I'm Inspector…"

"I know who you are," replied Duncan Bell brusquely before Carmichael had an opportunity to finish his sentence. "You were on the TV news bulletin about twenty minutes ago. Is there any news?"

Bell's question was asked in such a way that Carmichael's train of thought moved instantly from the old man's flamboyant attire and returned to the reason for his call.

Carmichael shook his head. "I'm sorry, I've nothing new I can tell you," he remarked sympathetically. "But, I'm very confident we will find her soon."

"Do you really think so?" Bell enquired, his voice shaky as he spoke, but at the same time sounding fortified by the prospect of a positive outcome.

The last thing Carmichael wanted to do was to give Duncan Bell false hope, so he chose to ignore his latest plea. "May I come in?" Carmichael asked.

"Of course, how rude of me," replied Bell, who pulled the door open wider to allow his visitor to enter his imposing white marble hallway.

"I wanted to have a chance to talk with you directly," Carmichael remarked as soon as they were inside and the door had been closed behind them. "I know you've already spoken to my officers and given a statement, but I thought it would be good for us to talk, too."

"Of course," replied Bell for a second time. "I'll be only too pleased to answer any of your questions if it will help you find Hayley." As he spoke, Bell stretched out his long sinewy arm towards a door behind Carmichael. "Please go through into the autumn room."

Carmichael gave a faint smile, turned and walked through the open doorway into Duncan Bell's autumn room. Once inside, Carmichael selected the nearest of the three lavish sofas and plonked himself down in the middle. He waited a few moments to allow his host to be seated before he started his questioning.

"What sort of person is Hayley?" Carmichael asked.

Duncan Bell considered the question for a few seconds before responding. "I'd describe her as a classic 'earth woman'," he replied. "She is a caring person who has devoted her life to looking after other people, most especially my two children and, of course, me, too."

Carmichael smiled. "I understand Mrs Bell is forty-eight," he said, eyes fixed firmly on the elderly man.

"Yes," replied Bell without any hesitation, "and we've been married just over twenty-five years."

"Really," remarked Carmichael. "So Mrs Bell was in her early twenties when you married?"

"Yes," replied Bell once more, although this time less enthusiastically. "Hayley was just twenty-three when we married."

"And you would have been?" Carmichael enquired.

"I was fifty-one," Bell replied. "Not that I see it's of any relevance to the disappearance of my wife."

Carmichael smiled once more. "It's just background, so I can get a fuller understanding," he added in an attempt to reassure Bell. "I also understand that you've been married before?" Carmichael remarked.

Duncan Bell looked somewhat indignant at the question, but replied quickly enough. "There have been three Mrs Bells," he remarked straightforwardly. "Is that of any relevance to your investigation?"

"As I've indicated already, I just want to make sure I have a full background on Mrs Bell," Carmichael replied with a reassuring smile.

"Well, I don't see my previous marriages having the slightest relevance to the fact that Hayley is missing," remarked Bell angrily.

"Did Mrs Bell have any special friendships?" Carmichael asked, deliberately leaving his question vague.

Bell, hands tightly clasped together in front of him, eased back into the sofa. "I see," he remarked. "Because Hayley is almost thirty years younger than me, you think she may have run off with a younger man."

Carmichael smiled again and gave a slight shrug of his shoulders. "That wasn't what I was suggesting," he remarked firmly. "But, as I say, we have to explore all possibilities."

"Well, she hasn't," replied Bell sharply. "We are still very much in love, Inspector Carmichael. I don't know what has happened with Hayley, but I can assure you she has no lover."

Carmichael paused for a few seconds before continuing his questioning.

"Can you tell me about your first two wives?" Carmichael asked.

"I'm not sure what relevance they have on Hayley's disappearance," Duncan Bell replied curtly. "But, as it happens, the first Mrs Bell did abscond. Pamela ran off with a close friend of mine over thirty-five years ago. Apart from some minor communications to sort out the divorce, we've not spoken since and I haven't set eyes on her since the day she left me. Then there was Claudette, the mother of my two children, she unfortunately died very unexpectedly of a brain haemorrhage when she was in her early thirties."

As he spoke, Duncan Bell stared wistfully into open space. "In short I've been blessed to have three great loves in my life," he remarked. "But, sadly, two left me too soon, which, as I am sure you can imagine, Inspector Carmichael, is why I'm so concerned about Hayley."

Carmichael nodded. "I understand," he replied as sensitively as he could.

"I'm also told that Hayley was the nanny to your children when your second wife was alive?"

"Yes," replied Bell sharply, the question having clearly rubbed him up the wrong way. "I can see you've done a great deal of research on me already, Inspector."

"It's just normal procedure," Carmichael replied. "We have to be thorough in situations like this."

"Like the half-a-dozen men who turned my house upside down were, I suppose," Bell replied angrily, his vexation clearly evident on his face.

"What do you think has happened to Hayley?" Carmichael enquired, realising it may be wise to move his questioning on.

Duncan Bell looked completely taken aback at being asked such a question. "Is that not your job to discover why she's missing?" he retorted loudly, his tone now one of extreme exasperation.

"Yes, it is," Carmichael replied calmly. "And it may well be that your wife has been taken against her will, however, she also may have decided to leave of her own accord, so it would be of great help if you told us of anything that might have caused her to take off." As he finished his sentence, Carmichael looked directly into Bell's eyes.

"There is no reason whatsoever for Hayley to desert me," Bell replied resolutely, his voice now raised and decidedly loud. "I am convinced that poor Hayley has been abducted or harmed in some way and, to be honest with you, Inspector, I'd feel much more reassured if you would concentrate your efforts trying to find her rather than investigating me and asking irrelevant questions."

Carmichael nodded gently before suddenly rising to his feet. "I'll take no more of your time, Mr Bell," he announced. "Be assured we are doing all we can to find your wife and I'll make sure you are kept totally in the picture as and when we have any news."

Duncan Bell seemed shocked that their meeting was coming to such an abrupt end, but at the same time appeared relieved. "I'll show you out," he remarked before quickly getting up to his feet and heading towards the door.

Carmichael followed a couple of steps behind his host as they departed from the room and walked briskly down the marble hallway. It was only once they reached the front door and Bell had opened it wide that Carmichael managed to look the old man in the face again.

"You mentioned you have children," Carmichael remarked.

"Yes," Duncan replied, "I've a son who lives in Vancouver, he's a lecturer at the university. I've also a daughter, she's just become a mother to her second child. She and her husband live in Brisbane in Australia."

Carmichael nodded gently. "Have you informed them about Hayley's disappearance?" He enquired.

To Carmichael's surprise, Duncan appeared to be irritated at being asked the question.

"Not as yet," Duncan retorted. "I didn't want to concern them unduly, but I have to confess that I may need to reconsider, since it's clear you and your team are making little, if any, progress."

Carmichael resisted the urge to respond directly to Duncan's remark, albeit that he found the insinuation insulting.

"One last question," he announced as soon as he'd crossed over the threshold and could feel the cold December air against his face. "Do you and Mrs Bell have any life insurance policies?"

Duncan Bell's facial muscles tightened and his lips pursed, indicating to Carmichael that his question had really struck a nerve. "My father was an insurance agent, Inspector Carmichael, so it's in my DNA and I have many policies and endowments. And, yes, these do include policies on both our lives, just like millions of other people. But, to be frank with you, I cannot recall how much the policies are for or the date when I took them out. Do you want me to check them for you?"

Carmichael could not be sure whether Duncan Bell had expected him to consider his words a genuine offer, but he decided he'd take them as such. "If that's not too much trouble," he replied calmly with a smile, taking out a business card from his pocket and handing it to the visibly-incensed, elderly gentleman. "If you could call me and give me the details of the life insurance policies and confirm when they were taken out, that would be most helpful," he added.

Bell's face was sullen and grey, and it was clear to Carmichael that the elderly gentleman was livid at the implication of this request. However, this didn't cut any ice with Carmichael. In his eyes he had every right to understand how much, if anything, Bell would receive if his wife was found dead.

For a few seconds Duncan Bell glared at him, then without uttering another word, he turned away from Carmichael and went back inside the house, slamming the front door behind him.

As he reached his car, Carmichael looked back at the house and, again, could have sworn he saw another slight movement of the blinds in the same upstairs window, but he couldn't be certain.

Chapter 10

"What an odious man," sneered Duncan Bell loudly, as soon as he was inside the house with the front door safely closed behind him. "Now, where's that blasted policy?"

Shaking with rage, the irritated old man stomped down the hallway and flung open the door to the winter room, the room where most of his papers were kept.

Still muttering under his breath, he crouched down in front of the large oak cabinet, one of his oldest pieces of furniture. Turning the key in the lock to release the door, he pulled out a pile of documents and transported them over to his oak desk. After three further trips, Duncan Bell finally managed to empty the contents of the cabinet and relocate them on his desk.

With a huge sigh, he sat down and started to go through the papers, something he hadn't done for many, many years.

* * * *

It wasn't difficult for Cooper to locate Melissa McManus and Tori Hunt, the two eighteen-year-olds who'd been in carriage two on the 10.37pm train that left Kirkwood for Southport on Friday evening. Both had been born and bred in Much Martin and, in such a small village, it took him less than ten minutes of asking a few locals to learn their names and addresses. It was Melissa he called upon first, at her home just twenty yards from the train station.

"Yes, we were on that train," the diminutive young woman with large brown eyes confirmed, "but that lady wasn't in our carriage," she continued when Cooper showed her the picture of Hayley Bell. "I do recognise her, as I've seen her about the village, but she definitely wasn't in our carriage and she didn't get off at Much Martin with us."

Tori Hunt, who Cooper talked to twenty minutes later, gave an almost identical story. "When we got on, there were only three other people in the carriage," she told Cooper. "They were all men and they all got off at Barton Bank."

"So after Barton Bank it was just you and Melissa in the carriage?" Cooper asked.

"No," the chubby, red-haired young woman replied. "There was one other man in there, but he got on at Barton Bank. I'm positive there wasn't a woman in our carriage other than Melissa and me."

Having completed his discussions with the two young women, Cooper clambered back into his beaten-up Volvo which he aimed in the direction of Kirkwood.

* * * *

After spending over an hour poring through his papers trying to locate the insurance policy, Duncan Bell sighed, leaned forward in his chair and flicked open the flap on the old red folder he'd extracted from his locked desk drawer. He tipped out the contents onto the desk and started to look intently at the letters and photographs now strewn in front of him.

He didn't notice the door open and was totally oblivious to the presence of anyone else, until their shadow fell upon the items in front of him.

"Oh, it's you," he remarked, almost dismissively, as

63

he looked up from his desk, while at the same time swiftly gathering up the letters and photographs and stuffing them haphazardly back into the file. "I completely forgot about you. You can blame that damn policeman for that."

Chapter 11

It was exactly noon when Carmichael arrived home. As he slowly strolled up the short steps leading to his front door, he could feel a few drops of icy rain against his face. He quickly turned the key in the lock and rushed inside to avoid getting too wet.

"Hello," he shouted loudly down the hallway. "I'm back."

After hanging up his coat, Carmichael walked slowly down the hall to the kitchen, the most likely place he expected to find Penny. When he discovered nobody in the kitchen, he walked back down the hallway and opened the door into the sitting room, one of the three other rooms on the ground floor.

The first thing he noticed was that the TV was on. Then he spotted Audrey, sleeping soundly in one of the large, high-backed armchairs. Carefully, he turned on his heels and made as quiet an exit as he could, gently closing the door behind him.

Having managed to escape without waking his aunty, Carmichael proceeded to wander down the hallway to the room they'd always jokingly referred to as the parlour, a description the estate agent had given the room when they'd first come to view the house, five years earlier.

Again, the TV was on and, again, the room had only one occupant, his son, Robbie.

"Where is everyone?" Carmichael enquired.

Robbie looked over at his Dad. "Well, Great Aunty Audrey is next-door, asleep," he replied. "Mum and Jemma have gone to the shops and I expect Natalie is at the stables with that horse, as usual," his tone as disparaging as always whenever he mentioned his little sister.

Carmichael smiled. "So you drew the short straw," he remarked.

Robbie hadn't been keen to remain in the house with his Great Aunty Audrey when his mother had suggested it earlier, but was now able to see the funny side. "Absolutely," he replied. "And, luckily, she dozed off about twenty minutes after they'd gone, so I've been able to escape in here for the last hour or so and watch some telly in peace."

"What have they gone to buy?" Carmichael asked his son. "I thought your Mum had bought just about everything she needed for Christmas."

Robbie shook his head despairingly. "Apparently there's a shortage of sprouts so they've gone shopping to make sure we have some for Christmas dinner."

"What!" Carmichael exclaimed. "We live in an area surrounded by farms with fields full of sprouts. If there are shortages it will be in the cities. We'll be alright. Anyway, apart from me and your Mum, I didn't think anyone else liked sprouts and we can always have some frozen ones. I'm sure there are loads in that massive freezer your Mum keeps filling up."

Robbie shook his head slowly and theatrically. "Oh no, Dad," he replied knowingly. "Great Aunty Audrey says that Christmas dinner isn't a proper Christmas dinner without fresh sprouts. Frozen ones are tasteless and have the consistency of rubber."

"So, your Mum's gone out to hunt down fresh sprouts to appease Audrey," Carmichael remarked.

"Precisely," Robbie replied with a sage-like nod of his head.

Carmichael puffed out his cheeks and plonked himself down on the sofa.

"Oh," added Robbie. "I better warn you that Aunty Audrey was less than impressed by your appearance when you did the press conference this morning about that missing woman."

"What!" Carmichael replied, his brow furrowed as he spoke.

"Yes," continued his son. "We all watched it together on the local news bulletin just before Mum went out. Great Aunty Audrey thought Chief Inspector Hewitt looked very smart in his uniform, but was very disappointed with how casually dressed you were."

"Oh, she did, did she?" replied Carmichael.

"She also mentioned that you needed a shave," Robbie added. "Mum thought it was quite funny, I'm not sure why."

Carmichael put his hands behind his head and looked up at the ceiling. "The next few days may be the longest of our lives," he muttered.

* * * *

By the time Cooper returned to Kirkwood police station, the team of PCs seconded to process the incoming calls had spoken to ten people who claimed to have been on Hayley Bell's train on Friday evening. Buoyed by the response, Rachel had already started to mark the seating diagram of the four-carriage Pacer 143 train to indicate where each of the passengers had sat during the journey.

"That looks impressive," Cooper remarked as he walked over to inspect Rachel's handiwork. "You can add Melissa McManus and Tori Hunt onto your diagram. They are the two women who were in Hayley's carriage, although they are both adamant they saw nobody fitting Hayley's description on the train."

"Are they sure?" Rachel enquired.

Cooper nodded his head. "Yes, they are positive that during their journey from Kirkwood to Much Martin, there were only ever three people in their carriage and they are certain that all three were men."

"I'm not surprised," Rachel conceded. "We've already had calls from two of those men. Independently, they both said that apart from your two young ladies, there were no women in their carriage at all, and one of them travelled all the way to Southport."

Cooper shook his head. "It doesn't make sense," he remarked. "The CCTV footage shows Hayley getting into the second carriage."

"Unless," replied Rachel, who was still formulating as she spoke. "What if Hayley didn't stay in that carriage?"

"Why would she do that?" Cooper enquired. "Why would she go into another carriage?"

Rachel shrugged her shoulders. "I do it all the time," she replied. "Once I'm on a train, I quite often will walk up through the carriages until I find a place to sit."

"But looking at your seating plan, the carriage she got on must have had plenty of empty seats," Cooper added.

"You're right," Rachel conceded. "In fact, based upon the CCTV footage, when Hayley got into that carriage we know that there was only one person in it. The two men I talked to and your two ladies all got on after Hayley. So there would be no obvious reason for her to walk into another carriage. However, if she did, none of the people we've spoken to would have seen her."

Cooper nodded. "That makes sense," he agreed. "And, if you're right, it means that it's the people in carriages one, three and four we need to talk to."

Rachel nodded. "Probably three or four I'd say," she remarked. "I doubt Hayley would have got into a carriage and then walked back in the direction she'd come from. That wouldn't make any sense at all."

"So have any of the people from carriages three and four who called in said they saw Hayley?" Cooper asked.

Rachel shook her head. "I'm afraid that's where the whole theory breaks down," she replied despondently. "We've spoken to ten people who claim to have been on the train and not one of them says they saw her. And, what's more puzzling is that between these ten people we have all four carriages covered."

"And, including Melissa McManus and Tori Hunt, that's a dozen people we've spoken to who were on that train and not one of them saw her," added Cooper.

"I know, it's just bizarre," Rachel conceded. "It's as if she just disappeared."

Cooper looked at his wrist watch then scratched his head. "We've got our briefing with Carmichael in just under three hours," he remarked, "and I'd like to be able to give him some positive news. Let's complete your diagram, as best we can, based upon the conversations we've had with the other passengers. If we can indicate everything we know, it may help us come up with a better theory than Hayley Bell just disappeared."

"I totally agree," Rachel replied. "But he also asked me to check into the death of Duncan Bell's last wife. I think Carmichael has the idea that her death might have been something to do with a life insurance policy he'd taken out on her, and I think his logic then suggests that the disappearance of the current Mrs Bell may be for the insurance, too."

Cooper shrugged his shoulders. "Sounds a bit of a stab in the dark to me," he replied. "I know the boss has a pretty good track record with his hunches, but this one sounds a little far-fetched. I'm sure if he was here, Carmichael would tell us to focus on the train, so let's do just that. If he doesn't agree I'll tell him it was me who decided."

Rachel nodded. "The train it is then," she said before picking up a blue marker and walking over to the plan of the four carriages.

Chapter 12

Aunty Audrey was still sound asleep at 2.30pm when Penny and Jemma sauntered through the front door.

"Did you manage to locate any elusive sprouts?" Carmichael enquired as his wife and daughter entered the kitchen.

Penny held up a blue plastic bag which was weighed down with what Carmichael assumed to be sprouts. "Of course," she replied, as if there was never any prospect of her returning without achieving her goal. "Our Christmas dinner will now be complete."

"And all our meals for a week after, judging from the amount you've bought," Carmichael replied, mockingly.

"Well, the farm only sold them in kilos so I bought two to make sure we had enough," replied Penny.

Carmichael shook his head. "So how's Audrey been?" he enquired.

Penny pondered the question for a few seconds, which was time enough to choose her words carefully. "About the same," she replied, which was as positive and tactful as she could be.

"That bad," replied her husband, with a grimace. "Well, the good news is she's still fast asleep in the other room, so I suggest you enjoy the peace and quiet while you can."

Penny smiled and kissed her husband's forehead. "We watched you on TV earlier," she remarked. "You were very good, sounded very commanding."

"Even though I looked untidy compared to the shiny, well-groomed Chief Inspector Hewitt," retorted Carmichael.

"Ah," Penny replied. "She mentioned it, did she?"

"No," replied Carmichael. "I've not had that pleasure, yet, given that she's fortunately been asleep since I got back, however, your son has informed me about her comments."

Penny looked back at her husband disapprovingly. "He's my son, is he," she replied, before allowing a tiny smirk to appear on her face. "Actually, I thought you looked quite rugged," she then added, before planting another kiss on his head.

"Have you found that woman yet?" Jemma enquired from the sink as she started to fill the kettle with water.

Her father shook his head. "Not yet," he replied reflectively. "However, I'm going back to the station for a briefing with the team at five, so hopefully we'll have had some calls from the public by then."

"What!" exclaimed Penny. "You're supposed to be on leave now. Can't anyone else handle the case?"

"It looks like my long lead up to Christmas might have to take a bit of a back seat," Carmichael replied. "Until we know for certain that Hayley Bell is safe, there won't be many of us able to enjoy an easy time, I'm afraid."

* * * *

It was exactly 23.2 miles from Carmichael's house in Moulton Bank to the police station car park at Kirkwood. Under normal circumstances the journey would take him between thirty and forty minutes, depending on the traffic and weather. Carmichael had left home at 4pm precisely, expecting to be able to arrive at least twenty minutes before the 5pm briefing was due to start. However, what should have been a leisurely, relaxing, relatively short journey became anything but, given

71

the fact that he got stuck behind a tractor for five miles which was travelling at no more than 25 mph.

It was therefore 5.05pm when Carmichael's BMW finally glided into his parking space, and he was fuming.

"What a bloody journey," he remarked as he strode hurriedly into the incident room. "Bloody tractors."

DS Cooper, DS Watson and DC Dalton were all waiting patiently in the room. They all knew Carmichael hated anyone being late for his meetings and had learned by experience that if he called a meeting for 5pm, what he meant was that it would start at 5pm on the dot and he expected the team to be there well before that start time.

As Carmichael marched to the front of the room, Watson leaned over and made a comment in Rachel Dalton's ear, a comment that was clearly a dig in some shape or form at their boss and one that made the young DC put her hand over her mouth to stifle an embarrassing giggle and prevent her being seen by Carmichael.

"Right," remarked Carmichael, who turned suddenly to face the team. "Let's get started."

Carmichael noticed the expressions on the faces of Dalton and Watson, and guessed that something had been said, but chose to ignore them and press on with the meeting.

"Rachel," he announced loudly. "I see that you've not only posted the diagram of the seating plan of Hayley Bell's train, but you've also made some detailed notes against it. Can you explain what you've done?"

"Of course," Rachel replied dutifully, getting up from her seat and walking over to the board.

"The train is quite an old one," she said. "It's called a 143. Normally the service from Kirkwood to Southport is made up of just two carriages. However, as we saw from the CCTV, on Friday when Hayley boarded, there were four carriages."

"Why was that?" Carmichael asked.

"They apparently wanted to do some maintenance on a couple of carriages in the Southport workshop, so they added them on when the train had arrived at 10.20pm," Rachel replied.

"I wondered why they had such a large train when there were clearly only a couple of dozen passengers at the most," Carmichael remarked. "How many people have come forward so far to say they were on the train?"

"We've had a fantastic response," interjected Cooper. "We've heard from twelve people already and, based upon what they've told us, we believe that we know roughly how many people used the train, where they got on, where they got off and which carriage they were in."

"Really," Carmichael remarked. "I'm amazed that you've had such a good response from the public. It must have been the way Chief Inspector Hewitt explained everything."

Rachel smiled. "Based upon the information we received from the twelve people we've spoken to, we believe that there were no more than twenty or twenty-one people on the train, including Hayley Bell," she continued.

"Why twenty or twenty-one?" Carmichael enquired.

Rachel quickly glanced over at Cooper.

"Rachel and I have spent this afternoon talking again to the twelve people who've come forward," Cooper confirmed. "We asked them to confirm where they got on, where they got off, which carriage and which seat they sat in. Also who else was in their carriage and, as far as they could recall, who else got on and off at each of the stations when they were on the train."

"Based upon what the twelve people told us," continued Rachel, who was clearly excited about the results of their conversations, "we've updated the chart."

Carmichael looked closely at the fruits of their labours.

"But that doesn't answer the question," he remarked. "Why twenty or twenty-one?"

Rachel again looked across at Cooper, clearly wanting him to reply.

"The feedback we received was pretty comprehensive," Cooper stated. "But we've only documented on the chart, the locations of the passengers on the train and where people got on or off when the people we spoke to were either totally confident about what they remembered, or their comments matched what others told us."

"So much so," continued Rachel, "that we feel we have a pretty accurate and clear picture of how many people got on or off at each station and where they sat on the train."

At that point Cooper frowned. "But there are a few things we have a problem with," he continued, choosing his words carefully.

"Which are?" Carmichael enquired, his tone demonstrating that he was desperate to get the information out of his two officers.

"Firstly, from what we have been told, seven people including Hayley got into carriage two, but only six got off the train out of carriage two. The one that didn't being Hayley."

"OK," Carmichael remarked. "So Hayley must have got off the train out of another carriage."

"That was exactly what we first thought," Cooper replied. "However, not one person we've spoken to can remember either seeing Hayley on the train or getting off the train, and we've spoken to people from every carriage."

Carmichael's brow creased as he considered what Cooper had just told him. "The other issue is the discrepancy we have between the total number of people who we've calculated getting on the train against the ones that got off," Rachel interceded. "We count twenty getting on in total and twenty-one getting off."

"But none of the twenty-one has been identified as Hayley Bell," stated Watson, who, like Carmichael was trying hard to make sense of what he was hearing.

"Correct," replied Cooper.

"So if the information you have is correct," Watson continued, "Hayley Bell disappeared as soon as she got on the train, but two people who never got on the train got off it!"

With embarrassed looks on their faces, Cooper and Dalton exchanged a quick glance. "Unfortunately that's about the long and the short of it."

"Then what you've been told can't be right," remarked Watson. "It's got to be inaccurate."

"I agree with Marc," Carmichael replied. "You've both done a great job, but we need to talk to the other people on the train as what you have so far doesn't pass a common sense test."

Rachel Dalton glanced sideways at Cooper.

"I agree," Cooper grudgingly replied with a sigh and a reluctant shrug of his shoulders.

"Hopefully," Carmichael added, "given the strong coverage by the local media, we'll be able to locate the remaining nine or ten people tomorrow. Can you take care of that, Paul?" he continued, looking directly at Cooper.

"Of course," replied Cooper.

Carmichael then turned to face Rachel Dalton. "Did you manage to find out anything about the death of Duncan Bell's second wife?"

Before Rachel had a chance to say anything, Cooper piped up. "We took the decision to focus all our energies on mapping out the passenger movements. I thought that needed to be the priority."

Carmichael nodded. "You did right," he acknowledged. "But I went to see Duncan Bell earlier and I had an uneasy feeling about him. I agree that he does seem genuinely worried about his wife, but I still think he's not all he seems."

"Did he mention anything about his children?" Rachel enquired.

Carmichael rubbed his hand across his chin. "He did," he remarked. "He has a son in Vancouver and a daughter in Australia, but he maintains he's not yet informed them about their stepmother's disappearance."

"That seems a bit strange," Rachel replied.

"Unless they're not close," Cooper interjected. "My mother's got a sister who she's not spoken to in donkey's years. These things happen in families."

Watson nodded avidly. "If they were estranged it would explain them living so far away, cos let's face it, you couldn't move much further away."

"And I guess it's up to Duncan Bell who he tells," Cooper continued.

"Unless he's bumped her off," Watson quickly retorted.

Realising the conversation was going off-track, Carmichael cleared his throat. "So tomorrow, Rachel," he said firmly, "I want you to delve into Duncan's past. I'm keen to know about both his two previous marriages. He told me his first wife, Pamela, ran off with a friend of his. I know this would have happened decades ago, but try and trace her if you can. He also confirmed that his second wife, Claudette, died of a brain haemorrhage about twenty-five years ago."

"Will do," replied Rachel.

"Actually, that reminds me," Carmichael remarked. "Bell said he'd call me to confirm the policy he has on Hayley's life. If he hasn't called me by the end of the day, can you pick that up with him, too, please?"

"Yes, sir," replied Rachel compliantly.

"So, that's you two sorted out for tomorrow. That just leaves you and me, Marc," continued Carmichael.

"What have you got in mind?" Watson enquired.

Carmichael smiled. "I think you and I should spend tomorrow talking to the ladies Hayley had dinner with on Friday. If they are her friends then I'd imagine one of them might hold the key to understanding what happened to her."

Watson nodded. "It's fine with me," he replied, "but I thought you were supposed to be on leave."

Carmichael gave a faint shrug of his shoulders. "I am," he replied. "But I doubt I'll be able to relax very much until we've made a bit more headway, so I'm afraid, guys, I'm with you all on this one, at least for the next day or so."

Chapter 13

Monday, 24th December

Carmichael looked up at the kitchen clock feeling very satisfied with himself. It was 8.30am and he'd managed to prevent a repeat of the previous morning's bottleneck by telling Audrey, the night before, that she needed to avoid using the bathroom between 7.30am and 8.15am.

Sitting alone at the kitchen table, drinking a mug of coffee, Carmichael thought long and hard about the case.

He'd instructed Watson to collect him from his house at 8.45am, so he had the luxury of fifteen minutes to mull things over.

Despite the fact that Cooper and Dalton had not spoken to everyone who'd been on Hayley's train, Carmichael was sure the two officers would have been meticulous in their efforts to identify all the passengers. Had it been Watson who'd been managing this exercise, Carmichael might have been less confident, but with Cooper and Rachel Dalton handling the proceedings, he knew they'd have been very diligent in identifying and double checking the exact stops where everyone had boarded the train, which carriages they had sat in and at which stations they'd disembarked. So although there were still another eight or nine people they needed to talk to, Carmichael's sense was that enough people had been spoken to, for at least one person to have noticed Hayley in their carriage. Consequently, their inability to do so seriously bothered him.

What also troubled Carmichael was the fact that Duncan Bell had still not called him with the details of the life insurance policy he'd taken out on his wife. In Carmichael's mind this hesitancy in coming forward was an indication that Bell had something to hide.

Unable to make any meaningful headway in his deliberations, Carmichael gulped down what remained of his coffee and, after placing the empty mug on the draining board, collected his jacket and walked down the corridor to the front door.

When Carmichael opened his front door, as he'd expected, Watson was waiting at the end of the driveway, his car engine running.

As he strolled down the path, Carmichael once again felt a twinge of remorse at leaving the rest of the family to look after Aunty Audrey on Christmas Eve. He'd fully anticipated Penny to be less than impressed when he'd mentioned he was going to have to work that day, but the reaction of his usually unflappable and patient wife was certainly more exasperated than he'd expected, a clear sign of how increasingly stressed she was becoming because of Audrey's incessant moaning and criticising. And when Penny had pointed out, in no uncertain terms, that Audrey was his relative not hers, Carmichael's guilt had become acute and genuinely heartfelt. But, in his eyes, he had no choice. Audrey's visit was not initiated by him and he had a case to solve, so what else could he do?

In an effort to placate his wife, Carmichael had made a solemn promise that, after today, he'd delegate the responsibility for tracking down Hayley Bell to his team, and would switch off completely at least until after they'd safely had Christmas as a family and deposited Audrey back on the train to Milton Keynes. But although he'd made that assurance with true sincerity, he'd deliberately avoided telling his wife that should they find Hayley's body, and the case escalate to a murder hunt, Christmas for him would be cancelled as there would be no way he would be able to excuse himself from leading the investigation, promise or no promise.

"Morning, sir," Watson remarked chirpily as his boss climbed into the passenger seat.

"It's still bloody cold," Carmichael replied crabbily, "I hope most of this white stuff melts away soon, I'm already fed up with this awful weather."

"I think you may be disappointed," Watson replied. "The weather report reckons this cold snap is going to be with us for a least a couple more days. We may even get some heavy snow this evening."

"That's all we need," replied Carmichael gloomily.

"Which of the five ladies do you want to talk to first?" Watson enquired, sensibly wishing to change the subject.

Carmichael fastened his seat belt. "Let's try and speak to either Maxine Lowe or Hannah Ringrose first. Then we can do Belinda Bishop and Lesley Saxham. As for the other one that's on holiday in Devon…"

"Francis Scott," remarked Watson.

"Yes, Francis Scott," continued Carmichael. "Let's decide if we need to call her after we've spoken to the other four."

Watson nodded. "Well, in that case, I propose we do Hannah Ringrose first," he suggested. "According to the notes, she works as an internal sales agent at a double glazing firm this side of Kirkwood. Unless they've already finished for Christmas, I think we should be able to find her at work. Then it will be just a few minutes' drive to Maxine Lowe's house. She's a teacher at a primary school, so with the schools all broken-up for Christmas, I'd imagine she's at home."

"Sounds like a plan," replied Carmichael, who was impressed that Watson had clearly been putting a modicum of thought into the case himself that morning.

* * * *

Cooper arrived at his desk at Kirkwood police station just before 9am, which for him was late. His first thought was to check if anyone else had come forward following the press coverage. Tracking down twelve people the day before had been an unbelievable result, considering how empty the train had been that evening, so Cooper didn't expect many more would have made themselves known since the briefing on Sunday evening. But he was wrong.

"You'll never believe it, we've had five more calls," he announced to Rachel Dalton in amazement, when she arrived.

"Really," she replied. "That means there can't be more than two or three people left."

Cooper shrugged his shoulders. "I'm totally astounded," he added. "But I'm not knocking it. Hopefully, having spoken to these five, we'll have an even clearer picture of who was on that train and one of them will be able to shed more light on what went on that evening."

"Do you want any help calling them back?" Rachel asked.

Cooper shook his head. "No, I'll be OK," he replied. "Anyway the boss will be bent out of shape if you don't get him the details he's asked for about Duncan Bell's ex-wives."

Rachel shook her head and sighed. "I'm not sure this latest hunch of his is going to lead us anywhere," she remarked somewhat disparagingly. "I thought he was genuinely concerned about Hayley. And, to be honest, his previous wives have been out of the picture for decades. The first one left him before I was even born."

Cooper smiled. "You're almost certainly right, Rachel," he concurred. "But my advice to you is to get Carmichael the information he wants and let him find out whether it's relevant or not. Although you could maybe delay starting for ten minutes while you get me a coffee."

Rachel glared back at Cooper and then smiled. "Dream on," she replied, before sitting down behind her computer screen and starting her research.

* * * *

The offices of Brighterlight Double Glazing were situated a stone's throw from the centre of Kirkwood, on the third floor of what had originally been the town's council offices.

Having abandoned the car in the multi-storey car park opposite, Carmichael and Watson clambered up the steep staircase and pressed the intercom button next to the locked door with the small sign indicating that this was the home of Brighterlight.

"Have you ever heard of these people?" Carmichael asked as he waited for a response.

Watson shook his head. "No," he replied. "Can't say I have."

As he finished his sentence, the speaker next to the intercom let out a high-pitched noise before a female voice sprang forth. "Hello, can I help you?" she enquired.

"Hello, this is Inspector Carmichael from Lancashire Police. May we come in, please?"

The door emitted a loud click. "Come through, I'll meet you in reception," uttered the voice.

Before the door mechanism locked once more, Watson pushed it ajar, held it wide for Carmichael, and then followed his boss inside.

In keeping with the rest of the building, the passageway which led through to the reception area was dark, drab and in urgent need of a lick of paint and a fresher-looking carpet. In the corner stood a pathetic-looking artificial Christmas tree which gave every indication that it had seen multiple Christmases, as did the baubles and cheap ornaments arranged rather haphazardly on its sad, drooping branches.

"Not much of an advert for a company attempting to sell home improvement products," Watson remarked derisively.

Carmichael turned his head around and smiled broadly back at his sergeant. "I suspect they don't invite many customers to the office," he replied. "At least, for their sakes, I hope they don't."

As soon as the officers reached the end of the corridor, Carmichael and Watson were welcomed by a casually-dressed, slender brunette in her early thirties with shoulder-length hair and a warm smile. "Hello," the woman greeted them, her right arm stretched forward to shake Carmichael's hand. "I'm the supervisor here at Brighterlight, how can we help you?"

Carmichael returned the supervisor's smile and shook her hand firmly. "I'm Inspector Carmichael and this is my colleague, Sergeant Watson. We'd like to talk to Hannah Ringrose, if that's possible."

"That's me," replied the woman, her smile still shining out from her friendly face. "Is this about Hayley?"

Carmichael nodded. "I know you've already given us a statement, but we'd like to ask you some more questions, if we may."

Hannah Ringrose smiled. "Of course," she remarked. "We don't have much in the way of spare offices here, I'm afraid, but there's a small breakout room over there we can use, if that's OK." As she spoke, Hannah pointed behind Watson to a half-glazed door.

"That will be perfect," Carmichael replied.

Carmichael and Watson entered the room. As Hannah had intimated, the room was indeed small, little more than three metres square, with no windows and just four low, threadbare, soft seats.

"Can I get you some drinks?" Hannah politely enquired, her smile still intact.

"Actually that would be very nice," Carmichael replied. "I'll have a coffee with one sugar, please."

"And I'll have the same," added Watson, with a smile.

Hannah Ringrose scurried out of the room leaving the two officers alone.

"Well she's not what I was expecting," Watson remarked.

Carmichael frowned. "What do you mean?" he enquired, although he had a good idea what his sergeant was thinking.

Watson leant back in his chair. "I was expecting the reading circle to be made up of middle-aged women who looked like librarians. She's certainly a pleasant surprise."

Carmichael laughed. "So don't you think attractive young women read?" he said mockingly.

"I know they read," replied Watson, who didn't appear the least bit embarrassed. "But I didn't expect good-looking women to have to waste their time attending reading circles. It's so…"

"So what?" Carmichael added, when his sergeant appeared to be struggling to find the right word.

"I don't know," Watson continued. "It's what I'd expect bored and frustrated middle-aged housewives to do."

Carmichael shook his head in despair. "You're priceless," he remarked just as the subject of their conversation re-entered the breakout room holding a tray with three plastic cups and a plate of mince pies precariously perched on top.

"The coffees are all the same," Hannah remarked. "And please help yourselves to a mince pie, we've got boxes of them in the office to eat."

Carmichael carefully took two of the cups and passed one over to Watson. "Thank you," he remarked before placing his scalding-hot cup on the small table beside his chair and helping himself to a mince pie from the tray.

"How can I help you?" Hannah Ringrose asked as she sat down opposite Carmichael.

"I'd like to understand more about Hayley Bell," Carmichael replied. "What sort of person is she?"

"I'm probably not the best person to ask," Hannah remarked. "I only know her through the reading group, but I'd say she's a kind, caring and friendly person."

"Not the sort of person to just up and leave then?" Carmichael added.

Hannah shook her head. "No, I'd say that would be way out of character," she replied. "But who knows what's going on in people's lives; maybe she has just run off."

"And when you saw her at the Italian restaurant on Friday," Carmichael continued, "how did she seem to you?"

Hannah shrugged her shoulders. "Just like normal," she replied. "She seemed very happy."

"How long have you been a member of the reading group?" Watson enquired, his mouth releasing a few crumbs from the mince pie he'd just bitten.

"About nine months," Hannah replied, turning her head to face Watson. "Max and I joined together."

"That's Maxine Lowe," Watson confirmed, his attention slightly distracted as he attempted, in vain, to catch more crumbs as they descended from the corner of his mouth, down his front and onto the carpet.

"Yeah," said Hannah who, by the small grin on her face, found Watson's inability to manage to eat and talk at the same time entertaining.

"And how often does the reading group meet up?" Carmichael asked, his eyes darting in Watson's direction to demonstrate his displeasure.

"Once a week," Hannah replied. "We meet on Tuesday evenings at Hayley's house."

"Always at Hayley's?" Carmichael enquired.

"Yes," Hannah replied. "It's quite an atmospheric house, so the group always meets there."

Carmichael nodded. "I can imagine," he remarked. "So which room do you use in the house?"

Hannah chuckled. "Normally it's in either the autumn or the spring room, but we've also been in the summer room a few times, if the book we are talking about is an upbeat, happy sort of read."

"And do you often discuss upbeat books?" Watson enquired.

"Hardly ever," Hannah replied with a wry smile. "And, to be honest, when we do it's usually me that chooses them."

"What about the winter room?" Carmichael asked.

Hannah shook her head. "No, I've never been in the winter room. I think that's Mr Bell's private study. I doubt he lets many people in there."

"Do you know Mr Bell well?" Carmichael asked, latching on to Hannah's previous comment.

"Not really," replied Hannah, as if she was reluctant to say more.

"I believe he's very keen on the arts," Carmichael continued. "Did he never get involved with the reading group?"

For the first time since they'd been in the company of Hannah Ringrose, the demeanour of the young woman seemed to alter to one of nervousness rather than confidence. "No," Hannah replied firmly. "To be honest I've never been that comfortable when he's there. I'm not trying to suggest anything, but he is a bit... well, peculiar."

"How do you mean?" Carmichael probed.

"Well, a bit creepy," Hannah replied. "He's never done anything, and I'm sure he's nothing to do with Hayley's disappearance, but he is a very strange man."

"You don't like him then?" Watson remarked.

Hannah's smile returned to her face, but this time it was a forced smile. "I don't really know him," she replied. "But I have to be honest and say I'm always slightly uncomfortable when he's around."

Carmichael nodded. "I understand that on Friday evening, you and Maxine both took a train from Kirkwood to Blackpool. Why did you do that?"

"We went out on the town," replied Hannah. "We met up with our other halves at a pub just by Barn Lane train station and then we went on to a few clubs in Blackpool."

"So when did you hear about Hayley being missing?" Carmichael continued.

"It was when your colleagues contacted us on Saturday," Hannah replied. "But as I told them, I have no idea what has happened to her."

Carmichael took a sip from his coffee cup. As soon as it hit the back of his throat, he decided he wasn't going to finish it. It was hot, as he liked his coffee, but was most certainly a cheap brand, too cheap for Carmichael to drink. He stood up. "We'll let you get back to your work," he remarked with a smile. "You've been very helpful."

Once again a natural beaming smile returned to Hannah's face. "If I think of anything that may be helpful I'll let you know, Inspector Carmichael," she remarked. "But I really have no idea what happened to Hayley on Friday evening."

Carmichael nodded and headed towards the door.

"What book is the group reading at the moment?" Watson asked.

"We've not got another meeting now until the first week in January," Hannah replied. "But the book we're going to discuss then is called *The Husband's Secret*, it's by an author called Liane Moriarty."

"Is it any good?" Watson enquired.

"I've not started it yet," Hannah admitted.

"And who chose that one?" Carmichael asked. "Actually it was Hayley, I think," she replied.

Chapter 14

"What did you make of Hannah Ringrose?" Carmichael asked, once he and Watson were safely inside the car.

"She's a good-looking girl," replied Watson, without any hesitation.

Carmichael raised his eyebrows and slowly shook his head. "Is that all you've got to say about her?" he enquired despairingly.

Watson shrugged his shoulders. "I'm not sure she told us that much, other than she finds Mr Bell a bit creepy," he replied. "Just like Rachel did."

"Yes," Carmichael agreed with a sage-like nod of his head. "He does appear to have that effect on young women."

"The other thing that really struck me," Watson added, "was how unconcerned she was about her friend being missing. As she's a fellow member of the reading group I expected her to show some anxiety, but she didn't. Although with the difference in their ages, maybe they just aren't that close."

Carmichael shook his head. "You're right, Marc, she did seem quite blasé about Hayley's vanishing act, but I don't buy that they weren't close. I think she's more likely to be unconcerned because she knows Hayley is safe somewhere. That would be my take on it."

"Possibly," said Watson, although his facial expression suggested he wasn't convinced.

"Anyway," continued Carmichael, "let's go and talk with Maxine Lowe. Maybe she will show a little more anxiety about the plight of Mrs Bell. If she's a primary school teacher she's sure to be a more caring soul, don't you think?"

Watson frowned and started up the engine. "Under no circumstances would I describe most of my old school teachers as caring," he remarked pointedly. "So I'll reserve judgement on Maxine until we meet her, if you don't mind."

Carmichael smiled. "Very wise," he replied, before turning his head to look out of the side window, signifying to Watson that he wanted to think rather than talk.

* * * *

"My guess is that they're coming to you next," said Hannah down the telephone. "Just thought I'd give you a heads-up."

Maxine Lowe shuffled nervously as she listened to her friend. "I think I should tell them," she whispered, trying hard to prevent her partner hearing what she was saying by facing away from him. "It might be important."

Hannah Ringrose sighed deeply. "It's up to you, but if you take my advice you'll just keep quiet about it," she replied irritably. "It's almost certainly irrelevant and you'll have to do loads of explaining to Pete if it comes out."

Maxine considered what her friend was saying for a few moments. "Maybe you're right," she conceded reluctantly. "But I'm not comfortable about it, Hannah. What if it is important?"

"My advice to you," added Hannah calmly, "is to do what I did. Just smile sweetly and answer their questions, but don't offer up anything else."

* * * *

Deep down, Penny understood why Steve felt he had to go to work. She'd been married to a policeman long enough to know how things worked within the force and she also knew what Hewitt was like. However, she was still pretty peeved at being left once more to be nursemaid and the main recipient of the comments and complaints from someone who wasn't even related to her. Nevertheless, Penny was determined not to allow Audrey to wear her down and, buoyed by the fact that Steve had promised faithfully to leave the investigation in the hands of his team after today, she resolved to battle through the day with a positive smile and sunny disposition, regardless of what Audrey threw at her.

Her resolve had been first tested when the old lady arrived at the breakfast table mid-morning. "I hope you don't mind me saying," she said in her thick Scottish accent, "but that mattress on my bed is very hard. Would it be possible to swap it for one a little softer?"

Penny took a deep breath and manufactured the best smile she could under the circumstances. "I'm not sure what we can do about that, Audrey," she replied as calmly and politely as possible. "Let me think for a few moments."

"Also," continued Audrey, totally oblivious to the dumbfounded looks on the faces of Penny and her two eldest children, who like Penny had already eaten, "would you mind if we had the radio on while we eat breakfast. I do like to listen to Ken Bruce in the morning. He's no Jimmy Young, but I do like him."

Penny ignored the childrens' looks of trepidation, switched on the old radio that she'd had in the kitchen for years, and twiddled with the tuning knob to find Radio 2.

"There you go," she remarked in triumph when she found the station just as Ken Bruce announced it was time for *Popmaster*.

"I think there are too many questions about modern music on *Popmaster*," Audrey proclaimed. "If they'd stick to music no later than the Sixties it would be so much better."

"What would you like for breakfast today?" Penny enquired, trying hard to change the subject.

"What have you got?" replied Audrey.

Penny took another deep breath to maintain her poise. This was the exact same response she'd had from Audrey the day before when she'd asked the self-same question. "Well, we've got cereal, toast, I've got some eggs and bacon and there's also some muesli."

At the sound of the word muesli, Jemma shook her head rapidly. "Sorry, there's no muesli left," she remarked apologetically. "I had the last out of the box."

"Do you know, dear," Audrey replied, her tiny dark eyes fixed in Penny's general direction. "I'll just have a fried egg sandwich this morning, like I always have."

Penny smiled. "No problem," she remarked.

"And a cup of tea, too," Audrey added. "If that's not too much bother. One sugar and maybe not as strong as the ones you've made me before, as I don't like strong tea."

Penny could feel her neck getting warm, but she was determined to retain her composure. "No problem," she remarked for the second time before turning towards the cooker.

"What is that infernal game you're playing, child?" Audrey piped up as soon as Penny's back was turned.

"It's called Candy Crush, Great Aunt," Natalie replied. "You have to match three candies in a row, which makes them disappear and you get points. Then, once you've got a certain amount of points, you move to a new level."

"I'm not sure what purpose that has?" Audrey remarked disparagingly.

"It's just a game, Audrey," replied Penny, her voice showing signs of her resolve cracking. "It's very popular."

"Do you want a go?" Natalie enquired, moving her tablet towards her elderly relative.

"Maybe later," replied Audrey, somewhat dismissively. "I'd like to listen to Ken Bruce now, if that's alright with everyone."

Penny cracked an egg and, with significantly greater vigour than normal, despatched the contents of the egg shell into the frying pan. "Just so I've got this correct," she added, "you like your eggs well cooked on both sides but the yolk still runny?"

"That's correct, dear," replied Audrey. "But I just want one egg. If I have two it will play havoc with me later."

****

Maxine Lowe's small terraced house was located in a short cul-de-sac just off Southport Road, one of the busiest roads in Kirkwood.

"Do you know, I didn't even realise this road existed," Watson proclaimed as he slowed the car down to try and find a parking space. "I must have driven past it thousands of times over the years, too."

"Just stick it over there, Marc," instructed Carmichael, who pointed to a smallish gap between two parked cars.

Had he been alone, Watson would have probably driven a little further down the road to try and find a bigger space, but he wasn't about to tell that to the boss, so pulled up beyond the space and then slowly but carefully manoeuvred the car back into the small gap.

"Perfect," remarked Carmichael, who'd been impressed by the apparent ease with which his sergeant had managed to execute the tight parallel-parking task. "Now, let's go and see what Maxine Lowe is able to tell us."

As the two officers strolled up the short path leading to the house, a young woman's face appeared in the window surrounded by flashing Christmas lights.

"That must be Maxine," Carmichael remarked. "At least she's home."

There was no need for them to ring the doorbell, as the woman in the window opened the front door before either of them had the chance to arrive.

"Can I help you?" the woman remarked, the slight reddening on her young fresh face indicating she was flustered.

Carmichael smiled in an attempt to ease her anxiety. "We're from Lancashire Police," he advised her while at the same time holding up his ID card. "We'd like to ask you a few questions about Hayley Bell."

The young woman brushed her long, blonde hair away from her eyes with the palm of her left hand and held it there. "Of course," she replied rather nervously, "come in!"

Carmichael and Watson walked in through the front door which led directly into a tiny living room, only big enough to hold a two-seater settee, one rather battered armchair and a tall, but decidedly thin, Christmas tree, decked with a multitude of flashing fairy lights and decorations. In the far corner of the room, steep wooden stairs led upwards and facing them, an open doorway led through to an even smaller kitchen.

"Sorry about the mess," Maxine apologised, as she quickly gathered up a mound of folded ironing piled on the settee. "Can I get you some tea?"

"No, thank you," replied Carmichael, who attempted to make himself comfortable on the badly-sprung armchair. "We won't take too much of your time, we just have a few questions we'd like to ask you."

Realising there were only two places available, both of which were on the settee, Watson stretched out his arm in the direction of the sofa. "Please, do sit down, Mrs Lowe," he said.

"I can get a chair from the kitchen," Maxine replied, taking a step towards the open door.

"No," remarked Watson firmly. "I'm absolutely fine standing."

Maxine Lowe stopped in her tracks and then quickly took the few small steps to the sofa and plonked her tiny frame down.

"Actually, it's Miss," she added, rather apologetically, as she looked up into Watson's face. "Pete and I live together, but we're not married."

Watson smiled. "Sorry, my mistake," he replied.

Carmichael waited a few seconds to allow Maxine, who looked extremely agitated, to make herself as relaxed as she could, before starting his questioning.

"Tell me how long you've known Hayley Bell and how you came to join the reading group?" he enquired.

"Not that long," Maxine replied. "It was in early April of this year when Hannah and I joined."

"And did you know any of the members before you joined?" Carmichael added.

"Oh no," replied Maxine, still acting as if she was terrified. "I met Hayley in the local library one lunchtime, we got talking, she was very nice and well, the upshot was, she told me she was in a reading group and asked me if I'd like to join."

"And you brought Hannah with you," Watson interjected.

"Yes," replied Maxine. "Hannah and I were at school together and she's a big reader, so I thought it might be good if we both joined."

"And you like it in the group," Watson added.

"Like it, she's obsessed with it," remarked a tall, dark-skinned young man who entered the room through the kitchen door. "Every Tuesday and every Thursday evening, she's there without fail."

"This is Pete, my boyfriend," Maxine confirmed before adding, "These are police officers, Pete. They're here about the disappearance of Hayley from my reading group."

"If she's any sense she'll have done a bunk from that weirdo she lives with," Pete remarked, before heading over to the front door. "I'll see you at about seven, Max," he then added before nodding quickly at Watson and making his exit out of the house.

"He's on afternoons this week," Maxine explained. "He works at the printing place over in Rainford Road."

"Still working on Christmas Eve?" Carmichael remarked, his head swivelling as he spoke to make eye contact with Watson. "It's comforting to know it's not just the police who have to work right up to Christmas, Sergeant Watson."

Watson smiled back, but didn't bother to respond.

Maxine smiled back too, albeit a nervous smile. " Pete's company have a big print job on that's a few days behind schedule, so they're all having to work right up to Christmas this year and, to make sure it's finished, be back again on Thursday."

Carmichael turned to face Maxine. "What sort of person is Hayley?" he asked.

"She's a lovely lady," replied Maxine. "I really like her and I'm very worried about her because she's not the sort of person to just up and leave. She's far too dependable."

"I thought you didn't know her that well?" Carmichael added.

"I don't really," replied Maxine. "But I cannot see her running off without telling someone."

"Like her husband," Carmichael added.

Maxine paused for a few seconds as if she was pondering how to respond. "Yes, she'd surely have told him if she was going away," she said.

"Maybe it was him she was running away from?" Carmichael suggested. "What did Pete mean when he called him a weirdo?"

Maxine, for the first time, smiled. "Ignore Pete," she said. "He's never been there. I've described it to him, so he thinks it's a mad house."

Carmichael smiled. "It's certainly different," he confirmed. "As is Duncan Bell. What do you make of him?"

Maxine's gaze dropped to the floor and she shrugged her tiny shoulders. "I've only spoken to him on a few occasions," she replied. "He seems OK, I suppose."

Carmichael's eyebrows rose. "I got the impression Hannah wasn't that keen on him," he remarked.

"Well Hannah's often very quick to make judgements," Maxine replied. "I prefer to wait until I know someone better."

Carmichael nodded. "So you've no idea what might have happened to Hayley," he continued.

Maxine shook her head. "No, I'm afraid I don't."

"When you saw her at the Italian restaurant on Friday, how did she seem?" Watson asked.

Again, Maxine shrugged her shoulders. "Just normal," she replied. "She seemed quite relaxed and happy. In fact she seemed really happy, come to think of it."

"Hannah told us that you and she took a train together from Kirkwood on Friday after the meal," Carmichael remarked.

"Yes, we went out on the town in Blackpool," replied Maxine. "We met up with Pete and Hannah's boyfriend, Andy, at a pub close to Barn Lane train station and then we went clubbing."

Carmichael paused for a few seconds before standing up. "Thanks for your time, Miss Lowe," he said. "If you do hear anything from Hayley, or if you think of something that you feel may be relevant, please call either myself or one of the team at Kirkwood police station."

"Of course," replied Maxine, who shot up from the settee, her face showing clearly her relief that they were leaving. "I'll show you out."

As the two officers followed Maxine over the few short paces to the door, Carmichael stopped for a moment.

"There is just one thing more I'd like to ask you," he said in a calm, quiet voice. "Your boyfriend mentioned that you go to the reading circle on Tuesdays and Thursdays. But Hannah told us that the group only meets on Tuesdays. What happens on Thursdays?"

Maxine's cheeks flushed and her expression left Watson and Carmichael in no doubt that the question had made the young woman feel decidedly uncomfortable.

"You're right, Inspector, the reading group does just meet on Tuesdays," Maxine confirmed. "On Thursdays I tend to stay late at school to prepare the following week's lessons and then, afterwards I'll usually go out for a drink with a few other teachers."

From the questioning expressions on the two officers' faces, it was clear to Maxine that she needed to elaborate more.

"Pete's quite possessive," she added rather uncomfortably. "He doesn't like me socialising with my colleagues when he's not there, so I've been telling him I'm at the reading group."

Carmichael smiled. "To be honest, Miss Lowe, any secrets you have from your boyfriend are no concern of ours," he replied, to allay the clearly mortified young woman's feelings. "As long as there's nothing you're keeping from us which may have a bearing on Hayley Bell's disappearance, then I don't need to know the details of what you get up to on Thursdays."

Maxine smiled momentarily, but looked nervous as she watched the two officers leave her house, before closing the door behind them.

"So, on Thursday evenings she plays away with one of her colleagues at school," remarked Watson insensitively, as soon as the pair were inside his car.

"That's certainly how it looks," replied Carmichael with a faint disparaging shake of his head. "Not that it's any of our business, Marc."

Chapter 15

DS Cooper replaced the handset of the phone in its cradle and leaned back in his chair. "I don't know how they did it," he remarked with astonishment, "but Hewitt and Carmichael must have broken all the records for galvanising public support. I've now spoken to almost everyone who was on that train on Friday evening."

"So what conclusions have you come to?" Rachel asked excitedly.

Cooper rubbed his chin. "Unfortunately, I'm as baffled now as I was last night. It's as if Hayley Bell vanished as soon as she went through the doors of the second carriage at 10.32 on Friday evening," he replied disconsolately.

"What makes you say that?" Rachel enquired.

"As I say, I've spoken to sixteen of the passengers and not one remembers seeing a woman fitting Hayley's description either getting on or getting off the train," said Cooper. "I've talked to at least three people from each of the four carriages and nobody remembers seeing Hayley."

Rachel Dalton gazed back at Cooper with a look of bewilderment. "That's impossible," she replied.

Cooper shrugged his shoulders. "I know," he said. "And what's even more bewildering is that, including Hayley, I'm now convinced there were twenty people who got on that train at either Kirkwood or one of the four stations between Kirkwood and Southport, but I'm equally certain that twenty-one people got off and none of them was Hayley."

****

Carmichael and Watson had grabbed a sandwich from a cake shop just around the corner from Lesley Saxham's house and had parked up to have a quick lunch before calling at her door.

"What did you make of Maxine, then?" Carmichael asked, referring to the young woman they'd just spoken to.

Watson took another bite of his sandwich while he considered his answer. "Maxine Lowe certainly seemed more concerned about Hayley than Hannah Ringrose," he replied. "But I'm not sure either of them knows what happened to Hayley."

Carmichael nodded. "They seem an odd pair," he remarked. "I know they are about the same age, but I'd never have put them together as likely friends. Hannah seems so confident and assured, while Maxine appears to be a complete wreck."

Watson laughed. "Maybe it's their different characters that make them so chummy. You know what they say about opposites attracting."

Carmichael bit into his sandwich. "Maybe," he replied, although his tone suggested he wasn't convinced.

"I'm more surprised about Maxine having some secretive liaison with one of the teachers every Thursday evening," Watson continued. "I'd not have put her down as the unfaithful type."

"And what does an unfaithful person look like, Marc?" replied Carmichael rhetorically. "But I get what you mean, I suppose."

"And Maxine didn't actually go out of her way to deny anything improper," added Watson. "That's what I'd expect most people would do in her circumstances."

Carmichael nodded. "True," he conceded. "But everyone's different, I guess," he added.

For the next few minutes the two officers finished their sandwiches in silence, each one taking the opportunity to deliberate on the events of the morning.

"I just hope Cooper and Rachel are making more headway than us," Carmichael finally said as he screwed up the empty paper bag in his hand and stuffed it in the pocket on the door. "Anyway, let's go and talk with Lesley Saxham. Maybe she can give us more of a clue about what happened to Hayley."

* * * *

Rachel Dalton had spent the morning gathering as much information as she could about Duncan Bell and his two previous marriages.

She'd managed to discover that he'd married twenty-one year old Pamela Newsome when he was thirty-five. The couple were married for five years before they divorced. Then, just under a year after his divorce from Pamela, Duncan Bell had married for a second time, to a twenty-three year old called Claudette Cotterill. They were together for nine years and had two children, James and Suzanne. Claudette had died from a brain haemorrhage when she was just thirty-two, as Norfolk George had correctly informed Carmichael. Shortly afterwards Duncan, then fifty-one, had wedded Hayley, who was spookily also in her early twenties when they married.

With Bell's second wife dying of natural causes, there wasn't any police record of her death, so, conscious of Carmichael's keen interest in the alleged life insurance policy, Rachel was doing a check to find out if such a policy had existed and, if so, to ascertain how much Bell received after Claudette had died. However, by lunchtime, and much to her frustration, she'd heard nothing.

"Apart from all his wives being in their early twenties and much younger than him when he married them, I've not found anything too remarkable about Duncan Bell," Rachel announced. "Although Duncan certainly doesn't let the grass grow between marriages."

"What do you mean?" Cooper enquired.

"Well there was less than a year between him divorcing wife one and marrying wife two," Rachel replied, "and, as the boss mentioned yesterday, it wasn't even six months after wife two died before Bell married Hayley."

Cooper considered Rachel's remark for a few seconds. "It does seem quite quick," he conceded. "But it's not unlawful. I guess he just got over them quickly."

Keen to have a break, Rachel stretched then stood up. "Do you want anything from the canteen?" she enquired.

Cooper shook his head. "No, I'm fine," he replied. "I'm going to shoot off in a minute to have a chat with the train driver again. I'm hoping he can shed some light on how it could be that more people got off the train than had boarded, because it's beating me, that's for sure."

Rachel smiled. "Have fun," she remarked light-heartedly as she walked past Cooper's desk.

"I will," replied Cooper sullenly.

Rachel was just a couple of paces from the door when Cooper lifted his head from the notes in front of him. "Have you heard from Duncan Bell about the life insurance policy on Hayley?" he asked.

Rachel stopped in her tracks and turned back to face him. "No," she replied. "He's not called me and Carmichael's not been in touch, so I guess the boss still hasn't heard anything from Bell, either."

"In that case," Cooper added, "I suggest you make contact with Bell again to get the details. At the briefing last night, Carmichael seemed very keen to know what's in that policy and was more than a little annoyed about Bell's failure to call him. If I were you, I'd follow that up as a priority. I'd imagine the boss will be less than enamoured if he doesn't have all the details by the time of our next briefing."

Rachel gave a faint-but-knowing nod of the head.

"Good point," she replied. "I'll make that my first job after lunch."

****

Lesley Saxham greeted Carmichael and Watson warmly. "Whatever I can do to help, I will," she announced once the two officers had introduced themselves, had been ushered into her cosy, warm living room and had been provided with a hot cup of tea and some chocolate digestive biscuits. "I'm very concerned about Hayley," she continued, as her piercing bright-blue eyes, amplified by her thick glasses, fixed their stare on Carmichael's face. "She's certainly not the sort of person to leave suddenly without telling anyone. She's far too level-headed and I cannot believe she'd ever deliberately create a situation whereby her friends and family would be sick with worry."

"Then what do you think happened?" Carmichael enquired.

"I can only conclude that something sinister has happened to her," replied Lesley, in a way that suggested she'd thought long and hard about the situation, but, at the same time, was uneasy having to admit her conclusion. "Is that how you see it, Inspector?"

Carmichael gazed back at the rather untidily-dressed, middle-aged woman. "Obviously we cannot rule that out as a possibility," he replied candidly. "However, we've absolutely no evidence to suggest any foul play, so we are continuing to investigate every possible scenario."

"Of course you are," replied Lesley. "And quite right, too."

Although they'd only met a few minutes earlier, and she was clearly not the most glamorous of women, Carmichael could not help feeling warmth towards Lesley Saxham. In contrast with Hannah Ringrose, Lesley demonstrated obvious concern about her missing friend and unlike Maxine Lowe, she appeared to be able to have a rational conversation without

102

any nervousness. In fact Carmichael's immediate impression of Lesley was that she was undoubtedly an intelligent, articulate, pragmatic individual, and the sort of person the Inspector tended to admire.

"Tell me a little about the reading circle?" Carmichael asked. "I believe there are just six of you in the group?"

"Yes," Lesley replied. "There are just six of us, all ladies, with of course a shared passion for reading. However, we all tend to like very different books, which, to be honest, makes for a healthy debate about the books we're reading and even more about what the next one should be."

Carmichael smiled. "And I suspect the fact that the six of you are of different ages makes the discussions even more interesting," he added.

"Absolutely," remarked Lesley with a massive grin on her face. "There are such varied tastes within the circle. The two youngsters always chose modern, what I would call throw-away reads; chic-lit and books that have recently been adapted for TV or cinema being the norm. Hayley and Francis, who are a good few years older than Hannah and Max, more often than not, select murder mysteries. Francis favours the grittier authors like Mo Hayder and Patricia Cornwell, while Hayley is into the cosy murder mysteries, with more of a plot and less blood and gore."

"And what about you and Belinda Bishop?" Carmichael enquired. "What are your tastes?"

"We're a little older still," replied Lesley with a warm smile. "So we tend to gravitate to completely different genres. I love reading the classics; Dickens, Hardy, the Brontes or the war poets like Frost and Owen. Belinda's more attracted to nonfiction; real crime stories, history books and biographies being her main penchant."

"Would you say that Hayley is closer to Francis Scott than she is to either Hannah, Maxine, Belinda or yourself?" Carmichael asked.

Lesley ran her hand through her wiry, grey hair. "I've never really thought about that," she replied. "We all get on fine, but I suppose we do tend to function in pairs, driven, I suspect, by age, with Hannah and Max, then Belinda and I, and Francis and Hayley. So, to answer your question, I'd say, yes, Hayley is closer to Francis than any of the rest of the circle."

Carmichael glanced over at Watson before continuing the discussion.

"And how long have you known Hayley Bell?" he enquired once he'd returned his gaze upon Lesley Saxham.

"Well I've known her since before she was married to Duncan," Lesley replied. "So over twenty-five years. She was just plain Hayley Frazer back then."

"That's right," Carmichael remarked, keen to pursue this line of discussion. "I was aware that Hayley was the nanny to Duncan's children by his second wife. Did you know the second Mrs Bell well?"

"Fairly well," replied Lesley rather wistfully. "Claudette's death was so sudden and so tragic."

"So I believe," Carmichael replied. "But I'm told Mr Bell married Hayley fairly rapidly. Is that correct?"

Lesley Saxham's eyes widened and she nodded as if to place some extra weight behind what she was about to say. "Within months," she confirmed. "It was frowned upon by many in the community back then, but, in fairness, they've been together, devoted to one another, for over twenty-five years, so I think the cynics of the time have been proved wrong."

"And is that what they are," Carmichael enquired, "a devoted couple?"

"Absolutely," replied Lesley without any hesitation. "That's exactly how I'd describe them."

"Did they ever argue or seem less than devoted?" Watson asked, his expression suggesting he didn't buy the fact that they could be so constant in their affections for such a long time.

"Never to my knowledge," replied Lesley. "But, of course, people like Hayley and Duncan wouldn't wish to make public any problems. That's not their way."

"So they could have had arguments?" Watson continued.

"They could, I suppose," replied Lesley. "But, as I say, these would have been behind closed doors and private. There's no way they would allow others to get a glimpse of any problems between them."

Carmichael smiled. "I understand," he remarked sagely. "And, in my experience, they're certainly not unusual in that respect. However, due to the nature of this enquiry and the need to locate Mrs Bell quickly, I'd hope you would call us should you remember any incident between them."

Lesley nodded and rolled her eyes. "Of course," she replied, as if the question was an insult. "But, if you think that Duncan has any involvement in Hayley's disappearance then I think you are mistaken. Duncan worships Hayley. There is no way at all he'd want her harmed."

Carmichael smiled again. "I'm not saying he did," he remarked reassuringly. "However any small disagreement may have a bearing on this investigation, so please tell me or one of my officers if you recall anything that may help us find Hayley."

As soon as he'd finished his sentence, Carmichael stood up to indicate the interview was over.

"Naturally," Lesley replied before rising herself and ushering the two officers towards the door. "I'll think long and hard, but I'm certain there's nothing I'm aware of that will help you, I'm afraid."

For a third time, Carmichael smiled before heading off towards the door, with Sergeant Watson following a few yards behind.

"Have a nice Christmas, gentlemen," said Lesley as she watched the officers stroll down her drive.

"You too," replied Watson, who half turned as he spoke and offered a friendly smile.

Chapter 16

Rachel Dalton was only away at lunch for twenty minutes, but when she arrived back at her desk, Cooper had already left to re-interview the train driver and had scribbled a note and left it propped up against her computer screen.

Hi Rachel,
After I've spoken to the driver I'll probably get down to Barton Bridge and have a look around. I think Hayley may have got off there.
See you later – and don't forget to chase Duncan Bell for details of the life insurance he took out on Hayley.
Paul

Rachel read the note before screwing up the scrap of paper up and throwing it in the bin at the side of her desk.

"I suppose I'd better chase up Duncan Bell," she muttered, picking up the phone.

* * * *

"I'm not sure any of the three women we've spoken to so far has any idea what happened to Hayley Bell," Watson remarked as soon as the two officers were inside his car.

Carmichael put his hands behind his head and stared in front of him. "You may be right," he replied before puffing out his cheeks. "What did you think of Lesley Saxham?"

Watson gave a faint shrug of his shoulders and the ends of his mouth turned down slightly. "She's pleasant enough, I suppose," he remarked rather nonplussed. "I liked her Christmas decorations more than the ones at Maxine Lowe's house and that miserable excuse of a tree at Hannah's office, but, to be honest, she wasn't much help. Mind you, in my view, neither were the other two we saw this morning."

Carmichael allowed himself a small smile. "I agree with you about the Christmas decorations and I would agree that they may not know what has happened to Hayley," Carmichael replied. "However, after speaking to the three ladies, I do feel I now know more about Hayley."

Watson said nothing, but his expression clearly indicated that he wasn't so convinced.

"But what seems certain," Carmichael continued, "is that if Hayley has deliberately done a runner then it's totally out of character."

Watson nodded. "I'd agree with that," he remarked. "I wasn't sure before, but I'm now starting to think Lesley Saxham may be right and something sinister has happened to Hayley."

Carmichael, his hands still clasped behind his head, turned his head to face his sergeant. "For some reason my gut tells me otherwise. But if she has fled, the question is what is she fleeing from or to?"

Watson started the engine. "Do you think it's her husband?" he enquired.

"I'm not sure, is the honest truth, Marc," Carmichael conceded, his hands now by his side. "If it is because of him, why now, just a few days before Christmas?"

Watson nodded as he listened to what his boss was saying. "Maybe something happened that pushed her over the edge," he suggested.

"Maybe," continued Carmichael. "But, if she has run off, I find it very hard to believe that none of her dear friends know about it."

"Me too," Watson replied. "But based on what Lesley just told us, Hayley's closer to Francis Scott than any of the others. So my guess is that Francis Scott is the one we really need to talk to."

"I fully agree," replied Carmichael with some certainty. "I reckon she will know."

Watson nodded. "But she's down in Devon, so it's not going to be easy to interview her until she's back."

"If need be I'll get the local police down there to bring her in to the nearest station and interview her over the phone," Carmichael added. "But let's get over and talk to Belinda Bishop first. You never know, she may be the person Hayley confided in."

* * * *

"Hello, this is Duncan Bell. I'm so sorry I'm not here to take your call. If you'd kindly leave your name and telephone number I'll call you back as soon as I am able," said the recording of Bell's voice on the telephone answer machine.

"Hello, this is DC Dalton at Kirkwood police station," said Rachel as slowly and as clearly as she could. "I'll try you on your mobile phone, but if we haven't spoken by the time you hear this message, can you please call me?"

Rachel sighed as she replaced the receiver and searched in her notebook for the mobile number she'd written down when she'd met Duncan Bell two days earlier.

* * * *

Belinda Bishop and her husband, Tarquin, lived in a grand, brick house surrounded by a well maintained garden, four doors away from the Bells.

Both well into their seventies, the Bishops were now retired. For over thirty years Tarquin Bishop had been in banking and had given up work early with a handsome pension. His wife had worked for HMRC, where she'd managed a team of fifty people involved in ensuring large businesses were not evading their full tax liabilities, a position which had gained her a reputation as a no-nonsense, effective operator.

Based upon the reports they'd heard from Cooper and Dalton, who'd met Belinda on Saturday, Carmichael and Watson were fully expecting Belinda Bishop to be an outspoken and potentially difficult individual to interview. And in that respect the two officers were not disappointed.

"Have you people not found Hayley yet?" Belinda announced loudly as soon as Carmichael introduced himself on the doorstep. "She disappeared on Friday evening, that's nearly three bloody days ago. You should have found her by now!"

Carmichael took a deep breath. "May we come inside?" he asked, as calmly as he could.

Belinda, nostrils flaring wide and head tilted back, threw open the door. "Go through to the lounge," she instructed. "Tarquin's already in there."

"Tarquin?" Watson enquired.

"My husband, of course," snapped Belinda, as if the question had been asked by an imbecile. "But God only knows why you're wasting precious time here. You should be out there finding the person who's taken poor Hayley."

Carmichael could feel his muscles tense, and the hairs on his arm bristled as he listened to the rude proclamations of the insufferable woman. However, he decided, for now, to allow Belinda to remain unchecked; a situation he wasn't going to allow to last too long once he and Watson were ensconced in her lounge.

* * * *

Cooper's conversation with the train driver lasted no more than ten minutes and, until his last question, it yielded nothing new in the way of information. However, something the driver said suddenly gave Cooper an idea, one that emphasised even more the need for him to get to Barton Bank as soon as possible.

Excited by the prospect of having a plausible reason for the disparity of passengers alighting and departing the train that evening, he rushed to his beat-up Volvo to make the twenty-minute drive to the small rural Lancashire village.

* * * *

In keeping with Watson's earlier observation, the improvement in the quality of Christmas decorations continued. Belinda's eight-foot spruce pine dominated her large entrance hall and eclipsed, by a country mile, anything Carmichael and Watson had previously observed that day. The impressive tree was complemented by tasteful and most-obviously-expensive, colour co-ordinated baubles, meticulously arranged on the bushy branches of the sweet-smelling pine.

"Nice tree," Watson remarked, as they walked past and into the lounge.

By the expression on her face, Belinda clearly welcomed the compliment, but her focus still remained on Hayley and her clear view of the police's inactivity, rather than the distraction of Christmas.

"So, tell me, what have you chaps uncovered?" she remarked brusquely, even before the officers had managed to do much more than acknowledge her husband, who remained seated in a large armchair.

"Good afternoon, Mr Bishop," said Carmichael, ignoring the discourteous comment made by Belinda and stretching out his hand in the direction of the still-seated, old gentleman.

"I'm DI Carmichael and this is my colleague, Sergeant Watson."

Tarquin Bishop rose from his chair, smiled briefly, shook Carmichael's hand warmly, and then, after nodding at Watson, returned the backside of his green corduroy trousers to the comfort of his armchair.

"You haven't answered my question," remarked Belinda, the indignation clear in her voice. "What progress have you made in finding Hayley?"

Carmichael looked around for a suitable place to seat himself.

"Not on the recamier," shouted Belinda, just as Watson was about to rest his behind on the crimson upholstery of the backless sofa. "It's an air loom, 200 years old and only recently restored. Sit on the davenport over there."

With a firm outstretched arm Belinda pointed directly at the sofa to her right. Dutifully Watson did as he was told, leaving Carmichael to sit in one of the many vacant seats in the room before responding to her earlier question. "I fully understand your concern, Mrs Bishop," he said in a calm-but-firm voice. "However, I think you'll find our conversation will be much more fruitful if you allow us to follow normal practices in these matters."

"Meaning what exactly?" replied Belinda sharply.

"Meaning we ask the questions and you provide the answers," Carmichael continued. "In my experience that's much more productive."

It was evident by her resentful expression that Belinda Bishop wasn't used to being told what to do, but Carmichael's words appeared to do the trick and she sat down without making any further comment.

"Have you known the Bells long?" Carmichael enquired.

"Donkey's years," replied Belinda. "Tarquin was Duncan's manager when he worked at Martins Bank in Kirkwood."

"Martins Bank?" Watson replied. "I've never heard of them."

"They were acquired by Barclays," Belinda replied, "in the early Seventies as I recall."

"Sixty-nine it was, dear," interrupted Tarquin. "All the staff were told it was a merger, but we all became Barclays. And it was the worst thing they could have done, in my opinion."

"So you knew Duncan Bell when he was married to his first wife?" Carmichael added.

"Even before that," Tarquin replied. "In fact, I was a guest at all three of his weddings. Isn't that right, Belinda?"

Belinda Bishop rolled her eyes skyward. "I'm not sure what relevance this has to Hayley's disappearance," she remarked acidly.

"So, the Bells have been long-standing friends of yours?" Carmichael continued.

"Well Belinda and Hayley are still very pally," Tarquin announced, "but I've had nothing to do with that man for years. Of course, I feel sorry for him and hope everything works out, and Hayley's found safe and well, but I'll not be going over to comfort him, that's for sure."

"So you don't get on," Watson remarked.

"No," replied Tarquin, sharply. "We damn well don't."

"Why is that?" Carmichael enquired.

"Because I found out that when Emily, my niece, was just seventeen and over here on holiday, that bloody Duncan seduced her," replied Tarquin angrily. "He must have been in his fifties then, too."

Taken aback at what he'd just heard, Carmichael turned his head in Belinda's direction.

"It was a long time ago, Tarquin," Belinda replied. "And Emily was just as much to blame. I've always believed him when he said she led him on and, let's face it, dear Emily's done little in her life afterwards to suggest she's a shrinking violet."

"It's not the bloody point," Tarquin responded. "She was my brother's daughter and in my charge. That excuse of a man took advantage of her. Thank God she wasn't made pregnant as a result."

Still shocked by what he'd heard, Carmichael remained looking at Belinda. "Was this when Duncan and Hayley were married?"

"Yes," replied Belinda. "It was just a year or so into the marriage. I think Duncan was still coming to terms with the death of Claudette and during the first two or three years of their marriage I think Duncan and Hayley did have some problems. But they worked through them and have been happily married for twenty-odd years now."

"Has Mr Bell had many affairs?" Watson enquired.

"No," replied Belinda swiftly. "To my knowledge that was the only one."

"Nonsense," Tarquin interrupted. "The man was always at it when he was married to poor Pamela and just because Emily is the only girl he's been caught out with since, it doesn't mean that he was faithful to Claudette, and who knows if he's had other affairs while he's been with Hayley."

"Does Hayley know about her husband and Emily?" Carmichael enquired.

Tarquin laughed. "Bloody well right she does," he replied. "After all, it was poor Hayley who caught them together in his precious winter room."

Carmichael and Watson exchanged a quick glance, both clearly intrigued by what they were being told. However, Carmichael was keen to bring the conversation back to Friday evening and to try and understand why Hayley had gone missing. "I understand that you caught a train to Moulton Bank on Friday after the meal in Kirkwood," he remarked. "Why did you do that given that you live in Much Martin? Why didn't you catch the same train as Hayley?"

113

"I stayed over at my sister's house," replied Belinda. "I try and get over at least once a week. She's got Parkinson's and she's finding it difficult these days."

"I see," replied Carmichael. "What time did you come home?"

"Well, it was at about ten the following morning," Belinda continued. "I was going to stay a bit longer, but I received the call from Duncan saying that Hayley had not arrived home, so I jumped in a taxi and went straight to their house. I was there with Lesley when your other colleagues called."

"You say they are a happy couple," Carmichael continued. "So, in your opinion, Hayley would have no reason to abscond?"

"None at all," replied Belinda. "I don't know what has happened, but she certainly would never leave Duncan."

"Do you agree?" Carmichael remarked, his question aimed at Tarquin.

"I honestly don't know," he replied. "But if she has buggered off, I certainly wouldn't blame her. The man's an arse!"

"Do be quiet," interjected Belinda, clearly exasperated with her husband. "Hayley did not make off, I'm certain of it, and…" the emphasis Belinda placed upon that word suggesting strongly she was about to let rip, once more, with a pronouncement in keeping with her character, "… I hope, Inspector Carmichael, you've abandoned the notion that Duncan has any involvement in Hayley's disappearance."

Carmichael took a deep breath. "Mrs Bishop," he said, his raised voice demonstrating his irritation, "I am conducting a missing person enquiry and it's paramount that we investigate all avenues. I fully appreciate you are concerned about the wellbeing of your friend; however, that does not entitle you to be rude and obstructive. For the final time, please can you just answer our questions?"

"Well said," remarked Tarquin, who evidently enjoyed seeing his wife admonished. "It's about time someone else, other than me, told you to shut up."

Although the expression on her face indicated she was outraged at being reprimanded by Carmichael, Belinda did as she was told and kept her mouth shut.

As if to emphasise his point, Carmichael paused for a few seconds before proceeding. "Do you know of anyone who would have taken Hayley against her wishes?" Carmichael enquired. "Has she any enemies?"

Belinda shook her head. "No, there's nobody I know of who would have done that," she replied. "Hayley gets on with everyone."

"What about one of those people she counsels?" Tarquin announced.

"What people?" Carmichael asked, his eyes opening wide.

"I don't know exactly who they are," continued Tarquin, who sounded very vague. "But doesn't she help addicts?"

Belinda rolled her eyes to the ceiling. "She did," she remarked, her patience clearly being tested to its limit. "But not recently. I'm certain Hayley stopped all that ages ago."

"What sort of addicts?" Watson enquired.

Belinda and Tarquin exchanged a look, but it was plain from the expressions on their faces that they didn't really know.

"You'd need to ask Duncan," replied Belinda, unhelpfully. "I think they were people with a variety of problems; drink, gambling, drugs. I think she did some counselling once they were recovering, but I'm really not sure."

Carmichael quickly glanced over in Watson's direction. "We'll leave it there, for now," he remarked before standing up from his seat. "We can see ourselves out."

Belinda Bishop elected to ignore Carmichael's comment and followed both officers out into the hallway.

As soon as Carmichael and Watson were out of the house and the front door had closed firmly behind them, Belinda let out an enormous sigh. "I need an enormous G and T," she muttered as she marched across the hallway and back into the lounge.

Chapter 17

"What a couple!" Watson remarked as the two officers wandered towards his car. "For a while in there I thought I'd been transported back, into a 1950s film."

Carmichael glanced sideways at Watson. "But Tarquin's last comment about Hayley being some sort of counsellor for recovering addicts is interesting. Nobody else has mentioned that."

Watson nodded. "Yes, you'd have thought her husband would have told us."

"That's exactly what I was thinking," remarked Carmichael, "and with his house being just a few yards down the road, I reckon we pay him a quick visit. I'd like to know more about what sort of counselling Hayley was doing."

Watson nodded and the two officers walked past his car towards The Laurels.

As they strode purposefully, Carmichael's mobile rang.

A quick glance at the screen indicated the incoming call was from DC Dalton.

"Hi Rachel," he remarked. "How's it going?"

The fact that his boss stopped abruptly and listened intently to what Rachel was saying indicated to Watson that she was giving him important news.

"We're on our way back," Carmichael announced down the phone. "Call Cooper and make sure he gets himself back too."

Without another word, Carmichael ended the call and looked directly into Watson's eyes. "Norfolk George has just brought a computer disc into the station," he informed his sergeant. "It's a video message from Hayley Bell."

* * * *

Less than an hour after receiving Rachel's call, the editor of the local newspaper, Carmichael and his three officers gathered around the monitor in the incident room ready to view the content of the disc.

"It's really short," Norfolk George remarked.

Rachel Dalton nodded before inserting the disc into the hard-drive and sitting down out of the eye-line of her three colleagues.

The familiar face of Hayley Bell appeared on the screen, silent at first and, apart from blinking, almost motionless.

"Hello, I'm Hayley Bell," she said, clearly unused to making video clips. "It's now Saturday, 22nd December. Here's today's newspaper." As she spoke, Hayley held a copy of the *Daily Mail* in front of the camera for a few seconds. The date clearly showed it was printed on Saturday, 22nd December. "I'm sending you this message to let you know that I'm safe and well and that I have no intention of returning," she continued in a calm, albeit slightly awkward, tone of voice. "I am looking to make a new life for myself and would ask you to please inform the police to stop their investigation as no crime has been committed. I apologise if I have inadvertently inconvenienced everyone, as that was never my intention. Also, please tell Duncan he must now live his life without me as I am not returning home."

The camera remained on Hayley's face for a few more seconds before the recording ended.

"You're not wrong, George," Carmichael remarked. "That was very short."

"But clear and to the point," remarked Watson. "She's done a runner and doesn't want to be found."

Cooper nodded. "It certainly looks that way and she's even had the sense to show a copy of Saturday's newspaper to prove it's a recent recording."

"How was the disc delivered?" Carmichael enquired.

"It was in my post this morning," replied Norfolk George.

Carmichael took a few seconds to consider what to do next. "Thanks George," he remarked looking straight at the old hack. "You can leave this with us. We'll take it from here."

Norfolk George's expression indicated quite clearly that he was unhappy at being asked to leave. "Are you going to make an announcement?" he enquired.

Carmichael remained impassive. "You've been around long enough, George, to know that I can't tell you too much," he replied.

"I will, however, let you be the first member of the press to know what we're doing when the time's right, but now's not that time."

Reluctantly, Norfolk George got up off his chair. "That's all the thanks you get for doing your civil duty," he mumbled under his breath as he departed through the door.

Carmichael waited until he was sure Norfolk George was well out of earshot. "We need to tie up the loose ends here," he remarked incisively. "I don't want us to be fooled into jumping to the wrong conclusion, but I think this message from Hayley Bell brings our investigation to a close."

"What loose ends?" Watson enquired, his brow furrowed to highlight his confusion.

"Most importantly, we need to confirm that this message is from Hayley Bell," Carmichael replied. "It certainly looks like the woman in the pictures we have, but, as none of us have ever met her, we need this verifying."

The team nodded as if to acknowledge and accept this was a necessity.

"I'll do that," remarked Rachel.

"Thanks," Carmichael replied with a faint smile directed at the young officer. "Ideally I'd like it to be Duncan Bell who makes that positive ID for us, but I'd accept verification from any of the other members of the reading group."

"I guess we need to provide Duncan Bell with an update, anyway," Rachel remarked. "So I'll try and kill two birds with one stone."

"I'll go with you," Cooper added. "It might be better if there are two of us there."

A faint grin appeared on Carmichael's face. "That just leaves a couple of other things we need to do," he remarked. "Inform Hewitt and then, once you two have managed to get the verification, inform the press, with Norfolk George being first in the queue. I'll take care of that."

The team nodded their agreement.

"It looks like we'll all be having an uninterrupted Christmas break after all," said Watson with a wry smile.

"Looks like it," Carmichael replied, who could picture the relief on Penny's face when she learned that he would be able to share the burden of entertaining Aunty Audrey over Christmas.

The meeting now over, the officers started to make moves to get out of the incident room and off home.

"By the way," Rachel remarked loudly at Cooper. "What was the big breakthrough you said you'd made?"

Cooper stopped what he was doing and perched himself on the corner of the desk. "It's now largely irrelevant," he remarked. "But I think I know what happened on Friday."

Carmichael and Watson, keen to understand the full details of what had happened, both stopped in their tracks and turned to face Cooper.

"Please, enlighten us," Carmichael insisted. "I'm intrigued to learn where Hayley got off the train and more curious to learn why nobody saw her."

Cooper, in typical laid-back fashion, seemed the least excited of all the officers in the room as he outlined his findings.

"Well," he started. "For ages I couldn't work out why, having spoken to almost all the passengers on the train, there was a discrepancy between the numbers of people we could account for getting on the train and those who got off."

As Cooper spoke, his three colleagues silently looked on with great interest.

"From their accounts and using the CCTV footage, including Hayley Bell, there appeared to be twenty people who got on the train that evening at either Kirkwood or one of the four stations between Kirkwood and Southport. However, again using evidence from the CCTV and the accounts of the passengers, it appeared that twenty-one people got off. And, to make matters even more confusing, not one of the passengers we'd spoken to could remember even seeing Hayley on the train."

"We know all that!" remarked Watson, who was clearly anxious for his colleague to be more forthcoming.

"Carry on, Paul." Carmichael encouraged his sergeant, while simultaneously shooting Watson a reproachful look.

"Well, obviously that couldn't be right," continued Cooper, his words being delivered in a slow but precise manner.

"Unless a passenger managed to clamber aboard while the train was moving," Rachel added.

Cooper smiled before continuing. "However, when I was interviewing the train driver, it actually struck me that it is possible for more people to get off than got on."

The frowns on the foreheads of Carmichael, Watson and Rachel Dalton seemed to suggest they were still perplexed.

"As I was talking to the driver," Cooper continued, "he reminded me of something we should have twigged all along."

"Which is?" Carmichael enquired, he, too, now starting

to get frustrated by Cooper's apparent inability to get to the point.

"That," continued Cooper, "the train had only arrived from Southport fifteen minutes earlier."

"We know that!" Watson remarked. "That train spends its life travelling from Southport to Kirkwood and back again."

"Exactly," Cooper replied. "So it's possible that someone who'd been on the train when it arrived at Kirkwood didn't get off. They just waited on the train until it pulled out of the station and back towards Southport. That would account for more people getting off than got on."

"But why would they do that?" Watson enquired.

"Because they'd arranged to meet Hayley," Carmichael remarked, as he realised the significance of what Cooper was saying. "To help her make good her escape."

Cooper smiled. "Exactly," he confirmed. "And, after going back to Barton Bridge, I also think I know who that person was."

Chapter 18

Having watched the recorded message from Hayley Bell, Hewitt listened intently as Carmichael provided a detailed update on their findings.

"So you think it was all meticulously planned by Hayley?" Hewitt asked.

"That's how it looks," replied Carmichael.

"Let me get this straight," Hewitt remarked. "Hayley's best friend, Francis Scott, leaves the restaurant with the excuse she has to go home early as she's travelling to Devon first thing the next morning."

Carmichael nodded, "That's correct."

"However," continued Hewitt, "she doesn't go home. Instead she travels to Barton Bridge, catches the train back to Kirkwood and waits on the train at the station. Somewhere along the way she gets changed into the joggers and a hooded top."

"That's correct," Carmichael remarked for a second time. "She then meets up with Hayley and gives her a similar change of clothes, which I imagine Hayley got changed into in the small toilet situated between carriage two and carriage three."

"Presumably Hayley would have changed into her joggers and hoodie before the train departed Kirkwood station?" Hewitt added.

Carmichael nodded his head once more. "I don't imagine it would have taken her that long to change. In fact, I expect she was already changed before most of the other passengers got on at Kirkwood. Several passengers reported seeing two females in carriage three get off the train at Barton Bridge, and we're now convinced that those women were Hayley and Francis Scott. What's more, one of them, most likely Francis Scott, had a rucksack which we believe she used to bring their change of clothing and to transport their other clothes off the train."

"And you're absolutely certain of this?" Hewitt enquired.

Carmichael shrugged his shoulders. "We're not 100% certain," he replied honestly. "However, Cooper managed to locate some CCTV footage from the supermarket car park next to Barton Bridge train station showing the two women getting into a red Fiesta. The footage isn't clear enough to make out all of the licence plate, however the first three digits match the licence plate of a red Fiesta registered to Francis Scott, so we're 99% sure we're right."

"It all seems very elaborate," Hewitt remarked, an element of surprise in his voice. "If she wanted to leave her husband, why would she go to such lengths? Surely she could have just got on a train without trying to disguise herself."

"That's a good point and one I've been asking myself," replied Carmichael. "And, at the moment, I have not been able to come up with a plausible answer."

"I suspect the only people who can answer that will be Hayley or Francis Scott," Hewitt added.

"Or the person she was running away from," replied Carmichael.

"I suppose that would be Duncan, the husband," Hewitt continued.

"Yes, that's my guess." Carmichael replied. "I can't be sure, but having met him, I can see why she'd want to get away."

Hewitt leaned back in his chair. "Good work, Carmichael," he remarked with genuine and unusual praise. "You and your team have done a great job. What's the plan from here?"

"Well other than Francis Scott being potentially less than honest when she spoke with DC Dalton on the phone, no crime appears to have been committed," Carmichael replied. "Cooper and Dalton are going to get verification that the woman who sent the recording is Hayley, although I'm certain it is and we will need to let Duncan Bell know his wife has simply absconded. Other than that, it's just a case of informing the press and tidying up the paperwork."

Hewitt nodded. "Well, you can let me and your team do all that," he remarked. "If I remember rightly, you're supposed to be on leave. Why don't you just get yourself home and enjoy Christmas with Penny and the family?"

It was extremely rare for Hewitt to be so considerate, so much so that his comments flummoxed Carmichael for a few seconds, but he quickly regained his composure. "That's very kind of you, sir," he replied with a smile. "If it's alright with you, I think I will."

With that, Carmichael stood up and walked over to the door. As he pulled the door towards him, he half turned, "Merry Christmas, sir," he remarked, before turning back and making a quick exit.

* * * *

Confident there was no longer any need for him to hang around, Carmichael returned to his office, grabbed his jacket and car keys and headed for the exit.

His intention was to call the team individually on his way home, however he was saved the job as he spied his three officers in conversation by Cooper's beaten-up Volvo.

"I thought you'd all be long gone by now," he remarked as he strode over to them.

"What did Chief Inspector Hewitt say?" Watson enquired.

Carmichael smiled and raised his palms upwards. "He was full of praise for everything this team's achieved," he replied. "So much so that he's told me I can resume my leave."

"I suspect Mrs Carmichael will be relieved about that," Rachel remarked with a warm smile.

"I suspect you're right," replied Carmichael as he walked past the three officers and towards his black BMW. "I'll leave the loose ends and the paperwork to you guys and I'll see you all after Christmas."

"Merry Christmas, boss," remarked Watson sarcastically.

Carmichael turned and smiled as he opened his car door. "Merry Christmas," he replied before clambering inside and heading out of the station compound.

* * * *

It was not yet five o'clock when Carmichael arrived home. Relieved and delighted that he would not be required to work during the Christmas festivities, Carmichael had managed to wind down completely during the thirty-three minutes it took him to drive the 23.2 miles back home.

However, his buoyant mood started to ebb, when he placed his key in the lock of the front door and remembered that Christmas this year included the pleasure of Aunty Audrey's company.

His loins fully girded in anticipation of hearing about Aunty Audrey's unwelcome comments and demands, Carmichael entered the hallway and shouted as merrily as he could, "Hi everyone, I'm back!"

When his announcement was met with an unusual silence, Carmichael's innate curiosity kicked in and he decided to investigate.

It took only two or three minutes before he located the family, all of whom were sitting happily together in the living room. Penny was reading a book with a large glass of white wine by her side, Jemma and Robbie were glued to an American comedy on TV and, at the far end of the room, Aunty Audrey was transfixed by the small screen of Natalie's tablet with the young owner snuggled close to her looking over her shoulder.

"Oh, hi, darling," Penny remarked when she saw him enter the room. "I didn't expect you back this early. How's the case going?"

When none of the other occupants of the room even acknowledged his presence, Carmichael walked the few short paces to where Penny was sitting and perched himself on the arm of her chair.

"It's all resolved," he replied, while nodding his head in the direction of Aunty Audrey. "Is everything OK here?"

Penny smiled broadly. "Let me make you a coffee," she responded, while simultaneously moving her head in the direction of the door and rising out of her seat.

"Fine," replied Carmichael who followed his wife into the hallway.

"What the hell's going on?" he whispered as soon as they were out of earshot. "It looks like…"

"It's a miracle," Penny interrupted. "Ever since Natalie showed Audrey Candy Crush, she's been hooked. It's all she wants to do. And, with her fully occupied, it's meant the rest of us can have some peace and at last start to look forward to Christmas."

"Has she been playing it all day?" Carmichael enquired.

"Well," replied Penny. "She picked it up as soon as the Ken Bruce show ended and, apart from the occasional toilet break and having her lunch, she's been totally engrossed. So much so that I don't recall her saying more than half a dozen words all day."

"Result!" announced Carmichael. "Let's hope her enthusiasm doesn't diminish between now and her going home."

"So the case is resolved!" Penny remarked as they reached the kitchen.

"Yep," replied Carmichael. "There are a few loose ends to tie up, but it looks like Hayley Bell simply ran away."

"What happened to her?" Penny enquired.

Carmichael poured himself a large glass of wine. "It would appear that, with the help of one of her friends, she just did a runner," Carmichael replied. "It was a well-planned exercise involving her getting changed into a hoodie in the toilet on the train, but the bottom line is she just absconded, so our misper's no longer a misper."

Penny's brow wrinkled. "Misper is an awful name," she remarked. "I don't see why you don't just call them missing persons."

Carmichael shrugged his shoulders. "It's just a nickname we use inside the force," he replied, as if it was of no significance.

"So how did the great Inspector Carmichael crack the case?" Penny asked mockingly, but at the same time grabbing her husband's arm affectionately.

Carmichael sipped from his wine glass. "To be honest, for once, I can't take any credit," he replied magnanimously. "It was Cooper's meticulous efforts that enabled us to find out why we didn't know where Hayley got off the train and how it was she hadn't been spotted. And Hayley also sent us a message on a computer disc telling us she was safe."

Penny's brow remained furrowed. "She plans and executes an elaborate disappearing act then, within days, records then posts you a message telling you she's safe!" she remarked, her tone one of bewilderment. "What made her do that?"

"We don't know," Carmichael replied. "It's all very strange if you ask me, but the bottom line is that she's safe. Apart from her friend misleading Rachel in an earlier statement, no crime has been committed, so it's case closed."

"I suppose it is," Penny continued, "but it makes no sense to me."

Carmichael pulled his wife close to him and kissed her brow. "Well, if you'd prefer I go back to the station and try to get to the bottom of it, I will," he added. "I just thought you'd prefer me home over Christmas."

Penny tilted back her head and stared into her husband's eyes. "I would," she said forcefully. "You're not going anywhere near Kirkwood police station until well after Christmas."

Chapter 19

Tuesday, 25ᵗʰ December

Carmichael gradually opened one eye. He had no idea what time it was, but didn't care, as he realised it was Christmas Day and, despite his worst fears over the last three days, he knew for certain he'd be able to spend Christmas at home with the family. With that pleasant thought in his head, he was determined to take full advantage of the rare luxury of waking up slowly.

His first sight, as he eventually managed to part his eyelids by more than a few meagre millimetres, was Penny, stood on tiptoes at the end of the bed gazing outside through the window.

"Merry Christmas!" he remarked as he pulled himself upright. "What are you doing?"

Penny half turned, her face beaming brightly. "It's snowing again," she declared. "It's actually snowing on Christmas Day. I can't remember it ever snowing on Christmas Day."

Carmichael smiled and shook his head. "You're more excited about Christmas than the kids," he teased.

Penny ignored him. "Come and look!" she exclaimed. "It's not just a few wispy flakes, it's snowing properly and it's sticking. It must be a foot deep already."

Carmichael dragged himself out of bed and joined his wife at the window.

"Merry Christmas," he repeated as he gently wrapped his left arm around her shoulders and kissed her tenderly on her warm forehead.

* * * *

With Aunty Audrey's preoccupation with Candy Crush, she hardly made a dent in the day's enjoyment.

Once breakfast was over and everyone had finished exchanging presents, Audrey sat quietly, in the corner, in an armchair she'd pretty much made her own property, her attention absorbed by the computer game. For Penny and the rest of the family this was perfect as it allowed them to spend the sort of Christmas they liked, playing silly games, enjoying an endless supply of rich tasty food and, in Steve's case, copious amounts of red wine, port and the odd bottle of beer. In short they had a marvellous day. The only noticeable exception was poor Mr Swaffy who remained banished to the garage. However, even his misery was somewhat lessened by the numerous lumps of turkey which Natalie surreptitiously ripped from the abandoned carcass in the kitchen and skilfully smuggled to her appreciative chum at every available opportunity.

To top everything off, Aunty Audrey even managed to pay Penny a half-compliment for the way she'd cooked their turkey dinner when, in her deep Scottish brogue, she announced to all that "apart from my own Christmas dinners, this is the best I've eaten since I was a child."

With the snow laying deep on the ground outside and the food and drink almost never ending, the day had gone as well as Penny could ever have dreamed. That was until the doorbell rang at 8.30 that evening and she caught sight of the expression on the face of Sergeant Cooper as he stood on her doorstep. A look that could mean only one thing, her husband's leave was over.

Penny left Carmichael alone to listen to the news his trusted lieutenant had brought him, but she knew it was unlikely to be good news.

"I'm sorry, Pen," he said remorsefully when he entered the lounge. "I'm going to have to go. It's Duncan Bell, Hayley's husband. He's been murdered."

Chapter 20

Although it was little more than ten miles from Moulton Bank to Much Martin, the journey down the snow-laden, windy country lanes took the two officers over thirty minutes.

When Cooper's trusty Volvo finally came to rest outside The Laurels, the imposing residence of the Bells, Carmichael could already see a number of vehicles at the scene, one of which was the unmistakable Land Rover belonging to Dr Stock, the most senior pathologist in that region of Lancashire.

Carmichael sniggered. "No doubt the good Dr Stock will have a few things to say about being dragged away from home on Christmas Day," he remarked before clambering out of the car and, without waiting for Cooper, marching up the snow-covered driveway towards the front door.

"The body's in the room at the end of the hallway," remarked a uniformed PC, who had been posted at the front door. "Dr Stock, DS Watson and DC Dalton are in there already."

Carmichael muttered, "thank you," as he marched on without bothering to make eye contact with the PC, who he recognised, but whose name he couldn't bring to mind.

As Carmichael entered the room, Cooper finally managed to catch up with him, having jogged up the drive and along the corridor.

"Good of you two to join us," remarked Stock derisively, as he spied Carmichael and Cooper out of the corner of his eye.

"So what's the story?" Carmichael asked, his question

aimed primarily at Watson and Dalton who had positioned themselves just a few paces inside the room.

"Cooper and I came over last night, as you'd told us, to give Duncan an update and see if he could confirm it was Hayley on the computer disc, but we couldn't get any answer," Rachel explained.

"I also came back this morning," Cooper continued. "But without any luck. I just thought he'd probably gone to stay with someone for Christmas."

Carmichael frowned as he listened to Cooper's rather unconvincing hypothesis.

"With his wife missing I can't see him going away," he said, the frustration and irritation palpable in his voice. "So who was it who found the body?"

"It was Belinda Bishop," Watson replied. "She was apparently concerned when he'd not arrived for drinks with the Bishops yesterday, so she came round and found him slumped over the desk with a dagger in his back."

"It's probably a letter opener," remarked Stock who had left the murder weapon in situ and was closely inspecting the entry wound, his small dark eyes just inches way from Duncan Bell's shoulder blades.

"And how long has he been dead?" Carmichael enquired, this time his question specifically directed at Stock.

"Hard to say," replied Stock, with a customary sharp intake of breath. "I'd need to take him back to the lab and look at him more closely before I could answer that with any degree of accuracy."

Carmichael took a deep breath. Of the numerous deaths that he had been called to investigate, he couldn't ever remember Stock being anything other than vague when he'd asked about the time of death at the crime scene. It had become almost like a game between the two of them, with Carmichael trying to get an instant idea of when the death had happened and the good doctor initially doing all he could to avoid saying anything that he couldn't back up with hard, irrefutable, scientific facts. "Are we talking hours or days?" Carmichael continued, in an attempt to give Stock plenty of wriggle room.

Stock lifted his head up and made eye contact with Carmichael for the first time since he'd entered the room. Then, after an admonishing tut and an incredulous, slight shake of the head Stock deigned to provide a guide to the waiting officers, "I'd say he's been dead for about two days," he announced. "But at this stage, I can't say more."

"Well, that narrows it down significantly," Carmichael remarked with an air of triumph. "I left him at around 11.30am on Sunday, so he must have been killed later that day or very early yesterday morning."

"I take it he was still alive when you left him," Stock added sarcastically, his gaze and apparent attention now refocussed back on Duncan Bell's body.

Carmichael ignored Stock's little jibe and took a few steps forward to take a closer look at the body.

"That's the lime-green shirt and those are the dark-blue trousers he was wearing when I interviewed him on Sunday," Carmichael remarked. "So it seems we're looking at a time of death on Sunday, sometime after 11.30am."

"Which would explain why he never called to tell us about the insurance policies," Rachel Dalton remarked. "Or why he didn't answer my calls yesterday."

Carmichael nodded. "So, presumably, Belinda Bishop has a key?" he remarked.

"She maintains she doesn't," replied Watson. "But she knows the code to the key safe on the wall next to the back door. That's how she managed to get in."

"Really," Carmichael replied. "Anyway, where is she?"

"She's in the autumn room," Rachel replied. "I left her

there with WPC Twamley. She was very distressed when I tried to talk with her before, so I thought I'd allow her a few moments to try and compose herself."

"Good idea," Carmichael replied, although it was clear his thoughts were elsewhere. "So am I right in assuming that this is the famous winter room?"

"I would have thought the rather large print of Monet's *The Road to Giverny* hanging over there on the wall would have told you that," remarked Stock who, for a second time, interrupted his examination of Bell's lifeless body to stare disapprovingly in Carmichael's direction.

"Is that what that is?" Carmichael replied without a hint of embarrassment at the derogatory implication in Stock's words.

"It's only one of the finest and most recognisable of Monet's paintings," Stock continued. "Did you never study art at school, Carmichael?"

"Well, I'll leave you to it, Stock," Carmichael replied, not wishing to share the details of the art classes he'd attended when he was a pupil at Watford Comprehensive, thirty years earlier. "I'll await your detailed post-mortem results with bated breath."

With that he beckoned his three officers to follow him into the hallway before leaving Stock and the forensics team to carry on with their painstaking examination of Bell and the winter room.

****

"What on earth were you two thinking!" exclaimed Carmichael angrily at Cooper and Dalton, as soon as they were in the hallway and out of range of Stock and the forensics team's hearing. "Were you not suspicious when Bell didn't answer the door? I know it's Christmas and you both want to get off and spend time with your families, but this is shoddy, guys."

Neither Cooper nor Rachel Dalton replied.

"In fairness," Watson chirped up. "As he was clearly murdered on Sunday, surely the fact that his body was found this evening, rather than yesterday or this morning, isn't going to matter that much."

Carmichael was having none of it. "That's not the point," he snapped back at Watson. "It's not acceptable for us to have left Bell's body here undetected for two days, especially when we'd asked him to provide us with information regarding his wife's disappearance. We should have been much more thorough."

Cooper nodded. "You're right, sir," he remarked. "I take full responsibility. You asked Rachel and I to talk with him, I'm the senior officer, so it's down to me."

Carmichael took a deep breath. "OK, we can't change history," he remarked. "And, to be honest, I'm annoyed at myself, too. I should have insisted we made contact with him on Monday when he'd failed to supply the insurance details as I'd asked him."

Carmichael paused for a few seconds before continuing. "Anyway, what's done is done, but for god's sake let's not make any mistakes finding Duncan Bell's killer."

Cooper nodded. "How do you want to play this?" he enquired.

Carmichael considered the question. "We're not going to achieve too much tonight," he reluctantly remarked. "So let's get together at 8am tomorrow, at the station, to try and work out a plan of action."

His three officers nodded, although, from the expressions on their faces, it was clear they were not happy about having to be in the office on Boxing Day morning. Their look of dismay wasn't lost on Carmichael, but was something he chose to totally disregard.

"But the priority has to be locating and talking to Hayley Bell," he continued. "She may not have anything to do with her husband's murder, but we desperately need to find her and talk to her."

"I agree," added Rachel. "And Francis Scott, too, given that she's been so instrumental in helping Hayley abscond."

"I want you two to get on to that right away," Carmichael commanded, his eyes directed at Rachel and Watson. "If need be get the local police in Devon to apprehend them, but, whatever you do, get them back to Lancashire tomorrow."

Rachel Dalton and Watson nodded, before heading off down the hallway towards the front door.

"What do you want me to do?" Cooper asked.

"Apart from driving me home later, I want you to keep close to Stock and his team," Carmichael replied, his piercing stare now fixed on his sergeant. "Make sure they stay focussed, we can't let the investigation get hampered just because it's Christmas. I need you to report back on anything they find, however small. Also, see if there's any evidence of anything being taken. This doesn't look like a burglary that went wrong, but let's not discount anything at this stage."

Cooper nodded and wandered back in the direction of the winter room.

"And I'll talk to Belinda Bishop," Carmichael muttered to himself, before striding off towards the autumn room.

* * * *

Carmichael always tried hard not to make snap judgements about people, but in truth he wasn't at all good at curbing his natural inclination to form an opinion based upon first impressions. When he'd previously met the Bishops, he'd very quickly made up his mind about the couple, and his take wasn't positive. With her haughty, loud-mouthed outbursts and liberally-dispersed opinions, Belinda had established herself, in his eyes, on a par with Aunty Audrey, an achievement that, prior to their meeting, Carmichael would have sworn impossible. Even her expression and the way she looked seemed rude and annoying to him, with her harsh, angular, sharp features and geometrical hair style only serving to complement perfectly her aggressive and overbearing personality. And, although Tarquin had been much more polite, he, too, had not done much to endear himself to Carmichael, who saw him as little more than a weak, cantankerous old fart, who'd clearly taken great pleasure in seeing his domineering wife being put in her place; a cowardly trait that didn't sit well with Carmichael.

Carmichael was, therefore, taken aback when he encountered the two on entering the autumn room.

Belinda looked nothing like the officious woman he'd met before, her painfully thin frame hunched up and slumped forward as she sat sobbing on the large ochre sofa, her hands in front of her being cradled tenderly by her attentive husband.

"I'm sure this has been a traumatic experience for you, Mrs Bishop," Carmichael said as sympathetically as he could. "But I'd like to ask you a few questions, if I may?"

"Of course," Belinda replied meekly, her moistened, frightened eyes peering up at him as she spoke.

"She's had a dreadful experience," remarked Tarquin, "so please be gentle with her, Inspector."

Carmichael, still somewhat surprised at the marked change in the demeanour of the Bishops, smiled. "I understand," he replied.

At that point Belinda raised her head and adjusted her posture, as if to prepare herself for the questions that were about to arrive.

Carmichael located an armchair close to where the Bishops were sitting and made himself comfortable. "First of all," he said, "were you together when you found Mr Bell?"

Belinda shook her head, but said nothing.

"No, Inspector," replied Tarquin. "My wife called me as soon as she'd made the 999 call. I shot across right away."

"So you were already here when the emergency services arrived?" Carmichael added.

"Yes," replied Tarquin. "I got here within a few minutes and the police and ambulance arrived about ten minutes later."

Carmichael nodded and turned his attention to Belinda, who was staring back at him, her red eyes surrounded with swollen, puffy skin. "So, in your own time, Mrs Bishop, can you tell me what happened?"

Belinda cleared her throat. "I'd invited Duncan over to join us for Christmas," she began, her voice faltering as she spoke. "With Hayley not being here and the children not coming home for Christmas, I thought it would be appalling for him to be left on his own on Christmas Day. But he said no, so I asked him to join us at six for a few sandwiches and a drink."

"And Mr Bell agreed he'd do that?" Carmichael enquired.

"Yes," Belinda replied. "But he didn't turn up, which is not like Duncan at all, he's always punctual."

"So you came over to see what was wrong," Carmichael remarked.

"Yes," Belinda replied once more. "But only after I'd tried to call him on the phone a couple of times."

"With no luck at all," interjected Tarquin.

"So what time did you get here?" Carmichael asked.

"It was around 7.30pm, I suppose," replied Belinda, although her words suggested she wasn't really sure.

"And do you have a key?" Carmichael added, even though he'd been told by Watson already that Belinda Bishop had used the key from the door safe to make her entry.

Belinda shook her head. "No," she replied, "however I know the code for their key safe by the back door. Hayley had told it me years ago, when they had it installed."

"Were you in the habit of using the key from the key safe to let yourself in?" Carmichael enquired.

"Absolutely not," replied Belinda, her normal aggressive demeanour appearing to have once more returned to her. "This was the first time I've ever used it."

Carmichael emitted a faint smile. "So tell me exactly what you did when you arrived at the house?" he asked, his tone calm and sympathetic.

Belinda sniffed loudly in an attempt to stem her tears. "Well, I rang the doorbell," she replied. "Then, when there was no answer, I walked round the side of the house and to the back. I tried the back door, but it was locked, so I removed the key from the key safe and walked back to the front of the house and opened the door."

Carmichael thought for a few moments. "Were there any lights on in the house?" he enquired.

Belinda shook her head. "No," she confirmed. "It was pitch black."

"So how did you manage to find your way around the back?" he asked. "It must have been very difficult to keep to the path."

Without looking up, Belinda stretched out her arm and pointed to a small table by the window. "I brought a torch," she replied. "It's over there."

Carmichael turned his head ninety degrees and spied the large, black, rubber torch standing upright on the mahogany table.

Carmichael turned his head to face Belinda's husband. "And you didn't accompany your wife when she came over?" he enquired, the inflection in his voice suggesting a degree of surprise. "Were you not worried about her going over to Mr Bell's house, when it was so dark, in all that snow and ice?"

Tarquin Bishop looked back at Carmichael with an expression of astonishment. "Belinda is more than a match for a bit of snow and ice," he replied dismissively. "And she had a torch!"

In similar circumstances, Carmichael couldn't see himself allowing Penny to have made such a journey by herself, but as he'd witnessed many times in the course of his work, relationships take many forms.

"And as you told me when we met before," Carmichael added, "you didn't care much for Duncan Bell."

Tarquin Bishop's neck stiffened and he straightened his back, as if to display to Carmichael that his comment had caused offence. "I hope you're not trying to imply that I had something to do with the man's death," he remarked irately. "I'm not going to pretend I liked him, but I didn't kill him."

Carmichael retained eye contact with the outraged face of Tarquin Bishop for a few seconds before returning his attention to Belinda. "Tell me what happened once you entered the house?" he enquired.

Belinda raised her head, looked directly at Carmichael and cleared her throat. "I called out for Duncan," she remarked. "But when there was no answer I turned on the kitchen lights and walked through into the hallway."

Carmichael looked intently at Belinda as she was speaking, his blue eyes piercing in their intensity.

"I kept calling as I went through the house and, as I entered another room, I'd turn on the lights and look to see if he was there."

"Did you not think that Mr Bell may have gone away?" Carmichael enquired.

Belinda shook her head. "To be honest, no," she replied without any hesitation. "Duncan had said he'd come over and Duncan always kept his word. I was sure something was wrong. In fact, I think I was expecting to find him dead, but from a broken heart or possibly having taken an overdose, or something. I never expected to come across the sight of him slumped over his desk and all that blood."

Carmichael nodded as if to encourage Belinda to continue, but when no words followed, he probed for more. "So how many rooms did you enter before eventually going into the winter room?" he enquired.

Belinda shook her head gently and smiled. "Only the ones that were en route between there and the kitchen," she replied. "I somehow knew he'd be there. It's where he always went when he wanted to be alone."

Carmichael smiled. "We men do like our sanctuaries," he remarked.

Belinda paused as if his words had resonated with her.

"Yes, I dare say you all do," she replied.

Carmichael gently rose from the armchair and looked down at the cheerless couple who remained seated together on the sofa. "I'll need you both to make formal statements before you leave tonight," he remarked. "I'll get one of the PCs to come in and do that. But, for the moment, I've no more questions for you."

Carmichael then turned and headed for the exit, but before he'd reached the door, he turned once more to face the Bishops. "You mentioned it was years ago when Hayley told you the code for the key safe," he remarked. "I'm surprised you remembered it."

A look of indignation appeared on Belinda's face. "1564," she announced firmly. "It's the year of Shakespeare's birth. I'm hardly going to forget the year England's greatest son was born, am I?"

Chapter 21

As Cooper's Volvo made the short journey back to Moulton Bank, Carmichael remained largely silent as he mulled over the circumstances of Duncan Bell's murder and quietly considered who had the motive and the opportunity to take the old man's life. He also thought long and hard about the movement he'd thought he'd seen behind the curtains when he'd been at Duncan Bell's house on Sunday. He couldn't be sure, but the more he thought about it, the more he was convinced that there was someone else there. And if there was, it was highly likely that the person behind the curtains had murdered Duncan.

By the time Cooper's car drew up outside his house, Carmichael had made little headway with his deliberations, much to his frustration. He was, however, certain that the man he'd met only once was more than capable of provoking feelings of dislike in those he encountered, which probably meant there'd be no shortage of potential candidates for his murderer.

"Do you think Duncan knew his killer?" Cooper enquired as Carmichael was about to open the car door.

Carmichael turned to face his colleague and nodded. "It's hard to be sure," he replied, "but, in my view, whoever plunged that letter opener into Duncan Bell's back had either been let into the house or had their own key. So, yes, I believe it's almost certainly someone close to the Bells."

"Me too," replied Cooper.

****

Having been together for over two decades, Penny could instinctively tell her husband's mood within seconds, and when he walked in that evening, it was no exception.

"You look tired," she remarked understandingly as she helped her husband with his coat. "I take it you'll be back in the office in the morning."

Carmichael nodded. "I'm afraid so," he replied with a slight shake of his head. "I've got a meeting with the team at 8am and I can't see me being home that much in the next few days."

Although she was disappointed, Penny saw no value in moaning and, after giving her husband a sympathetic smile and a warm embrace, looked up into his eyes. "At least the kids and I won't be alone," she remarked, much to Carmichael's surprise. "I got a call from the care home earlier, and it would appear that there's been a bad bout of food poisoning. Apparently many of the residents and half the staff are very unwell. They've asked if Audrey can stay here until Saturday."

"What!" replied Carmichael. "That's so bloody unfair."

Penny smiled. "We can't send her back there if everyone's ill," she replied.

Carmichael shook his head in disbelief. "I bet the troops aren't pleased," he remarked.

Penny shrugged her shoulders. "As you'd imagine, Robbie and Jemma aren't too impressed," she conceded. "But Natalie and Audrey both seem delighted."

"And what about you?" he enquired.

"Somewhere in between," she replied honestly.

Carmichael bent down and kissed his wife tenderly on the lips, "I'm sorry," he said with genuine remorse. "It's not been the best Christmas we've ever had."

Penny put on a forced smile, the one she used when she was trying to appear upbeat and stoic. "It's not been too bad," she replied reassuringly. "It's Mr Swaffy I feel sorry for. He's been banished to the garage for the last few days and the poor thing's going to have to stay there now until Saturday."

Carmichael smiled wryly. "I forgot about him," he remarked, "I bet he's sulking on his cushion."

Penny nodded. "I've put that old heater on in there, which has made it quite warm, but I do think he misses being allowed in the house."

Carmichael gave a faint shrug of his shoulders, as if to signify the helplessness of their situation.

"Do you want a drink?" Penny asked, tilting her head as if to point towards the kitchen.

Carmichael put his arm around his wife. "I could murder one," he replied.

Chapter 22

Wednesday, 26th December

With the snow thick and deep on the pavements outside and the desks, walls and ceilings of Kirkwood police station liberally decorated with cards and colourful festive decorations, there was still a strong feel of Christmas around the place. However, at precisely 8am, when Carmichael entered the room, the irritated looks on the faces of his three officers indicated quite clearly that they were sadly lacking in seasonal cheer.

"None of us want to be here," Carmichael remarked in an attempt to demonstrate that he was also frustrated at having to be working on Boxing Day. His effort didn't appear to have much of an impact, with not one of the three officers showing so much as a hint of a smile.

Carmichael allowed them a few seconds to sit down before he started.

"So what's the story with Hayley Bell?" he remarked, looking directly at Watson and Rachel.

"We spoke with her last night," Watson replied. "In fact we managed to speak with both Hayley and Francis Scott."

Carmichael had fully expected them to have struggled to find the dead man's wife so quickly, something his surprised reaction confirmed.

"Really," he remarked. "Were they together in Devon?"

Rachel nodded. "Yes, they were together in a cottage down there."

"And what was Hayley's reaction to the news about her husband?" Carmichael enquired.

Watson shrugged his shoulders. "Hard to say," he remarked rather unhelpfully. "She didn't cry or anything, but she did sound shaken by the news."

Rachel nodded. "Yes, I'd say she was shocked, but I wouldn't describe her as being distraught," she added.

"And what about Francis Scott?" Carmichael asked.

Watson and Rachel exchanged a quick look, both with a blank expression on their face. "The same as Hayley," replied Watson. "Shock, but not overly emotional about it."

Carmichael frowned as he listened. "I see," he replied, his mind clearly mulling over the significance of the indifference with which the news of Duncan Bell's death appeared to have been received by his wife and her friend. "So, are they coming back?"

Rachel nodded. "Yes," she remarked. "It was very late when we managed to talk with them last night, and they both maintained they'd been drinking. So the plan is for them to get a few hours' sleep and start back at about 7am today."

Carmichael nodded. "Well, at least that's something," he replied, the tone in his voice suggesting he was still uneasy about the relatively calm way the pair had seemed to take the bad news. "That's got to be about a five or six-hour journey, so they should be here around 1pm."

Watson shook his head. "Maybe, if they didn't stop," he remarked with a cynical smile. "I suspect the call of nature will make them have to break the journey. So I don't see them being here until at least 2pm, maybe even later."

"I agree," interjected Cooper. "If they're anything like my wife, I can't see them doing that journey without at least a couple of breaks."

Carmichael nodded. "Keep in contact with them,

Rachel," he instructed. "I want them to head straight here as soon as they arrive in Lancashire and, when they do, I want to interview them personally."

Rachel nodded. "Will do," she replied.

Carmichael then turned his head in the direction of Sergeant Cooper. "What about the crime scene?" he enquired. "Have SOCOs found anything of interest?"

Cooper shook his head. "Nothing noteworthy, as yet," he replied. "Stock's performing the autopsy this morning, so we should find out more from him and the forensics team later today. However, I think I may have discovered something that's significant."

"What's that?" Carmichael asked.

"I looked again in Hayley's bedroom and I couldn't find her passport," Cooper remarked. "It was certainly there on Saturday when Rachel and I had a look through her things, but its gone missing."

"What about her credit cards?" Rachel enquired.

Cooper shook his head. "They're still there, just as we found them on Saturday," he replied. "As far as I can see, it's only her passport that's gone missing."

"The only person that has any need of Hayley Bell's passport is Hayley Bell," Watson remarked. "So she's got to be our prime suspect."

"It makes sense," Cooper added. "It would explain why there was no forced entry."

"But we know she was in Devon with Francis Scott," Rachel remarked. "That's 300 miles away, she's hardly going to just pop in, is she, sir?" Rachel glanced at her boss, fully expecting him to agree.

Carmichael took a few seconds to consider the latest information before responding. "It does seem a long way for her to come," he agreed. "But it's not an impossible trip for her to make, I suppose."

"It would also explain why she wasn't heartbroken to learn about her husband's death," Watson added.

"I don't buy that at all," Rachel remarked firmly. "Surely, if she had killed Duncan, she would have put on an act trying to show she was upset. No, I think the simple truth is that she wasn't upset because she no longer has any feelings for him. Let's face it, she worked hard to plan her meticulously-executed getaway. That suggests to me that Hayley was a woman who wanted Duncan out of her life, so I don't think there was any love for him. That's why his death didn't seem to touch her."

"You make a fair point, Rachel." Carmichael announced. "And I'm also not totally convinced it was Hayley. However, she has to be on our list of suspects because, if she did come back to get her passport she could have killed Duncan at the same time."

"Do you know what I think?" remarked Watson rhetorically. "I think that despite her elaborately constructed escape plan, Hayley messed up. I think she forgot her passport, then, realising what she'd done, she came back from Devon, but was confronted by Duncan and, during the resulting argument, she killed him."

Carmichael shook his head. "That doesn't stack up, Marc," he announced. "Whoever killed Duncan did so in cold blood. We need to wait for Stock's post-mortem report, but it looked to me like he was stabbed in the back as he sat at his desk. His killing didn't strike me as something that occurred during an argument."

The room fell silent for a few seconds as everyone tried to put some logic behind what they knew.

"As always in these cases," Carmichael remarked, "we need to keep an open mind and consider who else had a reason and the opportunity to kill Duncan Bell. Let's start by drawing up a list of suspects, recording some facts and writing a few possible theories."

Carmichael didn't notice the smug looks on the faces of his three officers as their eyes connected for a split second. He had no idea that, prior to the meeting, they'd made a bet as to how soon it would be before Carmichael mentioned his trademark lists.

As Carmichael turned his back on them and started to write on the whiteboard, Watson pointed up at the clock on the wall and grinned widely at the others, knowing that his guess of six minutes was the nearest of the three predictions.

"Do you want me to be scribe?" Rachel asked, after rolling her eyes and shaking her head as if to register her displeasure at Marc for being so childish.

Carmichael, having just written Duncan Bell at the top of the white board, turned back and handed Rachel the marker. "If you don't mind," he replied. "After all, out of the four of us, your writing's the only one that's anything close to legible."

"And she can spell, too!" Watson added with a mischievous grin.

Chapter 23

It took the team no more than half an hour to debate and complete the task to Carmichael's satisfaction. On the board behind him, Rachel had carefully constructed three separate records. The first, written in red, contained the facts relating to Duncan Bell's death. The second, in green, was headed 'unknowns' and consisted of a series of hypotheses and unanswered questions. The third and final list, recorded in blue, was a roll call of potential suspects.

"OK, let's all take a few moments to go over them to make sure we all agree and we've not missed anything," Carmichael announced.

His three officers nodded compliantly. They'd been in this position countless times before on previous cases run by Carmichael, so they knew his methods by now.

"Which list do you want to talk about first?" Watson asked.

"We'll start, as we always do, with the facts," replied Carmichael, as if there wasn't any other way to start.

Without being asked, Rachel started to read out the six items on the facts list.

"Item one," she stated. "Duncan Bell died on Sunday sometime after 11.30am when you left him. Item two, whoever killed him either had a key or was let into the house as there were no signs of forced entry. Item three is that you think you saw a movement behind the blinds when you arrived and again when you left after interviewing Duncan

Bell on Sunday, which may have been the killer. Item four is that his body was found by Belinda Bishop, who came to the house after Bell failed to show for drinks at her house. Item five is that Belinda Bishop maintains she entered the house using a key from the key safe near the back door, and item six is that apart from Hayley Bell's passport, which was at the house on Saturday, nothing else appears to have gone missing."

"Not a huge amount of facts," remarked Carmichael rather gloomily. "But hopefully Dr Stock and the SOCO team will give us more information later in the day."

Without hesitation, Rachel started to read the list she'd written in green, under the heading 'unknowns', again a list of six recorded items.

"The first and most obvious one is who killed Duncan Bell?" Rachel announced. "We then have a whole list of questions, namely, who had access to a key to Duncan Bell's house? Who would Duncan have let into the house? Who had a motive to kill Duncan Bell?"

"By the sound of things there were a fair few," Cooper added.

"Then there's the question of who took Hayley's passport," continued Rachel. "And why?"

"If it wasn't Hayley, it has to have been someone getting it for her," Watson remarked. "It's of absolutely no value to anyone else."

"It's hard to argue against that, Marc," Carmichael concurred. "But, until we speak to Hayley, I'm not going to jump to any conclusions."

"That just leaves one other question," said Rachel, once Carmichael had finished talking. "Why Hayley went to such great lengths to plan and execute such an elaborate escape and, having done so, why she then sent us the disc informing us she'd simply run away?"

Carmichael nodded. "The only thing I'd like to add is why Tarquin Bishop allowed his wife to go to the Bells alone and in the dark. I find that quite strange."

Rachel picked up the green marker and added a seventh item to the unknowns list.

"That just leaves us with our suspects," remarked Carmichael as he looked over his shoulder at the short list of three names they'd compiled. "Only three at the moment, but I suspect this may grow quite rapidly as I'm sure we'll find that Duncan Bell wasn't short of enemies."

The officers looked over at the list of suspects, which read as follows:

1. Hayley Bell (aided by Francis Scott)
2. Tarquin Bishop
3. Pete, Maxine Lowe's partner

"Remind me again," Rachel interjected. "Why have we included Maxine Lowe's partner?"

Carmichael shrugged his shoulders. "We can't call him a major suspect," he conceded. "But when Marc and I went to see Maxine the other day it was clear he had little time for Duncan Bell, so I think he needs to be spoken to and his whereabouts checked for the time period when we think Duncan was murdered."

"So what's the plan of attack?" Watson enquired.

"I want you to go and interview Maxine Lowe and her partner, Pete." Carmichael replied. "Also, get over and talk with Hannah Ringrose and Lesley Saxham. Take a softly, softly approach with the ladies from the reading group, just tell them that you're there to give them the bad news about Duncan, but see if they all have alibis. As for Maxine's partner, you can play that a little tougher, after all, he made no secret of his dislike for Duncan, so he needs to know he's being investigated."

Watson nodded. "No problem," he replied.

"As for you, Paul," Carmichael remarked, his eyes now fixed on Cooper. "I want you to keep firmly behind Dr Stock and the SOCO team. I want a report out of them, even if it's just a preliminary one and I want it today."

"What about us?" Rachel enquired.

Carmichael smiled. "You and I are going to hang around here until Hayley Bell arrives and, while we are waiting, I want you to tell me again what you uncovered about Duncan Bell the other day. My instinct is telling me that this was a murder fuelled by hatred, so the sooner we have a fuller picture of Duncan and his life the better."

Chapter 24

With Cooper and Watson now having departed, Carmichael and Rachel Dalton sat alone in the incident room at Kirkwood police station.

"How did you spend Christmas Day?" Carmichael asked the young DC.

"I spent it at my parents with my brothers and their partners," Rachel replied with a smile. "It was nice."

Carmichael had never met Rachel's family, but he was aware that she was from a very well-established and wealthy family in the area, so in his head he conjured up an image of her Christmas as being a huge family gathering in opulent surroundings with roaring open fires and tables overloaded with a variety of Christmas food, to almost Dickensian excess.

"So I take it there were a fair few of you then?" he asked.

Rachel pondered the question for a few seconds. "Fourteen, including my nieces and nephews," she eventually replied. "How about you, sir?"

"There were only six of us," Carmichael confirmed. "But that was plenty enough for me, I can tell you."

Rachel smiled. "I do like Christmas Day at home with my family," she added. "But, to be honest, I'm rather pleased to get away from them all for a few hours. It can get a bit hectic with so many of us."

"I know what you mean," Carmichael concurred. "Anyway tell me what information you found out about Duncan Bell?"

Rachel Dalton nodded and placed the notes she'd taken a few days earlier in front of her. "As we know, he was married three times," she said. "His first wife was called Pamela Newsome. They were married when he was thirty-five."

"How long were they married?" Carmichael enquired.

"The couple were married for five years before they divorced," Rachel replied. "Then, just under a year after his divorce from Pamela, Duncan Bell was married for a second time, to a lady called Claudette Cotterill. They were together for nine years and had two children, James and Suzanne. Claudette was the one who died from a brain haemorrhage when she was just thirty-two."

"Then he married Hayley," interjected Carmichael.

Rachel nodded. "Yes, Duncan married her less than six months after Claudette's death, as Norfolk George had indicated. He was then fifty-one."

"That's pretty much what we knew already," remarked Carmichael. "Did you manage to learn anything about Claudette's death and do you know whether Duncan's first wife is still alive?"

Rachel shook her head. "With Bell's second wife dying of natural causes, there wasn't any police record of her death," she explained. "And I couldn't find any information regarding the life insurance policy Norfolk George mentioned to you."

"What about the first Mrs Bell?" Carmichael enquired.

Rachel shrugged her shoulders. "To be honest, I didn't get around to finding out if Pamela is still alive," she confessed. "Do you want me to try and find her?"

Carmichael nodded. "I think we should try and locate her. I doubt she can help us much as they separated so long ago, but we should find her."

"I'll get on to it straight away," Rachel replied.

"Is that everything?" Carmichael asked, his tone suggesting he was less than impressed.

"Apart from all his wives being in their early twenties when he married them, I've not found anything too remarkable about Duncan Bell's previous marriages," Rachel announced.

Carmichael shrugged his shoulders. "I guess Duncan's not the first man to like younger women," he remarked. "I suppose it gives us a bit of an insight into the sort of man he was, but marrying young women, even when you're getting on a bit, isn't a crime."

"I know," said Rachel. "But it's just a bit strange for him to only ever marry women in their early twenties."

Carmichael smiled. "Believe me, Rachel," he remarked glibly, "I'm certain there are thousands of men out there who would see that as an achievement rather than a crime. What I find strange is what women in their twenties saw in him?"

Rachel forced a slight smile, but said nothing.

"Anything else?" Carmichael enquired.

Rachel shook her head.

Carmichael raised his eyebrows. "Keep digging, Rachel," he stated. "Duncan's death may well be linked to something that happened in his past."

Rachel nodded. "I will," she replied dutifully.

* * * *

Marc Watson had found it even more difficult to find a space large enough to park his car outside Maxine Lowe's house than he had two days earlier. But having found a spot and successfully managing to squeeze his car in, he strode quickly over the snow-laden path towards Maxine's front door. The freezing air filled his mouth and nostrils and, as he trudged, he found himself having to stoop to prevent the icy sleet, now almost horizontal, from stinging his face.

He rapped loudly three times against the frosted glass on the front door.

After a few seconds, it opened and the lofty frame of Maxine's boyfriend, Pete, stood looking down over him.

"It's Sergeant Watson from Mid-Lancashire Police," Watson announced with a smile. "We met briefly when I was here a few days ago. Do you mind if I come in?"

With a perplexed expression on his face, but without saying a word, the tall, young man took a pace back and gestured with his head for Watson to enter.

Watson rushed inside and wiped his feet on the door mat.

"Who was it, Pete?" Maxine enquired from the kitchen.

It was clear to Watson, from the way she'd asked, Maxine hadn't expected her boyfriend to have let the visitor into the house.

"It's one of those coppers from the other day," he replied, the word it's indicating to Maxine that their caller was still there.

Maxine appeared in the doorway between the kitchen and the lounge, her face looking as flustered as it had the last time Watson had called.

"What's happened?" she asked in a voice that suggested she was expecting bad news.

"I'm really sorry to disturb you both," said Watson in a calm, authoritative voice, "especially on Boxing Day, but I need to ask you both a few questions, if I may."

"Has Hayley been found?" Maxine enquired, her voice trembling as if she expected to be told her friend was dead.

"Yes," replied Watson. "Hayley's actually made contact with us and she appears to be safe and sound."

As his words passed his lips, Watson could see Maxine's face illuminate, as if all her worries had evaporated in an instant.

"Fantastic news," she remarked. "That's just brilliant."

For a few seconds more, Maxine's elated expression shone out, like a beacon of joy. However, that was short lived as she started to question why, if her friend was safe, a police officer had come to visit her on Boxing Day. The same thought had clearly crossed her boyfriend's mind, too.

"So what are you doing here?" he asked in a gruff, no-nonsense tone.

"May I sit down?" Watson asked. "There's been a development and I need to ask you both some questions."

* * * *

In the hour Cooper had stood in Dr Stock's pathology lab, the surly medic had made no attempt to hide his displeasure at having to perform his examination of Duncan Bell on Boxing Day.

"I've tickets at the Hallé this afternoon," he grumbled loudly as he looked intently at the entry wound in Bell's back.

"Classical music's not really my thing," Cooper remarked. "I'm more of a middle-of-the-road type of listener."

Stock peered up over his spectacles at the tall, middle-aged officer. "And what sort of artists do middle-of-the-road music?" he enquired with unrestrained derision in his voice.

"All sorts really," Cooper replied. "Genesis, Fleetwood Mac, The Eagles. I like other stuff, too, a bit of the old Northern Soul. I suppose anything with a catchy tune I can hum along to really."

Stock shook his head then turned his attention back to the corpse on the slab in front of him.

Chapter 25

The news of Duncan Bell's death came as a massive shock to Maxine Lowe, who was now seated on one of the small sofas in her tiny lounge.

"So how was he murdered?" she enquired.

"I'm sorry, I can't share that information with you, at this stage," Watson replied, "but I need to know if you know of anyone who may have had a reason to kill Mr Bell."

Without thinking, Maxine's eyes fixed themselves on her boyfriend, who hadn't moved more than a few inches since letting Watson into the house. Realising what she had done, Maxine turned her head to face Watson once more.

"No," she replied firmly. "I hardly knew him, so I've no idea who would have a reason to harm him."

Watson smiled before turning his attention to Maxine's boyfriend. "And how about you, sir?" he asked.

"Pete never even met Duncan," Maxine interjected.

"I only ask," continued Watson, "because when I was here with Inspector Carmichael on Monday, you did seem very hostile towards the Bells."

"Like Max says," Pete replied, "I never knew this Bell guy or his wife for that matter. All I know is what Max has told me about the house and they just seem a bit strange, especially him."

"In what way were they strange?" Watson continued.

Pete walked a few paces to the kitchen doorway and leaned against the doorframe, his arms folded in front of his chest.

"Just creepy, with his bloody mood rooms," he remarked. "I ask you, what right-minded person has mood rooms?"

Watson smiled. "I understand what you're saying, but surely having mood rooms is just being eccentric," he suggested. "It's not what I'd call creepy."

"Maybe you're right," Pete replied. "But to me it's bloody weird. Anyway do you have any objection if I get myself a beer? After all, it is my house and it is still bloody Christmas."

Watson shook his head. "Actually," he added as Pete started to turn to walk into the kitchen, "can I have a few moments alone to talk with Maxine?"

Pete turned back to face Watson, his eyes piercing and angry.

"Where do you want me to go while you two are talking?" he replied. "It's bloody freezing out there, and in case you hadn't noticed, we live in a two-up two-down. There's no bleedin' mood rooms here."

"Why don't you get a beer, Pete and go upstairs for a few minutes?" Maxine suggested. "I'm sure the sergeant's questions won't take long."

Watson nodded. "Just a few minutes, that's all."

Pete trudged into the kitchen, grabbed a beer bottle from the fridge, yanked the metal top off and stomped up the stairs, slamming the bedroom door once he'd reached the landing.

"I'm not sure why you need to talk to me while Pete's not in the room," Maxine remarked as soon as her boyfriend was out of sight. "I've no secrets from Pete."

Watson raised his eyebrows. "Really," he remarked, "except for what you do on a Thursday evening."

Maxine's face became ashen. "Keep your voice down," she whispered. "The walls here are paper-thin."

Watson nodded. "I want to know why Pete disliked Duncan Bell," he remarked. "I don't buy this jealousy bit, there's more to it than that, I know it."

Maxine slumped back into her chair. "It was nothing," she said, the palms of her hands raised upwards to reinforce her words.

"Then tell me," Watson replied.

"About six months ago," said Maxine, her voice hushed to prevent her boyfriend from hearing, "the stupid old fool cornered me when I was in their house. It was just before one of the sessions and I found myself alone with him. It was just for a few minutes, while Hayley went out for something, and well…" Maxine paused while she searched for the right words, "well, to cut to the chase, he put his hand on my knee and propositioned me."

"What do you mean he propositioned you?" Watson enquired.

"He offered her £200 for a quickie," Pete interrupted from his position midway down the stairs.

Neither Watson nor Maxine Lowe had noticed Pete as he'd slowly descended the staircase.

Angry that Pete had intruded on his private conversation with Maxine, Watson's initial impulse was to challenge the young man, but he quickly decided that his best course of action would be to ignore his indiscretion and just interview them together.

"And what did you say to Duncan Bell when he made you this proposal?" Watson asked the now very uncomfortable-looking Maxine.

"I told him to sod off," she replied, "in no uncertain terms, I can tell you."

"And did he?" Watson asked.

"Well he never tried it on again, if that's what you mean," Maxine replied. "But I always made sure I wasn't alone with him after that."

Watson turned his head to face Pete. "And what did you do?" he enquired.

Pete was now at the bottom of the stairs. "Nothing," he

replied with a shrug of his shoulders. "But I'm not happy about Max going over there twice a week, and she knows it."

Maxine shook her head slowly. "Nothing happened and I always made sure I was never alone with him so I was OK," she protested exasperatedly, as if it was the millionth time they'd had that discussion.

"Well it certainly won't now," remarked Watson, his eyes fixed upon Pete.

"Don't start making out I had anything to do with it," Pete remarked curtly. "I never topped the old perv. It was probably a husband or boyfriend of one of the other women he's been propositioning 'cos blokes like him will be doing it all the bleedin' time."

"Did Mrs Bell know about what he'd said to you?" Watson said, his gaze now back on Maxine.

She shrugged her shoulders. "I didn't have the heart to tell her," Maxine replied. "But I can't believe she didn't know what sort of person he was."

Watson thought for a few seconds before taking out his pocket book. "I need you both to now tell me where you were from 11am on Sunday through to mid-day Christmas Eve," he said. "Let's start with you, Pete."

* * * *

It took another hour before Stock finished his post mortem on Duncan Bell.

"Tell Carmichael that I'll get the report written up and email it to him later today," Stock announced in his normal pompous tone. "But because I know what he's like, you can inform him that the murder victim was killed by a single stab to the back, and with some force."

"So, presumably Mr Bell would not have known anything until it was too late," Cooper remarked.

Stock deliberated for a second. "The blade went straight through the heart," he confirmed, "so, in my opinion, death would have been almost instantaneous, sergeant. But I'd imagine whoever did it was known to the dead man."

"Why do you say that?" Cooper asked.

"Because the desk backed up fairly close to the wall and the entry to the room was opposite," Stock replied. "The murder weapon was Bell's own letter opener, which I'd assume was normally on his desk, so given there were absolutely no signs of a struggle, I'd say it's likely that the person who killed him was in the room, nonchalantly picked up the letter opener, walked behind Bell and just thrust it into his back."

"That supports Carmichael's gut feeling," Cooper announced.

Stock shook his head slowly. "Well, I'm certainly glad that I'm in tune with Inspector Carmichael," he replied in a sarcastic tone.

"Could it have been a woman?" Cooper asked.

"Possibly," Stock confirmed. "Anyone with a reasonable amount of strength could have done it, in my humble opinion."

Cooper thought for a few seconds. "And do you have a more accurate idea of the time of death?" he enquired.

Stock looked him square in the face. "I'd certainly say it was on Sunday," he remarked. "And, judging by the contents of his stomach and the degree of their digestion and subsequent decomposition, I'd say between 12 noon and 4pm."

"Thanks, Stock," Cooper remarked. "I'll get back and tell the boss. I hope you still manage to get to your concert."

Stock gazed up at the clock and figured that if he hurried he'd still be able to make it before the performance started.

"Have you ever listened to any Holst, Delius or Vaughan Williams?" Stock asked as Cooper reached the exit.

Cooper shook his head and half turned. "Can't say I have," he replied.

"You should try them, sergeant," Stock remarked. "You never know, you may find your musical tastes are more varied than you think."

"I will," Cooper replied. "Never let it be said I'm afraid to try something new. Actually, my niece got me listening to some Dizzee Rascal the other month, and to be honest, I thought it was OK. My wife wasn't too impressed and I probably wouldn't play it in the car, but I can understand why young people like him."

As Cooper departed, Stock closed his eyes and shook his bowed head mournfully. "Philistine," he muttered under his breath, "uncultured Philistine."

Chapter 26

Penny had not had the best of mornings. As was often the case, she hadn't managed to get back to sleep after Steve, in typical fashion, had woken her up rushing around the bedroom as he sorted himself out before heading off to the office. She knew he'd never admit it, but Penny was convinced his noisy early morning departures were a deliberate ploy to ensure she, too, wasn't able to enjoy a little more unbroken sleep, an uncharitable and totally unsubstantiated sentiment, but it was how she felt.

Following roughly forty minutes attempting in vain to try and get back to sleep, Penny decided to get up.

After letting poor Mr Swaffy out of his temporary prison and giving him his favourite breakfast, scrambled egg and Weetabix, Penny set about tidying up the lounge, which she'd uncharacteristically abandoned the evening before without performing her normal late night cleaning-up routine.

By 10.30am she'd completed her chores and started to wonder when Aunty Audrey and the other three would emerge.

Half an hour and a mug of coffee later, Penny decided she wasn't going to allow her husband's work or the lack of energy of the other people in the house to spoil her day. Grabbing the long, red lead from one of the kitchen drawers, she decided she'd take the dog for a walk in the deep, crisp snow.

Two minutes later, having put on her thick, warm coat and practical, but decidedly-unstylish, wellington boots, Penny attached Mr Swaffy to his lead, scribbled a note telling the team where she'd gone, plonked it in the centre of the kitchen table, closed the door behind her and marched down the path.

* * * *

"Thanks for the heads up, Paul," Carmichael remarked after receiving Cooper's call and getting an update on Dr Stock's preliminary findings. "We're not expecting Hayley Bell and Francis Scott for another hour or so, so why don't you speak with Marc and find out how he's doing with his three interviews. If, between you, you can get them cracked off in the next hour or so, you can help Rachel and I with the interviews here."

With the heavy, icy sleet belting down on the roof of his beaten-up Volvo, Cooper looked at the clock on the dashboard which read 11. 45am. "OK, sir," he replied. "I'll call him now."

Carmichael put down the receiver and eased himself back in his chair, his hands clasped together behind his head.

"Looks like Duncan was murdered within hours of me talking to him on Sunday," he told Rachel.

"Really," Rachel remarked.

"The question is," Carmichael added, "does Stock's news help us identify Duncan's killer in any way?"

Rachel ran her fingers through her hair as she considered what her boss had just said. "Well we're told that the winter room was his special room, and one that he kept fairly private, so the only assumption I'd put forward is that it must have been someone he knew really well."

"Cooper told me that's what Stock thinks, too," Carmichael confirmed. "So who's in the frame?"

"Well it can't be Mrs Bell because she was in Devon," Rachel replied. "But it could be a lover. I know he was in his late seventies, but I reckon this thing we've discovered that he had for younger women could still be a factor."

Carmichael looked across at Rachel with a frown so pronounced it looked like a deep, ancient scar on his brow. "I guess there could be something in what you're saying, Rachel," he remarked, "but I'd be inclined to focus more on his older friends and, as for Hayley Bell, we've only her and her friend's word that they were in Devon. Given that they have already led us a merry dance about her disappearance, why should we believe that they were in the West Country on Sunday?"

****

As soon as Cooper had finished his call to Carmichael, he called Watson, who had just arrived at Hannah Ringrose's apartment when his mobile rang.

"How are you getting on?" Copper enquired.

"I've been over to see Maxine Lowe and her boyfriend, Pete Thorn," Watson replied. "He's an odd guy, very aggressive and frighteningly protective of Maxine. Having spent a bit of time with him, in my mind he's certainly a potential suspect."

"Really," Cooper remarked. "Well, according to Stock, the murder happened on Sunday, in the early afternoon. Do you know the boyfriend's movements at that time?"

Watson looked down at the notes he'd taken. "He maintains that he was at work at Steadmans Printers on the Sunday, starting at 8am and finishing at 6pm, but until I verify that with his employers he's still at the top of my list."

"But does he have a motive?" Cooper enquired.

"Oh yes," replied Watson. "It would appear that Duncan Bell took a shine to Maxine. Apparently he propositioned her some time back. He offered her a couple of hundred quid. Pete

Thorn denies he did anything about it, but I don't buy that one bit. He's so possessive I'd wager any money he'll have tackled Bell over it, and I can imagine him being the violent type, too."

"Carmichael wants me to give you a hand," Cooper remarked. "Do you want me to talk to one of the other two for you?"

"Yes please," Watson replied. "I'm already at Hannah Ringrose's house, so I'll talk with her. Why don't you go over and have a chat with Lesley Saxham?"

"That's fine with me," said Cooper. "And when you've finished, the boss wants us to get back to the station to help him and Rachel with the interviews of Hayley Bell and Francis Scott."

"Have they arrived yet?" Watson enquired.

"No," replied Cooper, "but unless they've been held up on the road up from Devon, they've got to be less than a few hours away."

"OK," confirmed Watson, who felt smug that it was he who had the task of again interviewing Hannah Ringrose, the attractive, slim, young woman, rather than the older and, in his eyes, much less appealing, Lesley Saxham, who he'd palmed off on Cooper. "I'll see you back at the station later. Have fun!"

With the call now ended, Cooper started the engine of his old, but reliable, Volvo and headed off in the direction of Much Martin, wiper blades working at full tilt.

* * * *

For over twenty minutes, Carmichael paced up and down. Occasionally he'd stop for a few seconds to look at the notes Rachel had written earlier on the incident board, or stare impatiently out of the window at the icy rain as it beat against the glass and started to melt the snow-covered, noticeably-empty station car park.

"What's taking them so long," he muttered anxiously as the hands on the incident room clock indicated it was 12.35pm.

"Coming up from Devon, I suspect they could be a few more hours yet," Rachel remarked as tactfully as she could. "Do you want me to call them to see how they are progressing?"

"Yes," replied Carmichael. "Find out exactly where they are."

Rachel picked up her mobile and dialled Hayley's number.

"Hello, Mrs Bell," she remarked after just a few seconds. "We were wondering how your journey is going."

After a slight pause, as Rachel listened to Hayley's travel update, Carmichael heard the young officer remark, "That's excellent. If you're just coming up to the Thelwall Viaduct you should be here in an hour. When you arrive, ask at the reception desk for me, DC Dalton, I'll come and get you both."

By the time Rachel had ended the call, Carmichael had sat down and was looking far more relaxed.

"From what she said," began Rachel, "I would expect her to be here at about 1.30pm."

Carmichael smiled. "Good," he replied cheerily. "That gives us time to go down to the canteen and grab something to eat before we start the interviews."

"They've only a few sandwiches out of the machine," replied Rachel. "The catering people are off today with it being Boxing Day."

Carmichael smiled again, but this time more broadly. "After all I ate yesterday, a plain, ham sandwich is perfect for me," he remarked. "Are you going to join me?"

Rachel smiled and picked up her handbag. "A plain, ham sandwich sounds good to me, too," she replied.

Chapter 27

Watson pressed the shiny, silver button next to the name Hannah Ringrose then waited for either a voice to enquire who was calling, or the click of the latch to release the lock on the communal front door. As he waited, he straightened his tie and roughed-up his hair quickly with his fingers. He was looking forward to seeing Hannah Ringrose again.

After a few seconds, when neither voice nor click arrived, Watson repeated the process.

After a further two attempts, Watson pressed the button directly below, against the name A E Flanagan. This time the response was almost instantaneous.

"Hello," the speaker replied, in a diminutive weak voice, which suggested to Watson that A E Flanagan was an elderly lady.

"I'm sorry to bother you, Mrs Flanagan," he announced, his mouth a matter of centimetres from the speaker. "I was wanting to talk with your neighbour, Hannah Ringrose," he continued, "but there's no reply. I was wondering if you knew whether she'd gone away for Christmas?"

"I think she's in," the lady replied," and it's Miss Flanagan."

"Are you sure, because she's not answering the buzzer?" Watson enquired.

"No doubt she'll still be in bed," Miss Flanagan replied. "They didn't stop partying until about 3am so I'd imagine they're sleeping."

By the sound of her voice, Hannah's neighbour didn't seem to have appreciated the revelry of the previous night.

"I'm from the police, Miss Flanagan," Watson remarked. "Could you open the front door please, as I need to talk with Hannah."

"I don't know about that," replied the old woman. "How do I know you're the police?"

With cold, sleety rain now lashing down around him, Watson was keen to get inside. "I can show you some identification," he said, "but you'll need to come to the door."

"There's no need for that," replied the old woman, "just put it up to my window. My front room looks out where you're standing. With that the net curtains in the window to Watson's right were pushed a few inches and the wrinkled features on the face of an ancient lady peered out at him.

Watson smiled and took out his identity card, which he held up near to the window.

The old woman looked closely at it before releasing the net curtains and disappearing back into the room. A few seconds later there was a loud click which indicated that Watson had been sanctioned to enter the apartment complex.

Wet and cold, Watson rushed in before the door locked once more.

Hannah Ringrose's front door was only a matter of ten paces down the hall, which gave Watson a few moments to wipe away most of the icy droplets that had accumulated on his shoulders and clear away much of the slushy snow from the tops and sides of his shoes.

Expecting he'd need to make a fair amount of noise to rouse Hannah, if she had indeed been partying until the early hours, Watson rapped heavily on the door with the base of his clenched right hand. He waited for a few seconds before again banging as loudly as he could and followed this up by shouting, "Miss Ringrose, it's the police. Can you open the door, please?"

He was about to strike the door for a third time when he heard movement from inside the apartment, suggesting Hannah was making her way towards the door.

When eventually the front door opened, Watson was taken aback by the vision that confronted him. It was quite clearly the slender, brunette, whom he and Carmichael had interviewed on Monday, but, in a grubby, white onesie, with her hair somewhat dishevelled and the confident, warm smile absent from her now very pale face, Hannah Ringrose looked very different and far less appealing than she had a few days earlier.

"Oh, it's you," she remarked, brushing back her hair from her forehead, with no hint of the welcome smile presented when they last met. "Has that old bag next door been complaining about the noise?"

Watson shook his head. "No, I want to talk to you about something much more serious," he replied. "Can I come inside?"

* * * *

In contrast, Cooper's reception when he rang Lesley Saxham's doorbell was far more in keeping with the friendliness that normally flourishes at Christmas time. Having been welcomed with a kindly smile and invited in to join the half a dozen or so smiling friends that Lesley and her husband Greg had invited round for drinks and a sumptuous lunchtime buffet, Cooper had been ushered into a small, but tastefully furnished, side room. There he'd been given a glass of orange juice, a plate of assorted sandwiches and a fancy, petite cinnamon-encrusted cake which Lesley's husband had been given the credit for creating.

"So I assume you're here about poor Duncan," Lesley remarked as soon as the two of them were alone. "Belinda called me last night to tell me the terrible news. Was he really murdered?"

173

"I'm afraid so," Cooper replied.

Lesley Saxham was no longer smiling, instead she struck a more sombre demeanour more appropriate for the discussion she knew they were about to have. "I've known Duncan for years," she remarked. "It's hard to accept he's dead, and even more unbelievable to know that someone killed him."

Cooper nodded. "As you knew him so long, do you know of anyone who may have held a grudge or who he may have offended?"

Lesley shrugged her shoulders. "No," she replied. "Well not to the extent that someone would kill him?"

"So, he did have enemies?" Cooper enquired.

Lesley paused for a few seconds. "Well, not enemies," she replied. "Not to that extent, but he could be difficult and I'd imagine, over the years, he's had more than the odd spat with people. But not to the degree that someone would kill him."

"And what about his relationship with Hayley?" Cooper enquired. "Was that a good marriage?"

"As I told your colleagues, Inspector Carmichael and Sergeant Watson the other day, they seemed devoted," Lesley replied. "Do you think Hayley's disappearance and Duncan's murder are linked?"

Cooper shook his head. "Well the good news is that Mrs Bell is safe and sound," he replied. "So we don't think so."

"Where the devil was she?" Lesley enquired, her face beaming as if a huge weight had been lifted from her shoulders.

As they'd not yet spoken properly with Hayley, Cooper wanted to limit what information he shared about Lesley's missing friend.

"I can't really tell you too much," he replied, "but you'll be pleased to know she's safe and well."

"I understand," Lesley remarked with a knowing smile and faint nod of her head. "I expect there's much you need to establish first before you can be more forthcoming."

"Exactly," replied Cooper with a smile as he had a small nibble of one of the sandwiches which, up until that moment, had remained uneaten on his plate.

"Now going back to Duncan," he continued once he'd swallowed the tasty morsel, "we're led to believe that he was… how can I put it, fond of women."

Lesley smiled. "A roving eye," she remarked. "That's what my mother would have called it." As she spoke, a tiny grin appeared on her lips.

"Precisely," said Cooper. "Particularly for younger women."

Lesley nodded. "I'm not sure he's been as active in recent times," she continued, "but he was a terrible flirt when he was younger. His first two wives knew of it, I know, but, to my knowledge, he's mellowed with age and certainly since he's been with Hayley I've no knowledge of him straying. But, of course, he'd not confide in me."

"But being her friend," Cooper added, "surely Hayley might, if she suspected anything was amiss?"

Lesley considered his question," I'm not so certain she would," she replied. "It's more likely she'd tell Francis, I think, or even young Hannah or Maxine. I don't think she'd share that sort of thing with either Belinda or I."

"Why not?" Cooper asked.

"We never spoke about those sort of things," Lesley replied in a matter-of-fact way. "Our relationship wasn't like that."

Cooper, realising that his interview was about to end, took a bite of the cinnamon cake followed by a sip of orange juice.

"I've just a few questions I need to ask you," he said. "Firstly, can you tell me when you last saw Duncan?"

Lesley pondered the question. "It must have been on Saturday when you and that pretty young colleague came to Duncan's house," she replied. "I left at about 3pm. Yes, I think it must have been then."

"Also, can I ask whether you are aware of the combination for the Bells' key safe?" Cooper asked.

Lesley thought for a few seconds. "I've never had the need to use it, but I know it was 1564," she replied with a smile. "Shakespeare's birthday, Duncan's literary hero."

"One final question," said Cooper. "Can you tell me what you were doing on Sunday between the hours of 12 noon and 4pm?"

Lesley's smile evaporated. "You don't honestly think I killed him, do you?" she remarked with a degree of amazement in her voice.

"I have to ask," replied Cooper. "We have to be able to account for everyone's movements."

"I went for a walk on Sunday morning," Lesley replied. "I was probably back by about noon or 12.30pm, then I went to the supermarket to buy more food for Christmas. I'll probably still have the receipt somewhere, if that would help?"

Cooper nodded. "If you could get us that, it would be useful," he replied. "And when you were walking, were you on your own?"

Lesley smiled. "No, I took Bruno with me," she replied. "He's our Boxer. We went down to the river. It was such a wonderful, crisp, fresh morning."

"And did anyone see you when you were walking?" Cooper enquired.

"I'd imagine lots of people," Lesley replied, "not that I know any of them by name, but I see a lot of the same people down there every Sunday morning."

Cooper took a last bite out of the cinnamon cake. "Well, I'll leave you to your party," he remarked. "Thank you for your time, Mrs Saxham."

"Not at all," she replied. "Please finish your sandwiches and I'll look for that supermarket receipt."

Without waiting for a reply, she shot up out of her chair and made a rapid exit.

As he waited, Cooper demolished the plate of sandwiches and drained his glass dry.

"Here you go," Lesley piped up as soon as she set foot back in the room, "my receipt."

Cooper stood up from his seat and took the receipt out of Lesley Saxham's outstretched hand. It was for £135.96 from the most expensive supermarket in the region, about twenty minutes' drive away, with the time and date being 14.57pm on Sunday, 23rd December.

"Thanks," he replied. "As I say, it's just standard procedure."

"I understand," Lesley replied with a friendly smile. "You're just doing your job."

Chapter 28

Reluctantly, Hannah Ringrose had let Watson into her apartment. Having been woken abruptly by him hammering on her door, she was clearly annoyed and her general demeanour did little to hide the fact.

"Who the hell was that?" came a muffled male grunt, from what Watson assumed was the bedroom, as Hannah led him down the hallway.

"It's nothing, babe, go back to sleep," Hannah replied before closing the door and walking further down the hallway and into the lounge.

"Looks like you had a good evening," Watson remarked sarcastically as he followed her through and caught sight of the array of half-filled plastic beakers and paper plates, some empty, others with half-eaten reminders of the previous evening's festivities.

Hannah gazed back at the sergeant and forced a smile before grabbing a handful of paper plates off the only sofa in the room and pointing towards the space she'd cleared, her invitation for him to be seated.

"Thanks," Watson remarked before crunching his way across the crisp-and-peanut-festooned carpet and plonking himself down on the sofa.

"Can I get you a drink?" Hannah enquired, walking back towards the door.

Watson was feeling thirsty and, under normal

circumstances would have accepted the kind offer, but the state of the place suggested to him that no vessel he'd be given would be clean enough to drink from.

"No," he replied with a forced smile, "I won't keep you long."

"Do you mind if I get one?" Hannah remarked. "I've got the mother of all hangovers this morning, so I need a couple of aspirins pretty sharpish."

Watson looked up at her from the uncomfortable sofa. Her face was pale and the way she kept breathing in deeply through her nose suggested to him that she was certainly feeling worse for wear and possibly not far away from being physically sick.

"You go ahead," he replied as affably as he could.

Hannah didn't hang around. Within seconds she'd disappeared and, a few moments later, Watson thought he heard a retching sound emanating from the bathroom.

As he waited, Watson looked more closely around the dimly-lit room.

He wasn't averse to throwing a party himself and had been very hung-over after an all-night bash on more than one occasion. However, he couldn't ever remember waking up the next morning to the mayhem that surrounded him now.

It was only as his eyes became accustomed to the gloom that he suddenly realised there were two entwined bodies, fully clothed, in the corner of the room and bar the occasional whistling sound as one of them breathed a little louder than normal, they looked dead to the world.

He was still studying the sleeping pair when Hannah reappeared in the doorway, a pint glass in her hand fizzing like an experiment in a chemistry lab as her aspirins dissolved.

"Ignore Baz and Helen," Hannah casually remarked. "Baz drank a bit too much last night so they crashed out here. They'll be out for hours yet, I suspect."

Watson raised his eyebrows before turning back to face Hannah.

"I assume there's been some development with Hayley," continued Hannah.

Watson nodded. "Yes, there has," he replied. "We believe she's safe, but that's not why I'm here."

Hannah took a large gulp from the pint glass. "So, what's up?" she enquired.

"Her husband, Duncan Bell's been murdered," Watson replied, keeping a sharp eye on Hannah in order to gauge her reaction.

"Really!" Hannah exclaimed, in a manner that left Watson in no doubt that this was news to her. "How did he die?"

"The scene of crime officers and the police pathologist are still carrying out their investigations," Watson remarked. "But it looks like he was stabbed to death."

"Where?" Hannah enquired.

Watson chose not to answer her question.

"I need you to tell me where you were on Sunday," he remarked.

To Watson's surprise, Hannah smiled. "Am I a suspect?" she asked. "I am, aren't I? That's wicked!"

Watson was amazed. "This is a murder enquiry," he replied angrily. "It's not some game!"

Hannah took a deep breath and appeared to attempt to look serious.

"Sunday, Sunday," she muttered to herself as she tried to remember. "Oh, Andy and I went down to Buxton to see his parents for the day," she eventually replied. "We had an early Christmas there as they have flown off to Cape Town to spend Christmas with Andy's older sister and her new baby."

"What time did you leave?" Watson enquired.

"It would have been about 9.30am," Hannah replied. "And we got back here at about 10pm."

Watson smiled. "It's just a formality, but I'll need you to provide me with their telephone number, so we can verify what you're telling me," Watson remarked. "And I'll need Andy to confirm your story, too."

"Sure," Hannah replied. "Do you need him to do that now?"

Watson nodded and stood up. "It may save time if he does," he replied.

"Shall I fetch him?" Hannah asked.

"Why don't we go in and see him together," Watson replied. "I think that would be better."

In a manner more akin to a petulant teenager than a woman in her late twenties or early thirties, Hannah Ringrose stood up and led Watson towards her sleeping boyfriend in the bedroom next door.

* * * *

Penny's walk with Mr Swaffy took far longer than she'd anticipated, but even though it was 12.30pm when she returned, she had half expected her children, and possibly even Aunty Audrey, to still be in bed.

She was, therefore, taken by surprise as she trudged back up the path towards the house, when the front door flew open and the pallid, worried face of her youngest daughter, Natalie, still clad in her pyjamas, greeted her.

"Where have you been, Mum," she exclaimed loudly, "we've been trying to call you on your mobile."

In her earlier haste Penny had left her mobile behind, a fact she only realised at that moment.

"What on earth is the matter?" Penny enquired apprehensively as she strode more quickly towards her daughter.

"It's Aunty Audrey," came the anxious reply. "She's dying!"

Chapter 29

It was 12.30pm when Watson emerged from Hannah Ringrose's apartment into the freezing afternoon air.

To his delight, the sleety rain had stopped, but it was still bitterly cold and with the ground beneath him being thick with a mixture of snow, slush and ice, the sergeant was watchful where he placed his feet.

With Andy Partridge, Hannah's grumpy, hung-over boyfriend, corroborating her alibi for Sunday, Watson had seen no need to hang around and had made a hasty exit. With his positive first impression of Hannah now completely shattered, Watson was pleased to be able to head off back to Kirkwood police station and the opportunity to help Carmichael interview Hayley Bell and Francis Scott.

He gingerly picked his way over to his car, conscious of the hazardous conditions underfoot, trying hard not to take a tumble in his haste to escape.

Once at his car, he made no attempt to linger and, within seconds of closing the door, sped off in the direction of Kirkwood, the heater on full and the radio turned up loud to mask the noise of the fan as it ejected warm air onto his feet and face.

* * * *

As soon as she'd entered the house, Penny released her grip on Mr Swaffy's lead and threw off her coat.

She bounded upstairs, two at a time and rushed into Aunty Audrey's bedroom where Robbie and Jemma stood, worried expressions etched across their faces. Aunty Audrey lay in her bed, propped up by a large pillow, her ashen head wet with perspiration and her eyes rolled upwards to the ceiling.

"What's the matter?" Penny asked anxiously as she approached the bed.

"We think she's having a heart attack," Jemma replied fretfully. "I've rang an ambulance and it's on its way."

"Where's the pain?" Penny asked the old woman as she reached her bed.

Audrey turned ever so slightly to her side, as if to be more able to communicate.

"It's in my…"

Before she could finish her sentence, the quiet of the room was shattered by a loud, long, rasping sound coming from under Audrey's blankets.

As soon as they heard it, Penny's eldest children both edged back a pace and, to everyone's relief, the colour almost immediately returned to Audrey's face.

"Do you think you may just have wind, Audrey?" Penny enquired, even though to her it was obvious what the trouble had been.

Before the now more-relaxed-looking Audrey could reply, Natalie appeared at the bedroom door. "The ambulance is here," she announced excitedly.

Penny puffed out her cheeks and rolled her eyes skyward. "Fantastic," she muttered under her breath, as she realised she'd have to tell the emergency service it had been a false alarm.

* * * *

Totally oblivious to the happenings back at home, Carmichael entered the small private room located next to the main

183

reception at Kirkwood police station, with DC Dalton a few paces behind him.

"Good afternoon, ladies," he remarked with a wide, friendly smile as he strode resolutely towards the two nervous-looking, middle-aged women seated facing the entrance. "My name's Inspector Carmichael and this is DC Dalton."

Chapter 30

It was 1pm precisely when Watson and Cooper entered Kirkwood police station. The two sergeants had met in the car park and, having spent a few minutes updating each other on the findings of their respective interviews, they ambled casually into the main incident room.

"Good to see you both giving this case such urgency," Carmichael remarked, in a sarcastic tone.

Neither officer replied, they knew from experience that the best way to cope with Carmichael when he was being facetious was to say nothing.

Carmichael put his hands behind his head and leaned back slightly in his chair.

"So do you feel any of the people you spoke to this morning could be our killer?" he enquired, his question aimed at both officers.

"I think Maxine Lowe's boyfriend, Pete Thorn, has to be on our list," Watson remarked. "He's a strange guy, really hostile and incredibly protective of Maxine."

"Really," Carmichael replied. "Where did he say he was when Duncan Bell was murdered?"

"That's the snag," said Watson dejectedly. "He reckons he was at work on that day, starting at 8am and finishing at 6pm. I've not yet tried to verify this with Steadmans Printers, where he works, but if they confirm what he says is true then he's in the clear."

"And what would his motive be?" Rachel asked.

"Bell was a lech who'd tried it on with Maxine," Watson replied. "I'd say that would be more than enough to drive Thorn to violence."

Carmichael took a few seconds to take in what Watson had told him. "Anyone else?" he added, again his question aimed at both sergeants.

Watson shook his head. "I'm pretty certain that Hannah Ringrose isn't involved," he remarked. "She was in Buxton with her boyfriend's family all day. It couldn't be her."

"And they confirmed that, did they?" Carmichael remarked.

"Er, no," Watson replied. "But her boyfriend, Andy, did."

Carmichael nodded. "What about you?" he enquired, his eyes now fixed solely in Cooper's direction.

"I spoke with Lesley Saxham," Cooper replied. "She maintains that on Sunday morning she went for a walk with her dog until about noon or 12.30pm, then she went to the supermarket to buy more food."

"Did anyone see you when you were walking?" Carmichael asked.

Cooper smiled. "I asked her the same question," he replied. "She maintains there would be quite a few people who saw her. However, she wasn't able to name any of them, but reckons it's the same group of people she sees down there every Sunday morning."

"That should be easy enough to check out," Rachel remarked.

Carmichael shrugged his shoulders. "Maybe," he replied, his words delivered in a way that suggested he wasn't altogether convinced. "And did she have a receipt for the shopping?" he continued.

"Yes," Cooper replied, holding it up in his hand. "Here it is, timed at 2.57pm."

"It doesn't seem like you think she's our killer," Carmichael remarked.

Cooper shook his head. "We need to check out her story," he conceded, "but I don't see her being our murderer. She's no reason to kill him and, to be honest, she seems to be one of only a few people we've spoken to who appeared to like him."

Carmichael nodded.

"That's true," Watson concurred. "His only fans seem to be her and Belinda Bishop as far as I can see."

"You may well be right," Carmichael added. "Nevertheless, I want her story and the alibis of the others checked out meticulously. I don't want us to overlook anything by being misled by hunches. Let's do this as thoroughly as we can."

His three officers nodded.

"But those checks can wait a while as we've Hayley Bell and Francis Scott downstairs," Carmichael remarked enthusiastically. "And I want to know what they've been up to. Hayley's disappearance may have nothing to do with her husband's death, but both those ladies have a lot of explaining to do."

As he spoke, Carmichael could see a confused look on Watson's face. "What's the matter, Marc?" he enquired.

"It's just I'm surprised they'd managed to arrive yet," he replied, his forehead furrowed with lines of astonishment.

"Why do you say that?" Carmichael asked.

"Because it was on the radio, when I was driving back from my meeting with Hannah Ringrose, the M6 has been shut in both directions just south of Thelwall Viaduct for the last three hours. Apparently the roads are gridlocked. And coming up from Devon they'd have had to have gone that way, there's no other route. I thought they'd be stuck in the middle of it all."

Chapter 31

Watson switched on the recording equipment. "Interview with Hayley Bell, at Kirkwood police station," he said in a clear voice. "The time is 13.52pm. In attendance Inspector Carmichael, Sergeant Watson and PC Dyer."

As he finished his sentence, Watson gazed over his left shoulder in the direction of the tall, thin constable who stood stiffly at the door of the interview room.

"Why are you recording our conversation?" enquired Hayley, the intonation in her voice emphasising her apparent bemusement.

Carmichael looked up into her face. He'd found Hayley Bell to be more attractive and much younger-looking in the flesh than she'd appeared in the photographs he'd seen of her.

"You're not under arrest," he remarked, reassuringly, "so if you don't wish us to record the conversation we can turn off the machine. However, we've many questions to ask you and, with this being a murder enquiry into the death of your husband, it would help us enormously if we could capture your answers on tape. Is that OK?"

Carmichael stared deeply into Hayley's wide-open hazel eyes.

It took her a few seconds to reply. "Yes, of course," she responded. "I've no objections."

Carmichael gave Hayley one of his warmest smiles. "Before we start, I'd just like to express our deepest sympathy, Mrs Bell, for your sad loss."

Hayley nodded. "Thank you," she replied. "That's very kind of you."

"Do you have any idea who might have wanted to kill Duncan?" Carmichael enquired.

Hayley considered the question for a few moments. "With a couple of exceptions, I'd say pretty much everyone he met over the years will have harboured bad feelings towards Duncan," she replied in a clear-cut manner. "He could be quite hostile when the mood took him."

"I see," Carmichael replied. "Anyone in particular, or anyone lately?"

Again Hayley took a few seconds to think before answering.

"Nobody in particular springs to mind," she replied.

"Does that include you?" Watson asked.

Hayley allowed herself a small smirk. "Oh that would include me, too, sergeant," she replied candidly. "But I'm not the murdering type. I'm a healer not a fighter."

After a slight pause, Carmichael looked intently into Hayley Bell's eyes. "I'd like to know why you decided to leave your husband, and why it was you chose to do so with such melodrama?" he enquired.

Hayley Bell, who up until that point had been sitting upright, eased herself back a few inches on her chair.

"I've not loved my husband for many years," she announced in a calm and controlled voice. "I did once, but…" Hayley paused for a few seconds as she considered how to word her reply, "but the light in our relationship went out some considerable time ago."

"So why did it take you so long to leave him?" Carmichael asked. "And why did you decide to leave him now?"

With arms tightly folded, Hayley threw her head back and gazed up at the ceiling. "I suppose the truth is I didn't have the courage until recently," she replied. "But a few months ago I decided I had to get out."

"Was there any specific event that triggered this?" Carmichael asked.

Hayley's head lowered allowing her once more to look into the eyes of her questioner. "No one event as such," she replied calmly. "I'd just had enough."

"So why did you adopt such an elaborate means of escaping?" Carmichael asked.

"I'm a dramatic soul," replied Hayley. "The mystery I created amused me."

Carmichael frowned. "Amused you!" he repeated, his frustrated voice raised to leave her in no doubt about his feelings. "You've had my team running around for days trying to find you. Did you not realise that people would be worried?"

Hayley's face remained impassive. "To be frank, Inspector," she replied, "I didn't expect there to be any furore. What happened took me totally by surprise. But, once I realised my disappearance was front-page news, I quickly sent you the video message so that you knew I was well."

Carmichael paused for a few seconds. "Yes, you did," he conceded. "You did that on Saturday as I recall."

"That's correct," Hayley replied. "As soon as I heard a report of my disappearance on the radio."

"Where did you make the recording?" Carmichael enquired.

Hayley looked blankly back at him, her expression suggesting she failed to see the relevance of his question. "From the cottage in Devon, of course," she replied.

"At roughly what time did you make the recording, Mrs Bell?" Carmichael asked.

"I don't recall exactly," Hayley replied. "At about 2pm or maybe 3pm."

"So quite soon after you arrived in Devon?" Carmichael observed.

"Well, yes," replied Hayley, her face looking a little

bemused. "We'd decided to make the recording when we were in the car driving down, and we used Francis's camera."

"Why didn't you just call us?" Carmichael enquired. "Or why didn't your friend just tell my officer when they spoke on the phone, instead of making up the story that she didn't know where you were?"

Hayley ran her hand through her hair. "We didn't want to reveal where I was," she replied. "I know it was wrong and, in hindsight, very foolish of us, but we'd planned my escape for so long and with such care to prevent Duncan knowing where I was. We just couldn't risk him finding out."

"Why?" Carmichael asked. "What was it that made you so frightened of him?"

Hayley leaned back in her chair, her arms still folded tightly against her chest. "Duncan was a difficult man," she announced. "He was a domineering person who had to control everyone and everything around him. He would never have let me go without a fight, which is why my escape had to be so meticulously planned and executed. If he'd have known where I was he'd never have allowed me to live there in peace."

Carmichael listened intently to Hayley's explanation before turning his head to look at Watson. "What do you think, sergeant?"

Watson shrugged his shoulders. "To be honest, sir," he replied, "I'm not sure what to make of it all. I would, however, like to know when you posted the disc and why you decided to post it to the *Observer* and not here, to the station."

Carmichael turned and stared back in Hayley's direction. "Yes, I'd like to know that, too," he remarked.

"We must have posted it at about 4pm on Saturday," Hayley replied. "We wanted it to catch the last post. And we chose the Observer as we thought they'd not only show it to you, but also let the general public know."

Carmichael paused for a few moments before leaning forward towards Hayley Bell.

"Do you know what I think, Mrs Bell?" he remarked. "I don't think you ever went to Devon. I certainly don't think you made and posted the disc on Saturday and, based upon the tissue of lies you've been telling us, I'm sorely tempted to charge you with wasting police time or even perverting the course of justice."

Hayley Bell recoiled back into her chair, as if Carmichael's words had been delivered with a physical force.

"Are you calling me a liar, Inspector?" she retorted, her voice angry but still controlled.

By her reaction, Carmichael felt confident that his statement was either true or close enough to make no difference.

"Put it this way, Hayley," Carmichael replied. "Had we been talking to you in June or July, I'd be more inclined to believe that a disc posted in Devon on Saturday could arrive on the doormat of the intended recipient on Monday. Although to be honest, that's not a given and I suspect when we check we'll find out that the last post on a Saturday in rural Devon will have long gone before 4pm. However, even if there is a collection after 4pm, in my view, the chances of a letter posted on the last Saturday before Christmas being delivered on Christmas Eve, just two days later, is almost nil. Furthermore, my sergeant informed me earlier that the M6 has been shut for hours, so I have no idea how you and Francis Scott managed to get yourself here today if you've driven from Devon. So, to answer your question, yes, I believe you have been lying to us."

Hayley Bell swallowed hard. "I'm saying nothing more," she said, "not until I can speak to a solicitor."

Her reaction was music to Carmichael's ears, as it convinced him even more that she had been misleading them.

"As I said before," Carmichael remarked in a calm, controlled manner, "you are not under arrest. However, you are more than welcome to ask a solicitor to accompany you when we talk again. My sergeant and I are going to leave you for a few minutes and during that time I strongly recommend you consider carefully what you tell us from now on because, when we return, we will want you to make a full statement. If, in that statement, you deliberately withhold evidence or intentionally try and mislead us, I will press charges against you which, given this is a murder enquiry, could prove very serious for you, possibly leading to a custodial sentence."

Having delivered his message, Carmichael rose from his chair and headed towards the exit.

Chapter 32

Watson closed the door of the interview room behind him and strode quickly down the hallway after Carmichael.

"Why didn't you arrest her and start interviewing her formally?" he enquired with the perplexed look Carmichael had seen numerous times since he'd been at Kirkwood.

Carmichael stopped and half turned. "I want to give her a chance to reflect on her situation," he replied. "She knows we know she's lying, so my guess is, the next time we talk to her, she'll tell us everything. At the moment she's not being charged with anything. I reckon she'll see this as her chance to start afresh."

Having delivered his reply, Carmichael turned and continued to march swiftly down the corridor towards the annex attached to meeting room 2, where Cooper and Rachel Dalton were talking to Francis Scott.

"Unless *she* murdered her husband," muttered Watson, so quietly that only he could hear. "And my money's now on her being our killer."

****

Within a few minutes, Carmichael and Watson had located themselves behind the two-way surveillance mirror and were listening to the conversation in the room next-door.

"To recap, then," Cooper remarked, "you and Mrs Bell had planned the escape for weeks. Only the two of you were aware of what you were attempting and the plan was for Mrs Bell to eventually make her way to Brisbane to meet her stepdaughter and start a new life over there."

"That's right," responded the rather portly Francis Scott.

"So, when you left the restaurant on Friday, you drove to Barton Bridge, got on the train and headed back to Kirkwood, getting changed into a hoodie on the way," Rachel Dalton added.

"Correct," Francis Scott replied.

"You remained on the train at Kirkwood station and when Hayley Bell got on, you gave her a rucksack with her change of clothes, which she slipped into in the toilet," Cooper continued. "Then you both got off at Barton Bridge station and went back to your house for the evening."

Francis Scott nodded to acknowledge they'd relayed the story correctly.

"Then early the following morning, which was Saturday, 22nd December, the two of you headed off down to Devon to the holiday cottage," said Cooper. "Remind me again what time you set off, your route and the time it took you to get there."

"We left at about 7am," she replied, exasperation etched across her chubby face. "We took the M6 then the M5, we stopped at a services just north of the M5 junction and also one in Somerset. And we arrived at the cottage at around 2pm."

"And while you were on your way, you heard the news report about Hayley going missing on the radio," added Rachel, "which prompted you to record and send the disc to the *Observer*."

"Again, that is correct," replied Francis Scott.

"Ask her why they sent the tape to the *Observer*?" Carmichael muttered at the glass in front of him.

To his dismay, neither Cooper nor Rachel Dalton asked the question.

"Then, this morning, you set off at 6am to come home," Rachel stated. "You pretty much followed the same route, but in reverse, and you came straight here."

Francis Scott nodded slowly, but big nods to ensure they were noticed.

"And during the four days you stayed in Devon, you didn't leave the house other than to get some food," Cooper added.

"That is exactly as it happened," Francis Scott replied. "You've got it perfectly right. Can I go now?"

Cooper looked sideways at Rachel Dalton. "If you can just wait here one moment," he replied. "We'll find out how Inspector Carmichael is getting on with Hayley, but assuming they are finished, too, I'm sure we can let you go. If you can wait here, we'll not be too long."

Cooper stood up and, with a slight movement of his head, indicated to Rachel that he'd like her to follow him out of the interview room.

"Sounds like they've rehearsed their stories well," Watson whispered at Carmichael. "Even down to their travelling times."

"Did you expect anything less?" Carmichael replied. "A pair of minds that are capable of planning such a sophisticated escape are more than capable of agreeing and sticking to a script about their movements. And they could well have managed to fool us if it wasn't for the incident on the M6 today. No amount of preparation could have helped them plan for that eventuality."

As he finished his sentence, the door opened and Cooper and Dalton joined them.

"I'm not sure how much of our interview you heard..." Cooper remarked.

"Enough," replied Carmichael before Cooper could continue. "They've got their story off-pat, that's for sure."

"How did it go with Hayley?" Rachel asked.

"Fine until we broke the news about the holdup on the M6," Watson replied. "She's now saying she wants a solicitor."

Cooper nodded sagely as, in his eyes, that was a predictable response.

"So shall we go back in and tell her we know they didn't travel up from Devon this morning?" Rachel asked.

Carmichael shook his head. "No, play her along a bit longer. See what else she'll tell you. If she finds out we know she's lying she'll probably clam up, too."

"What sort of thing do you want her to talk about?" Rachel enquired.

"For a start, ask her why they sent the tape to the *Observer*," Carmichael replied. "I'd like to hear what she has to say about that as I'm certain it's something they hadn't planned on being asked."

"OK," Cooper replied.

"And," added Carmichael, as the two officers were making their way back to the door, "you should ask her about Hayley's relationship with Duncan."

"OK," replied Cooper again before he and Rachel Dalton exited the small room.

"Do you think Hayley and Francis killed Duncan?" Watson enquired as soon as he and his boss were alone in the small viewing room.

"I think they might have," replied Carmichael as he peered intently through the glass screen of the mirror. "They're certainly not all they seem, that's for sure, so who knows what they're capable of."

Chapter 33

Tarquin Bishop was surprised, when he opened his front door, to see Lesley Saxham shivering on his doorstep with a bottle of expensive-looking red wine in her hand.

"This is a pleasant surprise," he remarked.

"Didn't Belinda mention she'd invited me over?" Lesley asked, the look on her face indicating it was her turn to be a little shocked.

"Er, no," replied Tarquin. "When did she do that?"

"This morning," Lesley revealed, the small creases on her brow and the faint shake of her head indicating mild frustration. "She called me early this morning and asked me if I'd care to come over."

"Really," remarked Tarquin. "In that case you'd better come in." As he spoke, Tarquin opened the door wider to allow Lesley to slip inside.

"As it happens, I've not seen or heard from Belinda for a few hours," he remarked as he took the wine from Lesley and studied the label. "I've been out for a while myself, at the pub down the road. I've only just got back in, actually."

Lesley smiled. A knowing smile suggesting she could imagine how her friend's husband had spent the afternoon. "Is she in the sitting room?"

Tarquin shrugged his shoulders, "I expect so," he replied. "That's where she normally goes to get away from me."

As he spoke, Tarquin exposed a few of his yellowing teeth

in an attempt to feign a smile. However, his words were so close to what Lesley knew to be the truth that she ignored him and walked down the hall in the direction of Belinda Bishop's sitting room.

* * * *

Carmichael was in no great hurry to resume his interview with Hayley Bell. He was eager to listen to what Francis Scott had to say about Hayley's relationship with Duncan Bell, and what her answer would be when Cooper asked her to explain why they'd sent the disc to the *Observer*. He also figured another ten or fifteen minutes on her own, pondering her predicament, wouldn't harm his chances of getting Hayley to be more forthcoming.

Having sent Watson off to try and get more accurate details about the nature and timing of the incident earlier that day on the M6 at Thelwall, Carmichael sat quietly, alone in the annex, peering through the two-way mirror and listening intently to the discussion next-door.

"Of course, I'm very sorry that Duncan is dead," Francis announced, her words sincere enough, but delivered with little sentiment. "And to be murdered, too, makes it so much worse. However, I'd be lying if I said I liked the man. He wasn't a very nice person, in my opinion, he'd been a lousy husband to Hayley and, as far as I can make out, a failure as a father to those two poor children."

"Strong words," Cooper remarked. "What exactly was it that made him such an unpleasant person?"

Francis opened her eyes wide and puffed out her cheeks, as if she was finding it difficult to know where to start.

"He was a control freak," Francis announced. "He was a know-all, he was a bore and he was devoid of any trace of humanity."

Rachel Dalton recoiled a few inches back in her chair.

"We're also told he was a bit of a ladies' man, too," Cooper remarked. "Is that true?"

Francis laughed. "By that do you mean he was a sexist lech?" she retorted.

"I don't know," Cooper replied. "Is that how you'd describe him?"

Francis smiled. "Fortunately for me," she continued, "I was not blessed with the face, figure, or the demeanour that attracts that type of man, sergeant, so I cannot comment from first-hand experience. However, I think in his day, Duncan was actively promiscuous regardless of his marital status. And, although I'm sure of late his age almost certainly dampened his ardour and, I suspect, significantly diminished his success rate, to my knowledge he was still prone to foisting himself on some poor unsuspecting young thing, if he thought he stood a chance."

"And did Hayley know about this?" Rachel enquired.

Francis let out a huge belly-laugh. "Absolutely," she replied. "Why the hell do you think she was trying so hard to escape from him?"

"Well she's no need to escape, now," Rachel replied. "Now Duncan is dead, she's free of him."

Behind the glass, Carmichael smiled. He'd have been proud of delivering that line himself.

"One thing I cannot understand," Cooper remarked, "is why you and Hayley decided to produce and send out the disc? Surely having made such a detailed plan to get Hayley away and avoid being detected, the very last thing you'd want to do is to make contact a few days later."

On hearing the question, Carmichael watched Francis Scott with greater intensity. Her facial expression changed markedly and the slight shuffling in her chair suggested to him that she was uneasy.

"We hadn't expected Hayley's departure to become national news," Francis explained, trying hard to exude a degree of nonchalance. "We just didn't want you or anyone else wasting time or believing that a murder or kidnapping had taken place."

"Did you not realise that was exactly what would happen when you were concocting your plan?" Rachel remarked. "Surely you must have known the disappearance of a respectable woman on a train, without any apparent reason, was going to attract national interest and would be investigated by the police."

Francis Scott sheepishly shrugged her shoulders. "We didn't," she replied rather meekly. "Honestly, we never ever expected it to be front-page news."

"Tell me about that disc?" Cooper continued. "When did you record it?"

"As I told you earlier, we did it on the Saturday, as soon as we arrived in Devon," Francis replied.

"And you then posted it to the *Observer,*" Cooper remarked.

"Yes," replied Francis.

"Why the *Observer?*" Cooper asked. "Surely posting it to Duncan or to the police would have been the most obvious thing to do?"

Francis Scott shrugged her shoulders again. "We just thought the *Observer* would be more likely to make Hayley's message more widely known," she replied, her answer sounding to Carmichael like it came straight off the top of her head.

Cooper paused for a while before leaning back in his chair.

"Before answering my next question," he announced, "I'd like you to think very carefully about how you reply. I want you also to be aware that deliberately trying to mislead the police is a very serious offence."

Cooper looked deep into Francis Scott's eyes. "Tell me

truthfully where you and Hayley stayed over the last few days because we know for a fact it wasn't Devon."

Carmichael observed Francis Scott even more keenly. She was clearly shocked by Cooper's statement and was now very uncomfortable. She shuffled even more markedly in her chair. Her chubby, round face blushed bright-pink and, as she considered how to answer Cooper's question, a small trickle of perspiration rolled down the side of her temple.

After a few seconds Francis Scott leaned back in her chair and folded her arms.

"I'm not prepared to answer any more questions, sergeant," she remarked, her voice trembling as she spoke. "I'm tired after a long drive and I'd like to go home."

Despite several attempts by Cooper and Rachel Dalton to get Francis to continue answering their questions, the portly lady remained silent, arms folded tightly and her eyes fixed at a point somewhere above both officers' heads.

With little sign of her changing her mind, Cooper and Dalton ended the interview and switched off the recording equipment.

"Can I go now?" Francis asked abruptly, in an indignant tone.

"Please remain here for a few moments, Miss Scott," Cooper replied calmly. "We need to talk with the Inspector. We won't be very long."

The two officers stood up and made their exit, leaving Francis Scott alone in the interview room.

* * * *

After vacating his position behind the two-way mirror, Carmichael met the two officers in the corridor outside the interview room.

"What do you think?" Cooper asked.

"It's obvious she's lying," replied Carmichael. "But whether we have any real grounds to charge her or Hayley is less clear."

"Do you think they killed Duncan?" Rachel enquired.

Carmichael shook his head. "I'm not sure," he replied honestly, "but they're certainly lying about something. And if it's not to cover up for murder, I don't know why."

As the three officers talked, the irrefutable image of Marc Watson appeared at the end of the corridor, his face stern and his movement swift and purposeful. As the three officers saw him their conversation halted. He was clearly in a hurry, not a characteristic normally attributable to their colleague.

"What is it, Marc?" Rachel enquired as he got within a few metres of them.

"There's been another murder," he replied in a loud, excited voice.

Chapter 34

The forensics team were already at the Bishops' house when Carmichael and his three trusty lieutenants walked into the cosy, small sitting room.

"Where's Dr Stock?" Carmichael enquired when, to his surprise, it wasn't the familiar stature of the old forensic scientist, but a young woman he'd never seen before, crouched over the lifeless corpse.

"My name's Dr Wilczek," replied the young pathologist in a strong Polish accent, "but you can call me Irina."

"Isn't that a variety of potato," Watson remarked in a slightly louder voice than he'd intended.

"That's a wilja," replied the pathologist with a contemptuous grin. "I learned that very early after coming over here from Poland."

"Where's Dr Stock?" Carmichael enquired again.

"He's at a concert," replied Irina. "I'm covering for him."

"He made it, then," Cooper remarked with a wry smile. "He was moaning this morning that he had tickets, but might miss it."

Carmichael, who didn't seem too interested in the conversation, gave a faint shrug of his shoulders, advanced a few steps closer to the body and took a few moments to study the gaping fissure on Belinda Bishop's blood-stained forehead.

"I guess it's pretty obvious how she died," he commented, as he gazed upon the dead woman's bruised and bloodied head. "But have you any idea what weapon was used and when she was killed?"

Irina pointed towards the floor where a large brass poker had been abandoned, with clear traces of blood and hair smeared over its handle. "I strongly suspect that is our murder weapon," she replied rather sarcastically. "And I'd imagine she's been dead for no more than five or six hours max."

Carmichael looked at his wrist watch. "So no earlier than 10am," he remarked.

The pathologist nodded. "And my guess is that death probably occurred between 11am and noon. Although I won't know for sure until I do a full examination."

"That rules out Maxine Lowe or Pete Thorn," remarked Watson, "as I was with them, then. But it's well before Hayley Bell and Francis Scott arrived at the police station, so they could have easily murdered Mrs Bishop then driven over to Kirkwood, afterwards."

"They could," Carmichael replied, with a gentle nod of his head. "But let's not jump to any conclusions, not just yet."

"Of course," Watson agreed. "Mind you it's a good job we asked Hayley Bell and Francis Scott to remain at the station. Now we have two murders on our hands, both of which were committed when Hayley and Francis have very shaky alibis, our focus has to be on them."

Although he agreed, Carmichael was keen not to allow his bumptious junior officer to have the satisfaction of knowing his own gut feeling was in tune with his sergeant's assumption. "As I said, Marc," he remarked sternly, looking Watson square in the eye, "now's not the time for hasty judgements. We focus our effort on doing our job thoroughly, which means finding out the facts, and quickly."

Watson nodded, but said nothing. There was no way he was going to argue.

"So who found the body?" Carmichael asked.

"It was her husband and a lady called Lesley Saxham," replied the uniformed officer who'd been the first on the scene. "They're with WPC Twamley in the living room. They're both very shaken."

Carmichael looked at DC Dalton then motioned his head in the direction of the next room.

"Come on, Rachel," he remarked. "Let's go and find out some details from them."

"What about us?" Watson enquired, his eyes moving in the direction of Sergeant Cooper.

"I want you, Cooper, to get back to Kirkwood police station and charge Hayley Bell and Francis Scott with wasting police time. That should give us a reason to keep them there while we gather more evidence," Carmichael ordered. "But don't mention anything to them about Belinda's murder, allow them both to see a solicitor, but keep them apart and make sure they remain detained at the station."

Cooper nodded and, without uttering a word, made a hasty exit.

"What about me?" Watson asked.

"I want you, Marc, to take this officer and do a thorough house to house investigation," Carmichael replied. "I want to know if any of the neighbours saw anything or anyone suspicious in or around this house in the last five hours."

By the expression on his face it was clear that Watson, not for the first time whilst working under Carmichael, believed he'd been given the rough end of the stick. He was, however, smart enough to know it was pointless saying anything.

* * * *

For the second time in the space of two days, Carmichael found himself confronted with Tarquin Bishop and asking questions about a murder, only this time it wasn't someone he despised, but his wife.

"I'm so sorry," Carmichael remarked with genuine sincerity. "I know this must be a very difficult time for you, but can you tell me how you came to find your wife had been murdered?"

Tarquin Bishop looked totally confused and utterly disconsolate. "I don't understand who would want to do such a thing to poor Belinda," he muttered, his head bowed low as he slumped forward on the sofa. "I know the old girl could be a tad sharp, but she wouldn't harm a fly."

As he spoke, Lesley Saxham, her eyes also moist as if she, too, had been in tears, wrapped a consoling arm around Tarquin's back and rested a firm hand on his shoulder. "It's just so awful," she remarked in a hushed, perplexed voice. "It makes no sense."

Carmichael sat down in an armchair a matter of a metre or so away from the two dazed figures.

"So which of you found Mrs Bishop?" he enquired.

"Well, both of us," replied Lesley. "Actually, me first, I was the first one in the room, but Tarquin was just a few seconds after me."

"And at what time was that?" Carmichael asked.

"It was at about 2.30pm," Lesley replied. "Belinda had called me this morning and asked me to come over. I had lunch guests so I told her I wouldn't be able to come right away, but that I'd be over as soon as I could. Our guests left at about 2.15pm and I came over almost straight away."

"That's right," Tarquin confirmed, his voice quiet and trembling and his eyes fixed to the floor in front of him. "She arrived at about 2.30pm and we went through to the sitting room to find Belinda."

Carmichael paused for a few seconds before asking his next question. "When did you last see your wife alive, Mr Bishop?" he enquired.

Tarquin shook his head gently from side to side.

"It was this morning at about 10.30," he replied, although his words didn't sound in the least bit assured. "She wanted to read her book, so she went to the sitting room. I just pottered around for an hour or so then I went to the White Hart for a few pints."

"Did you not say goodbye when you left?" DC Dalton asked.

Tarquin looked up at her, his face indicating he was still stunned by the death of his wife. "I suppose I must have," he replied vaguely, "although I can't be sure."

"But you didn't see her after she went into her room to read," Carmichael confirmed.

"No," Tarquin replied. "I didn't see her until we went into her room and saw her…"

As he spoke, his voice broke and he cradled his head in his hands, sobbing like a baby.

"I know it's difficult for you," Carmichael remarked sympathetically, "but we really do need to put a picture together of what happened here today."

Tarquin, still sobbing, lifted up his head. "I understand," he replied.

"What time did you return from the pub?" Carmichael asked.

"About 1.15pm," Tarquin replied.

"So an hour before Mrs Saxham arrived," Carmichael remarked.

Tarquin nodded his head. "Yes," he replied, "but, to be honest, it seemed like it was only minutes before Lesley arrived, as I think I must have fallen asleep in my chair pretty much as soon as I got in."

Carmichael didn't find that particularly difficult to believe as, judging from the smell of whisky on his breath, Tarquin had quite clearly consumed a fair few drinks that lunchtime.

"Just a few more questions," Carmichael said in a firm-but-sensitive tone. "Can you think of anyone who might want to harm your wife?"

Tarquin shook his head. "Absolutely nobody," he replied in a clear, assured voice. "She had no enemies at all."

"And how was she since she discovered Duncan's body," Carmichael enquired.

"I'm not sure what you mean," replied Tarquin, his face screwed up as if he was bewildered by the question.

"Well, was she nervous or worried about anything?" Carmichael remarked.

Tarquin nodded. "Well she was certainly very quiet and unquestionably not her normal self," he replied. "However, having found the murdered body of her old friend yesterday, I hardly think that's an unexpected reaction for her to have."

"You're right, of course," Carmichael concurred. "In the circumstances that is quite understandable."

By the faraway look in Tarquin's eyes, Carmichael could see that his spirit was now clearly wrecked. He saw no value in asking any further questions and, with a quick movement of his head, indicated to WPC Twamley to take the dishevelled and broken man out of the room. "Why don't you go with WPC Twamley," Carmichael suggested, "and get yourself a cup of tea?"

With a faint nod of his head, Tarquin Bishop rose to his feet and, guided by the young WPC, shuffled out of the room leaving Carmichael and DC Dalton alone with Lesley Saxham.

"He's devastated," remarked Lesley sorrowfully. "I can't say I've ever seen him in such a mess."

"You mentioned you'd received a call from Belinda this morning," said Carmichael. "What time was that?"

"It was about 9am," she replied. "Belinda sounded very agitated, as if she had something important to tell me, but I'm not sure what it was."

"Why did you think that?" Carmichael asked.

Lesley paused for a few moments while she considered the question. "It wasn't so much what she said," Lesley replied, "but the way she was so insistent that I meet her."

"She didn't give you any clue at all what it was she wanted to talk with you about?" DC Dalton enquired.

Lesley shook her head. "No, I'm sorry, she didn't. I just wish I'd been more inquisitive on the phone, or that I'd rushed over there and then."

"And why didn't you rush over?" Carmichael asked.

"Because, as I said already, I had some guests coming over for lunch," Lesley replied, her response indicating some irritation. "I had food to prepare."

Carmichael nodded deliberately, as if to reassure her he wasn't implying anything. "I see," he remarked. "And do you have any idea why anyone would kill Belinda?"

Lesley Saxham shook her head. "I've no idea at all," she replied definitively.

"Tell me about her relationship with Tarquin?" Carmichael asked. "Was theirs a good marriage?"

"I think so," Lesley replied. "Although, as I told you last time, when you asked me a similar question about the Bells, who really knows what goes on inside a marriage."

"Who knows indeed," Carmichael replied.

"Are you finished with me?" Lesley Saxham asked. "It's just I'd like to call my husband and tell him what's happened and that I'm bringing Tarquin back with me."

"That's very charitable of you, Mrs Saxham," Carmichael observed.

"It's the least I can do," she replied with a faint smile. "After all, Belinda was one of my oldest friends."

"Of course," Carmichael replied. "But before either you or Mr Bishop go anywhere, you'll both need to give DC Dalton a full statement."

As he uttered his words, Carmichael stared at Rachel before rising slowly from his chair. "I'll see you back at the station at 5.30pm," he remarked. "I'll call Watson and Cooper to make sure they're there then, also."

"Right you are, sir," replied DC Dalton as she watched her boss leave the room.

Chapter 35

The last thing Carmichael wanted to see when leaving the Bishops' house was the posse of twenty-or-so reporters who were jostling for a good position outside the cordoned area at the end of the driveway, microphones and pencils at the ready.

"Bugger," he muttered in exasperation, knowing he'd have to pass through them in order to reach his car.

"Is there anything you want to tell us?" one reporter shouted out.

"Are these two murders linked?" shouted another.

"At the moment I can't share any information with you," Carmichael replied calmly as he swiftly tried to get beyond the zealous media scrum.

"Is it true that Hayley Bell's in custody, charged with the murder of her husband?" was one of several questions fired in Carmichael's direction as he elbowed his way through the tightly-packed news reporters.

Carmichael ignored all the questions and, despite his black BMW being almost surrounded, he managed to open the door and clamber into the driving seat.

"Is Hayley Bell still gambling heavily?" Carmichael heard one of the hacks shout out just before he shut the car door.

Before starting the engine, Carmichael peered out of the window to try and spot the reporter who'd posed that particular question, but in the confusion, it was impossible.

After pausing a few seconds, Carmichael started his engine and gently edged the car out of the throng. As soon as it was safe to do so, he rapidly changed up a couple of gears and sped off in the direction of Kirkwood police station.

****

On his way, Carmichael dialled home.

"I'm afraid it's going to be a late one," he advised Penny before the conversation had barely started. "There's been another murder."

"Who this time?" Penny enquired.

"A woman called Belinda Bishop," Carmichael replied.

"Is this murder connected with the other one?" Penny asked.

"It would be too much of a coincidence if it wasn't," he replied pensively. "I've got the team together at 5.30pm, I need to brief Hewitt before then and, as two of our main suspects are both already in custody at the station, I reckon it will be near midnight before we're through."

"Have you eaten?" Penny asked, a question she almost immediately regretted as it seemed such an inappropriate remark to make given all her husband would have on his plate, but it was the first thing she thought of.

Carmichael chuckled. "Not yet," he replied, "but I will. How's your day been?"

Penny toyed with relaying the story of Aunty Audrey's phantom heart attack, but decided that could probably wait. "Nothing too strenuous," she replied. "We've just been watching the films on TV, mainly."

"And Audrey," Carmichael remarked guardedly. "Has she behaved herself?"

"Still playing Candy Crush," Penny replied. "She's on level sixty or seventy now, quite the expert."

"I guess as long as it keeps her quiet and occupied we should be thankful," Carmichael replied. "Anyway, I'll have to go, I need to call Hewitt and fill him in on the latest murder."

"See you later," Penny remarked before turning off her mobile and picking up the half-full mug of tea from the small table next to her cosy armchair.

* * * *

Chief Inspector Hewitt was at home when Carmichael's call came through. Having listened intently to the detailed update, Hewitt cleared his throat in his customary, annoying, theatrical fashion. "So your main suspects are either Hayley Bell and her friend, or Tarquin Bishop," he remarked, more as a deduction than a question.

"We'll certainly need to investigate their movements at the time of the two deaths in great detail, but they're not our only suspects," Carmichael replied.

"So who else have you got?" Hewitt asked gruffly.

"There are the other members of the reading group," replied Carmichael, "and at least one of their partners has made it clear he hated Duncan Bell."

"But I thought you said he was being questioned by Watson when this latest death happened?" Hewitt retorted.

"The time of death still needs to be verified," replied Carmichael. "So I want to keep all my options open for the moment."

"That's fully understandable," Hewitt remarked. "But for heaven's sake make sure you focus initially on Hayley Bell, Francis Scott and Tarquin Bishop. From what you've told me, it's likely to be one of those three who you're looking for."

"I was planning to talk again with Tarquin Bishop in the morning," Carmichael replied, "but we'll be interviewing Hayley Bell and Francis Scott again this evening."

"Keep me abreast of your progress, Carmichael," Hewitt remarked, in a manner which indicated the conversation was about to end.

"I'll call you should we make a breakthrough," Carmichael announced calmly, pleased his update with Hewitt was over.

Without any further niceties, the line went dead leaving Carmichael less than ten minutes' drive away from the station, which was long enough for him to ponder two things. The first was just how he was going to go about conducting the interviews with the two ladies at the station. The second issue, which was uppermost in his mind, was whether there was any substance to the comment made by the reporter outside the Bishops' house, insinuating that Hayley had a gambling habit.

Chapter 36

Carmichael's team meeting commenced at precisely 5.30pm, the allotted time.

"How did you get on with the house-to-house?" Carmichael enquired, his eyes fixed firmly in Watson's direction.

"A complete blank," Watson replied. "We got no answer from most of the houses, presumably the occupants were visiting friends and family for Christmas, and where we did manage to speak to neighbours, none indicated seeing anything out of the ordinary. In fairness, the Bishops' house is quite hidden, so if someone had broken in, or had been acting suspiciously, it would be difficult to spot."

Carmichael's expression indicated his disappointment, but he elected not to ask Watson anything else.

"What about you, Rachel?" he enquired, turning his body a few degrees and pointing his bright blue eyes in DC Dalton's direction.

"Did you get Tarquin Bishop's and Lesley Saxham's statements?"

The young DC ran her fingers through her short, dark hair. "Yes," she replied before placing a copy of the two statements on the desk in front of Carmichael. "Tarquin Bishop maintains he fell asleep in the chair in the front room when he got home from the pub and it was not until Lesley rang the doorbell that he woke up. He claims he hadn't tried to find his wife when he arrived home and is, frankly, not quite sure exactly what time he did get back."

Watson smiled. "He was pissed, then, I take it," he observed.

Rachel nodded. "That would seem to be the case. I checked with the landlord of the White Hart," she continued. "He knows Tarquin well, he's a regular. He seems to remember Tarquin arriving at about 11am and leaving at about 1.30pm. The pub's about a fifteen-to-twenty-minute walk from his house, so I'd say Tarquin must have got back at about 1.50pm."

"About forty minutes before Lesley arrived," Carmichael remarked.

"Plenty of time for him to kill his wife," suggested Cooper.

Carmichael shook his head. "If our stand-in pathologist is right," he continued, "Belinda Bishop was already dead by the time he got back. She reckons the time of death was between 11am and noon, so if your publican is telling the truth, Tarquin Bishop is not the killer, as his wife was murdered when he was getting plastered in the pub."

"We can rule out Maxine Lowe and Pete Thorn," Watson added, "as I was with them at about that time."

"And Lesley Saxham maintains she had guests at her house until 2.15pm," Rachel added.

"So," Cooper announced, pointing up at the list of three names they'd drawn up in blue that morning when discussing Duncan's murder, "assuming we are looking for the same person for both murders, we appear to have just two names left."

"I know they never made the list," Watson added, "but if we are looking for the same person for both murders, we can strike off Hannah Ringrose and her partner, too, as they were in Buxton when Duncan was killed and I'm not sure whether they'd have had time to kill Belinda Bishop at 11am and get back to their flat by the time I arrived this morning."

"Which just leaves us with Hayley Bell and Francis Scott," Carmichael confirmed. "And I think it's about time we talked with those two ladies again, don't you?"

Chapter 37

Carmichael looked up at the large clock which hung on the wall directly behind Francis Scott's head; it indicated the time was 6.05pm. With PC Dyer stationed by the door, like a Buckingham Palace sentry, and with Cooper having set the recording equipment in motion and completed the niceties required before any formal interview could commence, Carmichael was ready to start.

"I'm not sure if your legal adviser has fully explained to you the gravity of the charge of wasting police time," he began in a calm but cordial tone, glancing in the direction of the young solicitor sitting to the left of Francis Scott, "but it's not a trivial offence, Ms Scott, especially given the serious nature of the crimes we are investigating."

"Crimes!" exclaimed Francis Scott insolently, "Hayley and I have done nothing wrong, we've committed no crime and, quite frankly, this trumped-up charge is an insult."

Carmichael looked to his left at the two-way mirror, behind which sat DS Watson and DC Dalton. He knew they would be listening intently to the grilling that was about to commence.

"Well, I'm pleased you've decided at least to engage with us," Carmichael remarked, his voice still controlled and his words delivered with a small, friendly smile. "Let me share with you what we know and then I'll give you a chance to be totally honest with us. How does that sound?"

Francis Scott gave a slight shrug of her shoulders, but said nothing.

"OK," Carmichael continued, his blue eyes fixed on the face of the woman less than a metre away from him, across the table. "We know that the disappearance of Hayley Bell was a very clever, carefully-planned exercise and it was meticulously executed by you and Mrs Bell. We also know that, despite telling us you drove up from Devon this morning, you did no such thing. What we don't know, however, is why, having taken so much trouble to plan Hayley's disappearance, you and Mrs Bell decided to send a video message via a disc to the local newspaper, just a day after you'd seemingly made a success of your vanishing act. Also, we don't understand why you sent it to the local newspaper rather than here."

Carmichael paused to allow Francis Scott to comment, however when it was clear she was going to remain silent, he continued.

"I also find it difficult to believe that the postal service, a few days before Christmas, would be so efficient as to deliver the parcel all the way from Devon in, effectively, one working day. In short, Ms Scott, other than to try and cover up the act of murder, I'm struggling to think of a reason why you and Mrs Bell would concoct such an elaborate escape plan and why you'd persist in lying to the police about your whereabouts in the last four or five days. Can you please help me understand what's been going on?"

Unmoved by Carmichael's words, Francis Scott eased herself slowly back in her chair and, after a faint glance to her left at her motionless solicitor, she folded her arms tightly and rested them on her chest.

"As I mentioned earlier to the sergeant here and the other officer, I've no comment," she replied with such cold arrogance it caused Carmichael to take a deep breath in through his nose as he tried to retain his composure.

"Let's leave it there, then," Carmichael remarked, much to the surprise of Francis Scott, the other three people in the room and the two watching from behind the two-way mirror. "You'll be detained here overnight and I'll interview you again in the morning. Maybe, after a good night's sleep in one of our cells, you'll feel more willing to talk."

"You're intending to hold my client overnight!" exclaimed the solicitor, his voice cracking as if the notion was mindboggling.

"Absolutely," replied Carmichael as he rose slowly to his feet. "I'm investigating two murders, so I'm in no mood to play silly games with your client."

Francis Scott's facial expression suggested she was shocked by Carmichael's surprise disclosure.

"There's been a second murder!" she called out. "Who else has died?"

Carmichael, who was now towering over Francis and her brief, frowned. "I think you've got this whole police interview procedure mixed up," he commented pointedly. "It's the police who ask the questions, you answer them."

After delivering his remark, Carmichael turned and, with Cooper close behind, made his way to the exit.

"Make sure Ms Scott is escorted to her accommodation for the night, PC Dyer," he instructed the still, statuesque officer posted by the door, before walking out into the corridor.

"Did you see the look on her face?" Carmichael asked Cooper as they walked briskly down towards interview room one.

"I did," replied Cooper. "If Francis knew Belinda Bishop was dead, she certainly did a great job of hiding it."

"That's exactly what I thought," remarked Carmichael. "But she's not going to tell us anything, not tonight anyway. She's sticking to their agreed script. But, based upon our last discussion with Hayley, I'm not sure she'll be so meticulous."

"Do you really think so?" Cooper asked, his tone suggesting he wasn't convinced.

Carmichael abruptly stopped walking, which took Cooper by surprise.

"No, not for certain," he replied, "but I'm about to find out."

Chapter 38

There was something about Hayley Bell that Carmichael found endearing. Although she was no longer in the full flush of youth, as his mother would have put it, she was still unmistakably attractive, and Carmichael imagined she would have been a stunner twenty years before. But it was not simply her looks he found appealing, it was more the powerful yet distinctly feminine persona and what was going on behind those mesmerising hazel eyes that fascinated Carmichael the most.

For this interview Carmichael asked Watson to accompany him, leaving DS Cooper and Rachel Dalton to watch from behind the glass.

"Have you thought through what we discussed earlier?" Carmichael enquired. "And have you had adequate time to consult your legal adviser?" As he spoke, Carmichael moved his eyes to his left where Hayley Bell's solicitor was seated.

"We have spoken," Hayley replied. "And whilst I have no idea why you have deemed it necessary to charge Francis and me with wasting police time, I'm prepared to co-operate fully with you in order to help you find whoever killed Duncan."

Carmichael smiled smugly and glanced momentarily at where he imagined Cooper to be sitting.

"That's excellent news," Carmichael replied, once his eyes had again met with those of Hayley Bell.

"So what is it you want to know?" Hayley continued, as if she was genuinely willing to provide honest answers to any questions Carmichael wished to throw at her.

Carmichael smiled back at the attractive woman on the other side of the desk. "Sergeant Watson," he remarked, his eyes remaining fixed on Hayley Bell. "Can you kindly pass over to Mrs Bell the report you have regarding the incident on the Thelwall Viaduct earlier today."

Watson released the document from his tight grip and slid it across the table in Hayley Bell's direction.

"Maybe you'd like to take a few moments to read it?" Carmichael suggested.

Hayley Bell picked up the report and examined its contents.

It took no more than two or three minutes for Hayley to place the report back on the table and push it back in Watson's direction.

"So, as you can see," Carmichael remarked, "as a result of an incident involving approximately thirteen vehicles, the northbound carriageway of the M6 at Thelwall has been closed since 9.52am. It reopened only two hours ago." As he spoke, Carmichael's eyes remained focussed on Hayley Bell. "With the extent of the delays, even if you had been able to exit the motorway, the diversion would have taken you over forty miles out of your way. As a result, as I'm sure you can understand, we don't believe it's possible for you to have got to the station at the time you did if you'd have been driving up from Devon."

Hayley Bell sighed gently, a sound of resignation that suggested to Carmichael she realised the substance of her previous story had been dealt a mortal blow.

"Look, Inspector," Hayley remarked with an air of guilt, "I admit we weren't in Devon, but, surely, not being entirely honest about where we were isn't such a major crime!"

Carmichael had no intention of allowing Hayley to try and control the conversation, so elected to avoid debating the point.

"So where did you and Francis Scott hide out when you went missing on Friday?" he asked.

"Before I answer that," Hayley remarked. "I want to make it absolutely clear that this whole thing was my idea and that Francis just helped me. She's not done anything wrong other than be a good and loyal friend."

Carmichael nodded. "I don't doubt her loyalty to you," he replied.

Hayley turned her head and made eye contact with her solicitor before returning her gaze to Carmichael.

"You're right," she said, her voice faltering slightly as she spoke. "Francis and I were staying in a cottage we'd rented in a small village near Kendal."

"Kendal!" exclaimed Watson, "but that's no more than an hour and a half away."

"It took us about two hours to get there," Hayley replied. "But, yes, we were quite close."

"Why on earth did Francis tell my officer that you were in Devon?" Carmichael asked. "And why, after you knew your husband was dead, did you keep up the pretence that you were in Devon?"

Hayley looked decidedly uncomfortable. She nervously ran her fingers through her hair and, for the first time, the gaze of her large hazel eyes moved from Carmichael to the table which separated them. "The plan was always for Francis to make out she was away in Devon," Hayley replied. "Therefore, when your officer called her she just told her that. And, after we knew that Duncan had been murdered, we decided it would be sensible to keep to that story, but add that I was with her, too. I know it sounds stupid, but we just thought if you knew we'd been less than honest about where we'd been staying, then that would throw suspicion on us."

"And presumably," continued Carmichael, "had there not have been an accident on the M6 today, and had we not been able to prove that you'd been lying to us, then you'd have maintained that story?"

Hayley once more glanced over at her solicitor before fixing her eyes again on Carmichael. "I suppose that's true," she replied sheepishly.

Carmichael raised his eyebrows, leaned back in his chair and took a deep breath. "So what else have you been less than truthful about?" he enquired sternly.

"There are a few other matters," replied Hayley, her gaze again lowered to the desk in front of her. "We didn't put the disc in the post as we told you. We hand delivered it through the letter box at the *Observer*."

"And when did you do that?" Carmichael enquired.

"It was very early on Monday," Hayley replied. "It was at about 5am, when we knew there would be nobody about."

"Presumably you chose the *Observer* as you knew there would be officers here around the clock and you didn't want to be spotted," remarked Carmichael.

Hayley nodded. "And possibly CCTV cameras, too," she admitted.

"And when exactly did you make the recording?" Carmichael enquired.

Hayley looked into his eyes, her face etched with guilt. "It was on Sunday evening," she replied.

"In your cottage in the Lake District," interjected Watson.

"That's correct," Hayley replied.

"What else?" Carmichael enquired.

Hayley Bell nervously fiddled with a small gold locket which hung around her neck on a gold chain. "I also went back to the house that morning," she said, her voice now showing the clear signs of her uneasiness. "I was only in there a matter of minutes, but I did go home."

"Why?" Carmichael enquired.

"To get my passport," Hayley replied. "As I knew that within hours everyone would know I was safe and well, I felt it would be a good idea if I had it."

"But why didn't you take it initially?" Watson enquired.

"Because when we planned my escape, Francis and I decided that I should deliberately leave it behind. In our original plan I wasn't intending to go abroad. However, I figured once people knew about the message on the disc, it might make sense for me to go abroad, maybe Australia to see Suzanne." said Hayley.

"But when you went back to the house, did you not worry about waking your husband?" Carmichael enquired.

Hayley nodded. "Oh yes," she said robustly. "But as I keep my passport in my bedroom drawer, and Duncan and I have separate rooms, I knew I'd be reasonably safe if I was quiet. Also, Duncan is a very sound sleeper, he takes a couple of sleeping tablets every night, so I knew I'd be pretty safe, but I was very nervous."

"And you took nothing else?" Carmichael asked.

Once more Hayley shook her head. "I was tempted to take my credit cards, but I decided you'd have noticed they'd been left behind so I didn't want to risk it."

"Risk us knowing you'd been back home?" Watson added.

"Yes," replied Hayley. "I thought we'd be pretty safe getting the passport, but I didn't want to risk taking anything else."

"So you had no idea when you entered the house that your husband was dead?" Carmichael remarked.

Hayley shook her head. "Absolutely not," she replied. "There's no way I'd have gone into the house if I'd known that."

"And when you were in the house did you enter the winter room?" Carmichael enquired.

"Is that where he was killed?" Hayley replied.

"Just answer the question, please, Mrs Bell," said Carmichael in a clear, authoritative tone.

"No, I did not," replied Hayley.

Carmichael looked over at Watson, whose expression suggested he was as flabbergasted at Hayley's revelations as he was.

"What else haven't you told us, Hayley?" he asked.

Hayley eased back into the chair. "I assure you, Inspector Carmichael," she replied, her tone open and sincere, "I have nothing more to add. I realise I should have been honest with you before, but when we talked earlier today, I was scared you may think I had something to do with my husband's death."

Carmichael glanced over at the clock on the wall, which indicated the time was 7.25pm.

"I think I'd like to stop the interview now," he remarked. "We can reconvene in the morning."

Hayley's eyes opened wide. "Am I free to go home?" she asked.

Carmichael shook his head. "I'm afraid not," he replied before rising to his feet. "We'll be keeping you in overnight."

"But, surely, wasting police time is not so serious as to warrant my client being kept in custody," the solicitor remarked.

"Under normal circumstances I'd agree," Carmichael replied. "However, I'm investigating a double murder and, as I'm not yet convinced your client is being totally honest with me, I'm not prepared to release either her or Francis Scott. Especially as they both have a talent for disappearing."

"Double murder!" exclaimed Hayley, her voice shrieking out the words.

"Didn't I tell you?" continued Carmichael with a smugness he couldn't conceal. "Today your friend, Belinda Bishop, was found murdered, too."

Hayley's eyes widened and her mouth opened. "Oh my god," she said, the shock etched across her face. "Who on earth would want to kill Belinda?"

"Who indeed?" Carmichael remarked. "But I'd certainly like to know your movements today which I'll read in the morning from the statement you'll be making to the duty sergeant tonight."

Carmichael didn't linger any further and, with Watson a few steps behind him, departed the interview room to join Dalton and Cooper in the adjoining annex.

Chapter 39

The four officers gathered together in the main incident room.

"What do you make of her story?" Cooper enquired, his question directed at his boss.

"I don't believe her," announced Watson, without waiting for Carmichael to share his opinion. "I reckon she killed him."

"What do you think, sir?" Rachel asked Carmichael. "Do you think it was her you saw behind the curtains on Sunday?"

Carmichael considered the question. "It could have been," he replied. "She could have been in the house when I met Duncan on Sunday, but, if she was, why would he have not said?"

"Maybe he didn't know she was there," suggested Watson. "She could have sneaked in and hid until you'd gone, then killed him."

Carmichael screwed up his face. "That may be what happened," he replied, "but I'm not convinced."

Cooper nodded. "And, like we saw with Francis Scott, if she knew Belinda was dead then she's also a brilliant actor," he remarked. "The look on both their faces when you told them was pure surprise, I'm certain of it."

Rachel nodded. "It was," she agreed. "I was watching Hayley at that moment. She was absolutely stunned when you told her."

"Maybe there are two killers," Watson suggested. "Maybe someone else killed Belinda, but Hayley and Francis have to be the prime suspects for Duncan's murder."

"Actually, that's an interesting point," Carmichael observed. "If you're right, Marc and it was Hayley who was in the house on Sunday, where was Francis?" I can't believe they both crept in without Duncan noticing. No, I think it was someone else I saw, if indeed there was anyone. It happened so quickly, maybe I was mistaken or maybe it was just a movement caused by a draught."

"Well, I don't buy that story of hers that she went over to the house at 5am to take her passport," Watson remarked, with conviction, "that would be such a risky thing for her to do. She knew Duncan was dead when she took that passport because she'd killed him."

Carmichael leaned back in his chair and glanced up at the clock.

"It's now 8.15pm," he remarked. "I don't think we're going to get anywhere further tonight. I suggest we all go home, enjoy what's left of Boxing Day with our families and reconvene tomorrow."

It was plain by the exhausted yet relieved looks on the faces of his three officers that they were only too happy to comply with Carmichael's latest instruction.

"What time do you want us to get together in the morning?" Rachel enquired.

Carmichael rubbed the stubble which was starting to poke through on his chin. "Why don't we do this?" he remarked. "In the morning you three check out our other suspects' alibis for both murders. Then let's reconvene here for lunch at 1pm, by which time I'll have managed to read Hayley's statement. I'll also interview both women again and I'll get someone from uniform to study all the CCTV tapes they can get hold of for Sunday and Monday to see if they can spot Francis's car in or around the area. Hopefully, between us, we'll have a much better idea of what the hell's going on here by the time we meet again tomorrow."

"Sounds like a good enough plan to me," Cooper remarked before grabbing his coat from the back of the chair.

"Me too," added Rachel as she picked up her bag and started to follow Cooper towards the door.

Watson slowly shook his head. "I admit we've not enough evidence to charge Hayley and Francis with the murders," he reluctantly conceded, "but I'm certain they're guilty."

"You may be right, Marc," Carmichael agreed, "that's why they're staying here, for now. Nevertheless, if we don't have anything more concrete by midday tomorrow, we're probably going to have to release them."

With another faint shake of his head, Watson grabbed his jacket and sloped off out of the office to join the other two, who were already walking away down the corridor.

* * * *

It was just after 9pm when Carmichael arrived home. The temperature had dropped considerably in the last few hours and, as he walked up the garden path, he could feel his feet slipping slightly with each step. He quickly opened the front door and rushed into the relative warmth of the hallway.

"Hi," he shouted as he removed his coat and hung it up on the coat hook high up on the wall.

When nobody replied, he walked the few paces down the hallway to the front room door.

"Oh hi," exclaimed Penny as her husband's head appeared round the door. "I was wondering when we'd see you."

Despite the fact that his three children and his aunty were also in the room, Penny was the only one to demonstrate the slightest bit of interest in his arrival.

Penny's warm welcome made Carmichael smile. "Do you want anything to eat?" she enquired, rising to her feet.

"That would be good," he replied. "It's been a full-on day, so I've hardly had time to grab anything."

"Let's go through to the kitchen," said Penny, a suggestion that sounded to Carmichael like she was relieved to have an excuse to escape from the others.

Once in the hallway, having shut the door behind them, Penny lovingly placed her arms around her husband's shoulders and planted a warm kiss on his lips.

"I'll have to come home late more often," he remarked.

"What do you mean?" Penny replied, "you're always coming home late."

Within a matter of minutes the pair were alone together in the kitchen, Penny busily making a massive turkey sandwich while Carmichael sipped steadily at the large glass of Pinotage he'd poured himself.

"So how's it been here?" he asked.

"Eventful," Penny replied. "Your Aunty thought she was about to die this morning, but, just as the ambulance arrived, we discovered she had wind!"

Carmichael almost choked on his wine. "You're having me on," he remarked. "You called the ambulance!"

"I was out," replied Penny. "It was poor Jemma and Natalie who did that."

"I bet the ambulance crew weren't best pleased," Carmichael replied with a smirk on his face.

"Actually they were fine," Penny replied. "I suspect they get that sort of thing all the time."

"How's the old dear now?" Carmichael asked.

"She's back to normal," replied Penny. "Eating everything that's put in front of her and sharing her robust opinions at every conceivable opportunity."

"And her wind?" Carmichael added.

"Fortunately we've had no repeat, as yet," Penny replied. "But the night is young."

Carmichael chuckled loudly. "I bet Saturday can't come quickly enough for you," he remarked.

"And for your children," Penny added. "I think even Natalie is now starting to lose patience with her."

Carmichael bit deep into the sandwich his wife had placed in front of him as they'd been talking.

"Anyway, how's the case going?" Penny enquired. "Do you have any idea who the killer is?"

Carmichael chewed and shook his head.

"Not really," he replied a few seconds later, having swallowed the mouthful. "We have Hayley Bell and her friend Francis Scott in custody, and Marc certainly thinks it's them, but I'm not so sure."

"Why?" Penny asked.

"Francis Scott's being very unco-operative," continued Carmichael, "which is often a sign of guilt. And Hayley has admitted she originally lied to us and that they were holed-up in the Lakes rather than in Devon. She's also admitted returning to the house. So, they're clearly not whiter-than-white and, at the moment, they are way-out-there as the most obvious people to have killed Duncan, but when we mentioned the second murder to each of them they were both genuinely shocked by the news. In short, I'm not sure it's them."

Penny picked up her glass of wine and sipped it for a few seconds.

"Don't take this the wrong way," she remarked, "but sometimes I think you can be taken in by women."

Carmichael frowned. "What do you mean by that?" he enquired, his voice sounding somewhat disconcerted.

"As I say, don't take it the wrong way, but you're not exactly renowned for being the best judge of when a woman is lying. I know the girls can sometimes hoodwink you."

"Can they now?" Carmichael replied, his tone still one of incredulity. "I see I'm going to have to be less trusting from now on with the ladies in this house."

Penny smiled. "Present company excepted, of course."

"Of course," replied Carmichael with raised eyebrows, before taking a deep swig of the blood-red liquid from his rapidly-emptying wine glass.

Chapter 40

Thursday, 27ᵗʰ December

It took Carmichael almost fifteen minutes to clear the thick ice encrusted on his windscreen and get on his way, a delay which annoyed him immensely.

He'd spent a restless night mulling over the case. Although he knew he could retain Hayley Bell and Francis Scott in custody for only a limited amount of time, and even though his head kept telling him to follow the plan he'd outlined to the team at the debrief the evening before, he could not help thinking that they were missing something obvious.

As his car reached the outskirts of Kirkwood, Carmichael's thoughts started to focus on Hayley Bell's reading group, and what an unlikely collection of women they were. Maxine Lowe and Hannah Ringrose seemed an odd pair within the group, as they appeared to him to have almost nothing in common with the other, older, women.

As he reflected upon this implausible alliance, he suddenly realised he was nearing Southport Road where Maxine Lowe lived.

Remembering that Maxine had told him and Watson that her boyfriend, Pete, would be working that day, Carmichael deliberated whether it might not be a good idea to pay her a visit while she was alone. He looked briefly at the clock on the dashboard, it was still only 8.15am.

"Why not?" he remarked out loud, before indicating and manoeuvring his black BMW into position to turn right into Southport Road.

* * * *

"This must have been a very stressful Christmas for you," remarked Aunty Audrey as Penny contemplated how she was going to get the old lady into an upright position in her bed without causing herself a serious injury. "Not only have you been virtually abandoned by Stephen over the last few days, but you've also had to put up with a silly old woman like me. And when you should be putting your feet up and relaxing."

Penny took a deep breath and gave out the biggest and brightest smile she could muster. Although she couldn't have put it more aptly herself, there was no way she was going to admit her true feelings to Audrey.

"Not at all, Audrey," she replied. "We've enjoyed having you with us."

"But I've been such a burden," Audrey continued in her broad Scottish accent. "Firstly, the scare when we all thought I was dying and now this blessed cramp in my legs. You must be counting the hours down to me leaving."

Penny took another deep breath before gathering all her strength to haul Audrey's considerable bulk from its half-lying, half-sitting position to one which would be more comfortable.

"I'm counting the minutes," she thought to herself as she made one last gargantuan heave.

"I'm sure I'll feel much better later," announced Audrey as soon as she was sitting upright. "But I think it's probably sensible if I stay here for the foreseeable future. I hope it's OK for me to have my breakfast here?"

Still out of breath, Penny moved a few paces backwards. "No trouble at all, Audrey," she replied again with the best smile she could raise. "Will it be an egg sandwich, as usual?"

* * * *

The look of astonishment on Maxine Lowe's face, when she opened the door, instantly told Carmichael that his decision to make a small detour that morning was the correct one.

"Good morning," he remarked with a faint smile. "May I come in?"

Maxine's right hand clutched the door firmly as her left hand rose slowly to cover her mouth, but not before her trembling voice said, "Don't tell me there's been another one?"

"No, no," replied Carmichael reassuringly, realising she was thinking there'd been a third death. "It's nothing like that. I just need to ask you a few more questions."

Maxine's face brightened and she actually managed a feeble smile. "But I've told you and the other officers all I know."

"That may be the case," Carmichael replied. "However, I need you to clarify a few things that you told Sergeant Watson and I the other day."

"You better come in, then," Maxine replied, as she opened the door wide to allow Carmichael to enter.

Carmichael smiled, this time a broader, more affable smile. "Thank you."

It hadn't occurred to Carmichael that Maxine would not be fully-dressed, but when she opened the door to let him in and revealed that she was still in her dressing gown, he did, albeit briefly, have a feeling of guilt at arriving unannounced so early in the morning.

237

"I'm sorry to impose on you," he remarked as he watched Maxine sit herself down in the centre of her tired-looking sofa, and arrange her dressing gown so the bottom of the garment covered her knees.

Maxine smiled. "No, that's OK," she replied. "What is it you wanted me to clarify?"

Carmichael sat down on an armchair a few feet away, which was the only other empty seat in the room, the rest of the sofa and the two chairs at the dining table being totally loaded with either neatly folded, but unironed clothes, or newspapers and magazines.

"I'm sorry," Maxine continued, seeing the look on Carmichael's face, "I'm a bit behind with my housework at the moment."

"That's no trouble," replied Carmichael. "I can assure you that if you came into my house it would look much more untidy than this." It was a lie he felt he needed to tell, but one that he knew Penny would lambast him for, if she could hear him.

Carmichael's bogus comment seemed to do the trick, and Maxine's oval face brightened. "I didn't offer you a drink. Would you like some tea?"

Carmichael shook his head. "No, I'll only take up a few minutes of your time, and then I need to head off." Another remark which wasn't necessarily truthful, but one Carmichael made to try and help Maxine feel at ease. "I wanted to talk to you about the proposition Duncan Bell made to you."

Maxine's cheeks blushed. "It was nothing, really," she remarked. "For some reason he clearly took a shine to me and, one evening when I was down there and Hayley was not around, he made a pass at me."

"A pass." Carmichael repeated. "Can you be a bit more specific?"

Maxine took a deep breath and puffed out her cheeks. "He was a silly old man who, for some reason, thought he stood a chance with me," she replied calmly. "He was absolutely harmless and I didn't feel in any way threatened. He just tried it on."

"But I suspect he made a pass on a few occasions," Carmichael remarked, "It was more than just one incident?"

"Yes, he did, he asked me on two or three occasions," replied Maxine.

"And on the final occasion he offered you money, too?" Carmichael added.

Maxine nodded. "Yes," she replied, "£200, to be exact."

"And I understand Pete was none too pleased," Carmichael continued.

"No, he wasn't," replied Maxine. "I knew as soon as I'd mentioned it that I'd made a mistake. I thought Pete would just laugh, with Duncan being such an old man, but he was very angry."

Carmichael looked directly into Maxine's eyes.

"But not enough to harm Duncan," Maxine quickly added. "Pete didn't kill the poor old devil, he wouldn't."

Carmichael continued to stare at Maxine. "In my experience, the behaviour of jealous people can be very unpredictable, Miss Lowe," he remarked.

"It wasn't Pete who killed Duncan Bell," Maxine replied firmly. "I know it wasn't."

Carmichael decided to leave that particular avenue of questioning and broach another subject entirely. "I'd like to talk to you about Thursday evenings," his piercing blue eyes fixed intently on Maxine's face as he spoke. "As I recall, on Monday, when Sergeant Watson and I spoke to you about what you get up to on Thursday evenings, you told us that you spend them with colleagues from school. Is that really what happens on Thursday evenings?"

Maxine didn't have to answer, the guilty look on her face signifying as clearly as any words could that she hadn't been telling the truth.

Chapter 41

With his mood buoyed significantly by the information he'd received from Maxine Lowe, Carmichael made the short journey from Southport Road to Kirkwood police station with a cheerful, smug smile on his face. However, his expression changed when his car pulled into the police station and he spotted Francis Scott being driven out of the car park in the back of a taxi.

Having abandoned his car in the first vacant space he could find, Carmichael burst through the door and marched towards the custody sergeant who, having seen Carmichael arrive, stood somewhat nervously behind the desk.

"What on earth is going on?" Carmichael enquired angrily. "Who the hell authorised the release of Francis Scott?"

"We tried to call you," replied the custody sergeant. "Did you not pick up your voice message?"

Carmichael took his mobile from his pocket and, as he did, could see the small, red, flashing light which indicated he had a voice message. "Damn," he muttered, as he realised his mobile phone was still on silent.

After quickly reactivating the ring tone, Carmichael returned his stare to the burly sergeant, their faces only half a metre apart. "So why have you released her?" he enquired for a second time.

"It's her father," replied the sergeant. "He's had a heart attack and is in Kirkwood Hospital. When we couldn't raise you I called Sergeant Cooper. He said we should let her go on compassionate grounds."

"I see," replied Carmichael who, whilst annoyed that she'd been released without his approval, knew that if he'd been there he would have made the same decision. "Has anyone gone with her?"

"We managed to speak with DC Dalton, who said she'd go to the hospital from home and meet Ms Scott there," replied the custody sergeant. "By the sound of it, the old man is in a bad way so we thought it best to let her meet Ms Scott at the hospital rather than delay things further by making her wait until DC Dalton got into the office."

Carmichael couldn't fault the logic, a fact that he signified with a few gentle nods of his head before heading off through the door and down the corridor.

****

Rachel Dalton had been sitting in her car with the engine running, waiting for the heater to clear the ice from her window, when she'd received the call from Cooper asking her to get over to Kirkwood Hospital and meet Francis Scott. As the hospital was only two minutes' drive from her flat, she'd arrived outside the private room in Nightingale ward a good ten minutes before Francis Scott scurried down the corridor.

With a worried look in her eyes, but without saying a word, the ashen-faced, middle-aged woman dashed past the young DC and into her father's room.

Not wanting to appear to intrude at such a difficult time, DC Dalton decided it would be best for her to take a seat in the corridor outside the old man's room.

****

Carmichael's first task when he'd left the duty sergeant was to grab himself a bacon roll and a steaming cup of coffee. His second was to instruct DC Dyer to acquire and study all the CCTV tapes he could find covering the vicinity of Duncan Bell's house for Sunday and Monday, to see if they could spot Francis Scott's car in and around the area.

Having eaten his roll and drunk his coffee, Carmichael then called Cooper. He wanted to make sure, now that Rachel Dalton was at the hospital, that between Cooper and Watson, they would be able to check in greater detail the alibis of Tarquin Bishop, Lesley Saxham and Pete Thorn, relating to Belinda Bishop's murder. He also told Cooper that he needed to make sure Watson didn't forget to contact the parents of Hannah Ringrose's partner to verify their claim that they were with his parents in Buxton when Duncan Bell was killed.

Carmichael also took the opportunity to advise Cooper of the information he'd gleaned from Maxine Lowe regarding what she really got up to on Thursday evenings.

With the call over and satisfied that everything was still going to plan, Carmichael picked up Hayley Bell's latest statement and started to read.

* * * *

Rachel Dalton could have been waiting no more than fifteen minutes before the door opened and the solemn face of one of the nurses emerged. Instinctively, Rachel rose from her chair. "Is he alright?" she enquired.

The nurse shook her head. "I'm afraid not," she replied. "Mr Scott passed away a few minutes ago."

Rachel remained standing as the nurse walked slowly away down the empty corridor.

After considering her options for a few seconds, Rachel decided to call Carmichael. She was just about to ring when the door opened again and a second nurse emerged; a larger, older lady than the first with a ferocious-looking face.

"Can't you read!" the nurse exclaimed loudly, pointing at a sign a few metres away from Rachel which had a drawing of a black mobile in a red circle with a red diagonal line dissecting the mobile in half. "No mobile calls allowed within the hospital."

Rachel didn't even consider arguing as she could sense the person reprimanding her was unlikely to be swayed.

"I'm sorry," she heard herself saying before scurrying away to find a safe place to make the call.

* * * *

It was precisely 9.15am when Carmichael entered the interview room.

"Good morning, Mrs Bell," he announced in a cheery tone. "I've just been reading your latest statement. I'm pleased you've at last decided to be honest with us."

Hayley smiled. Despite having had to spend the night in custody and, by amending her statement, admitting her earlier statement had been misleading, she still exuded an aura of confidence.

"As you've read my revised statement," Hayley replied in a manner verging on the arrogant, "I'm not sure there's much more to say."

"I disagree," replied Carmichael firmly. "It's much better, but I'm still not sure it's complete."

Hayley shook her head in an exasperated fashion. "Look, I've admitted that Francis and I were staying in a cottage we'd rented near Kendal," she remarked. "As I told you yesterday, I know it sounds stupid, but we just thought that if you knew we'd been less than honest about where we'd been staying, then that would throw suspicion on us."

"I understand that," replied Carmichael. "I don't condone you lying to us, but I do understand your reasoning. However, there are a few other things that still don't ring true."

"And what are they?" Hayley enquired.

"Your reasoning for making that disc," replied Carmichael, "and why you hand-delivered it to the *Observer* and did not post it to us, here."

"I thought I'd explained that yesterday, which I then confirmed in my statement to you," remarked Hayley in a forthright tone.

Carmichael retained eye contact with Hayley. "I don't believe you," he replied calmly and firmly.

"So, tell me what do you think happened?" Hayley enquired, her voice raised and angry.

Carmichael smiled. "I will," he added, again with a composure which suggested he wasn't idly fishing for information. "However, before I do, let me ask you something else. Tell me what you, Francis, Hannah and Maxine get up to every Thursday evening."

On hearing this latest question, Hayley looked visibly shaken.

"What do you mean?" she asked, almost as if she was trying to buy herself some time to think.

Carmichael smiled. "Maxine told me this morning what you four do every Thursday. I wondered why you hadn't mentioned it to me."

Hayley folded her arms tight to her chest. "I don't see what bearing those private sessions have in relation to my husband's murder!"

Carmichael looked sternly back at Hayley. "I think you should let me be the judge of that, don't you?"

Chapter 42

"Damn," Rachel mumbled when Carmichael didn't pick up the call in person and the dull, impersonal answering message he'd left started to kick in. She decided to ring off and call Cooper.

To her relief, DS Cooper answered the call within three rings.

"Hi Rachel," he said. "How's it going at the hospital?"

"He's dead," replied Rachel abruptly.

"Oh," replied Cooper. "So how's Francis?"

"I don't know," Rachel continued. "She's still in with him."

"So why are you calling me?" Cooper enquired, his voice sounding perplexed.

"I wanted to ask you what you think I should do with Francis?" Rachel replied.

There was a short pause as Cooper contemplated what advice to give his junior colleague.

"Have you spoken to the boss?" he enquired although, as soon as he'd heard the words coming out of his mouth, he realised that had Rachel spoken to Carmichael she would not have now been calling him asking for some guidance.

"His mobile's on voice mail," replied Rachel.

"I'd bring Francis back to Kirkwood, if I were you," said Cooper. "I think the boss will want to talk with her, particularly after what he was told by Maxine Lowe this morning."

"What was that?" Rachel enquired.

"She told him that she and two other members of the reading group meet every Thursday evening at Hayley's house for some sort of therapy session with Hayley," replied Cooper.

Rachel's forehead wrinkled as she tried to fathom out what Cooper was saying. "What sort of therapy?" she asked.

"For their gambling addiction," continued Cooper. "It would appear that Maxine, her friend Hannah and Francis are all gambling addicts. In fact, according to Carmichael, Maxine and Hannah were attending Hayley's counselling sessions well before they became part of the reading group."

"Do you mean like Gamblers Anonymous?" Rachel asked.

"I guess so," replied Cooper. "But with Hayley Bell providing the counselling."

"Does Carmichael think that this gambling development has any relevance to the case?" Rachel asked.

"I'm not sure," replied Cooper. "But he's going to talk with Hayley about it this morning and, if I know Carmichael, he'll want to speak with Francis Scott about it, too."

"I'd better bring her in, then," remarked Rachel. "I'll see you back at the station."

Cooper had no time to reply, for as soon as she'd uttered her last sentence, Rachel ended the call and headed back in the direction of Nightingale ward.

* * * *

Hayley Bell, arms still folded tightly and clamped against her chest, gazed upwards at the point where the dark-grey wall met the white ceiling. "I don't see it being of any significance whatsoever," she announced, "but, if you must know, it's true. Maxine and Hannah have had issues with debts caused by their gambling addiction. I've been working with them individually for nearly two years. They both joined my Thursday evening sessions earlier this year. It was about the same time that I

246

asked them to join the reading group, as I thought that getting involved in a new pastime would help them."

"And has it?" Carmichael asked.

"Absolutely," replied Hayley passionately. "To my knowledge, Maxine hasn't bet online for at least eighteen months. Hannah had a minor lapse about six months ago, but I think she's now also well on the way to getting her addiction under control."

"And can gambling addicts ever recover?" Carmichael asked. "Or are they like alcoholics and will always have the problem, even if they are able to manage it."

Hayley smiled. "It's very similar," she replied.

"What about Francis Scott?" Carmichael asked. "What sort of gambling was she into?"

"Francis is my star pupil," Hayley replied with a smug grin of satisfaction. "She was a desperate case when I first met her over ten years ago. She would bet on anything. But now she's a totally reformed character, in fact I ask her to attend the sessions now more as a role model for the others than to get help herself."

"I see," remarked Carmichael. "So are there other women in the group and is the group only made up of women?"

"Yes and yes," Hayley replied. "I only mentor women in my groups and we have two other ladies attending at the moment."

"I'll need their names and addresses, please," Carmichael stated.

"But why?" Hayley replied. "My sessions are supposed to be confidential."

"Mrs Bell," said Carmichael angrily. "Both these women have access to your house every week. I presume they knew your husband, too, so it's important we talk to them, if only to eliminate them from our enquiries."

Hayley shook her head. "I suppose I have no choice," she remarked frostily. "But, to my knowledge, neither knew Belinda Bishop, so I can't see how they can be realistic murder suspects."

"As I said to you earlier," Carmichael replied, "you need to let me be the judge of that."

* * * *

"Where's Ms Scott?" Rachel enquired, upon entering the small private room where the body of Francis Scott's father lay in the bed. The solitary nurse, who had been left to attend to the body, looked round at the clearly-agitated, young woman standing in the doorway.

"Who are you?" she asked.

"I'm DC Dalton, a police officer, I need to know where his daughter's gone."

The nurse shrugged her shoulders. "I've no idea," she replied. "She left about five minutes ago. She may be in the restaurant having a coffee."

"Where's that?" Rachel asked, her voice trembling as she spoke, but with a clear sense of urgency.

"If you go down the corridor to the end," replied the nurse, who pointed in the direction she meant, "then down two flights of stairs to the ground floor, it's about twenty metres down the corridor."

"Thanks," Rachel replied, before dashing out of the door and running as fast as she could in the direction of the hospital restaurant.

Chapter 43

It took Carmichael a further twenty minutes to satisfy himself that Hayley Bell had told him everything about her Thursday evening counselling sessions.

"So, let me get this right," he remarked, "you were once a gambling addict yourself, but for the last ten years, through your weekly sessions at your house, you've helped numerous people stop gambling. And, more latterly, with the support of Francis Scott, who is also a reformed addict to gambling, you've been helping Maxine Lowe and Hannah Ringrose."

Hayley gave a slight shrug of her shoulders. "It's a fair summary, I suppose," she replied, with a distinct lack of enthusiasm in her voice. "Although I prefer to call my sessions support and I'd never claim to have helped people stop gambling. I merely provide people who genuinely want to give up gambling with some tools to assist them in their efforts. An individual will only stop gambling if they have a real desire to do so."

"Or have run out of money," remarked Carmichael cynically.

"No, alas, in my experience," continued Hayley, "having no money is rarely in isolation sufficient impetus to stop gambling, if you're addicted."

Having been suitably corrected, Carmichael decided to bring some closure to this particular subject.

"But I am right in saying that you have been holding sessions in your house every Thursday evening for a considerable time?" Carmichael remarked.

"That's correct," Hayley replied.

"And did Mrs Bishop or Mrs Saxham know about these sessions and about other members of the reading group having gambling addictions?" Carmichael asked.

Hayley Bell shook her head. "Of course not," she remarked, as if the question had caused massive offence. "As I've told you before, Inspector, my sessions are all confidential. I'd never discuss them with anyone outside the group."

"Not even your husband?" Carmichael added.

"My goodness, no!" replied Hayley, as if the idea was totally preposterous. "I never discussed any of my ladies with Duncan."

"But he'd have known about Maxine and Hannah having a gambling addiction," Carmichael suggested. "He must have seen them in the house every Thursday and he must have known why they were there."

"I suppose he must have," conceded Hayley indifferently, "but I never discussed them or anyone else with Duncan, I can assure you, Inspector."

For a split second, Carmichael took his eyes off Hayley as he considered his options. "Going back to your latest statement of events," he remarked, "I think you've still omitted something of great importance."

"Really," replied Hayley, her voice loud, emphasising her clear irritation. "What am I omitting?"

Carmichael smiled. "The sequence of events doesn't make sense," he said. "I've been struggling with what you've been claiming and the timings just don't add up."

Hayley stared back at Carmichael, arms folded and eyes piercing in their intensity, indicating without any question, anger and resentment towards her interrogator. "Timings, what timings?" she replied.

"Having got to know you a little in the last few days," Carmichael continued, "and having more than a little admiration for the skill you demonstrated in the planning and execution of your disappearance, I cannot accept that, within two days, you would reveal you were alive and well so readily."

"I'm flattered, of course," replied Hayley self-righteously, "but I can't follow your logic."

Carmichael always relished pitching his intellect against his prey and, in the case of Hayley Bell, he could see he was up against an extremely smart and capable opponent.

"I believe that this was never your plan and that something happened to make you send that video message," Carmichael continued. "What was that, Mrs Bell?"

Carmichael paused to allow Hayley to comment. When she elected not to do so, he continued. "My guess is that you and Francis went back to the house on Sunday and you either killed your husband or, more likely, you found him dead. Is that what happened?"

Hayley remained impassive, but Carmichael could see in her eyes that she wasn't comfortable.

"I think the video message was sent after your husband was dead in an attempt to suggest to us that you had no idea he'd died and to provide some distance between you and Duncan's murder."

"Utter rubbish," Hayley replied. "And I'd very much like to see you prove that."

Carmichael smiled again. "Mrs Bell, I have my officers scouring CCTV footage of a ten-mile radius of your house on the day your husband was killed. They've not yet found anything, but there are dozens of cameras on the roads around your house and I have no doubt that, within a matter of hours, we'll locate an image of the car Francis Scott and you were driving when you came back on Sunday."

For a split second Carmichael thought Hayley Bell was about to admit she'd been lying and that she and Francis had returned on Sunday, but something seemed to prevent her from making that momentous leap. Instead she eased herself back into her chair. "I think you are playing games with me, Inspector Carmichael," she replied. "I suspect there are very few CCTV cameras near our house and I can assure you, even if there were, you wouldn't find any images of Francis's car, as it simply was nowhere near my house on Sunday."

The tension in the interview room was now high, something that Carmichael, in a perverse way, was relishing. In his eyes, Hayley's attitude and demeanour suggested his theory was almost certainly, in the main, correct. However, as yet he had no proof and, unfortunately, Hayley knew it.

"I'm going to release you now, Mrs Bell," he remarked. "You will, of course, be hearing from us about the serious charges we will be bringing in relation to the deliberate false statements you gave us previously. And, as soon as we find more evidence, we will want to talk with you again, but for the moment, you're free to go."

Hayley Bell appeared shocked by this sudden announcement, but took no time to get up out of her seat and start to walk to the door. Before leaving the interview room, she turned back to face Carmichael who, by now, was also standing. "I assume Francis is also being released," she remarked.

"Actually, she's already gone," Carmichael replied. "Her father was taken very ill earlier, so she was allowed to visit him in hospital."

"Oh, my goodness," remarked Hayley. "Is he alright?"

With a faint movement of his shoulders and with the palms of his hands facing upwards, Carmichael felt compelled to share the sad truth. "I'm afraid Mr Scott had a heart attack, I haven't had an update on his condition, but I'm told it's touch and go."

"Poor Francis," said Hayley. "I must go to her, she'll be devastated if he dies."

Without waiting for Carmichael to say anything more, Hayley Bell left the interview room and with Carmichael a few paces behind, strode briskly down the corridor.

* * * *

Out of breath and anxious, Rachel Dalton rushed into the hospital restaurant, her eyes scouring the tables and the small queue of people waiting to be served at the gleaming, stainless-steel counter. Francis Scott wasn't there.

"Blast it!" she exclaimed out loud, much to the wonder of an elderly lady stood by her in her dressing gown and slippers.

"Are you OK, my dear?" the woman enquired, her voice shaky, but her intentions unmistakably sincere.

"I've lost someone," Rachel heard herself saying, her eyes not having the luxury of exchanging even a moment's gaze with the old lady.

"Oh dear," came the reply before the tiny frame shuffled off towards the dinner queue.

Rachel took a deep breath and considered what her next move should be.

* * * *

As the taxi Francis Scott had hailed in the hospital car park sped out onto the A59, her mobile started to vibrate in her small handbag. Extracting the offending item, Francis could see that the name Hayley was illuminated in white letters on the small navy-blue screen.

Francis pressed the receive button and placed the mobile against her left ear.

Chapter 44

With the exception of Bruno, her beloved Boxer dog, Lesley Saxham had spent the entire morning alone at home. Her husband, Greg, had arranged to meet some of his closest friends at the golf club for nine holes followed by a bottle of fine red wine, an annual ritual which Greg and his friends had been observing on the day after Boxing Day for as long as Lesley could remember. This year, Greg had taken Tarquin Bishop with him on the basis that joining the group may, in some way, take poor Tarquin's mind off the tragic death of Belinda, even if only for a few hours.

Lesley was tired and welcomed an opportunity to be alone with her thoughts, so when the doorbell rang, for a split second, she seriously considered pretending to be out. However, something inside her told her that she needed to answer the door.

"Oh it's you," remarked Lesley as she opened the door wide. "I wasn't expecting to see you today."

****

As was customary, Carmichael's 1pm de-brief started at exactly 1pm.

"Who wants to kick off?" Carmichael enquired.

"It may be best if you start, sir," replied Cooper. "I think you've probably made the greatest breakthrough today."

Cooper hadn't deliberately tried to flatter his boss, but his words brought a self-righteous grin of satisfaction to Carmichael's face, suggesting he agreed wholeheartedly with Cooper's comment. "Very well," he replied. "I discovered from Maxine Lowe, earlier today, that her Thursday evenings are not spent with her work colleagues, as she told you and I, Marc, nor are they with a mystery lover, as you'd speculated. No, Maxine and Hannah are both gambling addicts who spend their Thursday evenings at Hayley Bell's house, attending counselling sessions which she conducts for a small group of women with similar problems."

"What!" exclaimed Watson, who was hearing this news for the first time. "They're addicted to gambling?"

Carmichael nodded. "I know," he replied, "it does sound bizarre. At first Hayley Bell wasn't keen to confirm this story, but it would appear that it's true."

"Well I'm amazed, I'd never have guessed that," remarked Watson. "Does Maxine's boyfriend know?"

Carmichael shook his head. "No," he replied. "He has no idea whatsoever as, according to Maxine, her gambling issues predate them seeing each other. Maxine is very worried about him finding out, too, which is why she tells him that she's at the reading group on Thursdays."

"Did you manage to find out if any of the other members of the reading group are ex-gamblers?" Cooper enquired.

"Good question," replied Carmichael. "According to Hayley, neither Belinda Bishop nor Lesley Saxham have any idea about the sessions she holds with Hannah and Maxine, however, Francis does. In fact, it would appear that Francis also had a gambling addiction many years ago and Hayley uses her as a role model for those people who want to make sure they stay away from gambling."

"So do you think the deaths are linked to this gambling addiction?" Rachel enquired.

"To be honest, I'm not sure," Carmichael replied. "However, we need to consider it as a possibility."

"I assume that there are other people who attend the sessions on a Thursday, too," Watson suggested.

Carmichael nodded. "Yes, there are and we'll need to talk to these people, as they may be linked to the two murders."

"What else did you discover from Maxine?" Rachel enquired.

"Nothing new, although she talked about Duncan Bell's unsuccessful passes at her," Carmichael replied, "the final one being the one with an offer of a fairly substantial payment. All of which Maxine turned down."

"And do you believe her?" Watson asked.

Carmichael pondered the question carefully. "Yes, I've no doubt he made the passes at her and I'm equally sure she turned him down flat," he replied. "I also got the impression she viewed Duncan as a silly, but harmless, old man. I don't think she saw his attempts to seduce her as being a threat in any way at all. In fact I think she found them a bit of a joke really."

"But as I found out, jealous Pete didn't share that opinion," interjected Watson. "He's still way up there on my list of suspects for Duncan's murder."

Cooper shook his head. "No, he's in the clear," he replied with conviction. "I talked with the boss at Steadmans Printers this morning. He swears blind that Pete was in work all day on Sunday. He is adamant that there was no way he'd have been able to slip out, travel nearly twenty miles and get back without his absence being noticed."

Carmichael nodded sagely. "He has absolutely no motive for killing Belinda Bishop either, so it looks like jealous Pete Thorn is off our list of prime suspects."

By the expression on Watson's face it was clear he didn't agree, however, he offered no further argument.

"Talking about alibis," continued Carmichael. "Did you check out the others we have on our list of suspects?"

"I also checked out Tarquin Bishop's story again for yesterday lunchtime with the landlord at the White Horse," Cooper continued. "The landlord confirmed what he told Rachel, that Tarquin arrived at about 11.30am and, after downing at least four double whiskeys, left at about 1pm. He says that Tarquin was completely smashed, which apparently is not uncommon."

"It ties up with his story to us and the reason why he may well have fallen asleep once he got home," Carmichael observed. "However, he could have still killed his wife either just before or just after he went to the pub."

Cooper nodded. "And of course we know he hated Duncan, so Tarquin has a motive for the first murder and only a partial alibi for the second one."

Again Carmichael paused for a few moments while he absorbed what his officers were saying. "What about the others?" he asked.

"I followed up Hannah Ringrose's alibi for Sunday," replied Watson. "It took me ages to get hold of them on the phone, but I managed to speak to Arnold Partridge, the father of Hannah's boyfriend, Andy. They are still in Cape Town, but he confirmed that they were both in Buxton in Derbyshire on Sunday, so there's no way either Hannah or her boyfriend could have killed Duncan."

"What about Lesley Saxham?" Carmichael enquired. "How did her alibi stack up?"

Rachel shrugged her shoulders. "That was going to be my job this morning," she replied. "But I had to drop that to go over to the hospital to be with Francis Scott."

"Who you lost," interjected Carmichael spikily.

"Yes," replied Rachel ruefully. "I'm sorry about that, sir. Uniform are out in force trying to locate her as we speak, so hopefully she'll be found soon. As soon as this briefing is over my plan is to get out there with them."

"For your sake I hope you do," replied Carmichael, his displeasure palpable in his voice.

Rachel was annoyed about letting Francis give her the slip and, as such, was keen to redeem herself. "I'll find her, sir," she pledged, her face pink with a mixture of anger and embarrassment.

"With Rachel otherwise occupied, did you guys have a chance to check Lesley Saxham's alibi?" Carmichael asked, his words directed at Cooper and Watson.

His two sergeants shook their heads.

"I need you, Marc, to get on to that this afternoon," continued Carmichael. "Is that clear?"

Watson just shrugged his shoulders. "That's fine," he replied. "I'm happy to check out her alibi with the dog walkers of the village. After what I've eaten this Christmas, a little exercise won't do me any harm."

"What about us?" Cooper enquired.

"We're going to check out a little hunch I've got," Carmichael replied, somewhat cryptically. "Having spoken again to Hayley Bell, I'm reasonably sure that, at last, most of what she's now telling us is correct, but I'm still convinced it's not totally true. I put it to Hayley this morning that she and Francis never planned to send the message to us on Monday. She denied it, but I could see she was lying."

"So what do you think their plan was?" Cooper asked.

"I'm not sure," Carmichael confessed, "but I think their little scheme was knocked sideways by them discovering Duncan had been murdered."

"Or they murdered him?" interjected Watson.

"They may well have murdered him," replied Carmichael, "but although Hayley is quite clearly an accomplished liar, I don't see her being our killer somehow."

"So what exactly are we going to do to move us forward?"

enquired Cooper, who was more than a little confused about the assignment he was being allocated.

Before Carmichael could answer, the door opened and WPC Twamley hurried into the room.

"I thought you should know, sir," she announced breathlessly. "We've just received a call. Someone else from the reading group you're investigating has been found dead."

Chapter 45

It was just before 2pm when Carmichael and his three officers arrived at Lesley Saxham's house.

As his car drew up, Carmichael could see there were already several SOCOs busying themselves within the confines of the cordoned-off driveway.

"Who reported the incident?" Carmichael asked as he ducked under the tape and strode purposefully towards the house.

"It was Lesley Saxham's husband," replied the PC who had been the first on the scene. "Apparently, he and a friend, a man called Tarquin Bishop, had been playing golf this morning and when they returned home at about 1.15pm they found the dead woman and the other badly-injured lady."

"So where's Mr Saxham and Mr Bishop now?" Carmichael enquired, just as he reached the open front door.

"Tarquin Bishop is still inside the house," replied the officer. "Greg Saxham went in the ambulance to the hospital with the injured woman."

Carmichael stopped in his tracks. "What!" he exclaimed. "His wife has been murdered and he goes to hospital with the woman who killed her?"

The PC looked confused. "No, sir," he replied. "It's a lady called Francis Scott who's been killed. By all accounts, Mrs Saxham managed to fight her off, but was badly injured in the struggle and it's Mrs Saxham who's been taken to the hospital."

The news of another violent death was quick to be picked up by the local radio station, who announced the incident at the end of their 2pm news bulletin.

"Penny!" hollered Audrey from her bedroom at the top of the stairs. "Did you hear that? It sounds like there's been another murder. Poor Stephen's going to be busy this afternoon, I reckon."

Tired of the continual stream of orders and pronouncements from on-high, Penny let out a gigantic sigh before picking up Audrey's tray of tea and chocolate biscuits. She started to clamber up the staircase, for what seemed like the thousandth time that morning.

"There'll be another murder for Steve to investigate soon if she doesn't shut up," Penny muttered under her breath.

****

Carmichael and his team entered the kitchen, the main focus of activity.

"Afternoon, Carmichael," remarked Dr Stock who was crouched beside the limp, bloodied body of Francis Scott. "Why is it all your murders come in clutches?"

Carmichael chose to ignore Stock's cynical words. "You don't have to be a forensic scientist to work out how this one died," he said as he stared down at the kitchen knife embedded in Francis Scott's chest.

"No," replied Stock, "I'm sure even Sergeant Watson could work that one out," a comment which brought a wry smile to the faces of Rachel Dalton and Cooper.

Unimpressed by Stock's latest statement, Watson folded his arms tightly and glared angrily back in the direction of the chief SOCO.

"No beautiful assistant today," Carmichael remarked. "Where's young Dr Wilczek?"

Stock looked up at Carmichael. "Have you taken a shine to Irina?" he replied. "Well I'm afraid you will just have to put up with me. Dr Wilczek's gone back to Poland for New Year, but I dare say I should just about cope on my own."

Carmichael surveyed the scene. "It looks like there was a hell of a struggle," he observed.

Cooper nodded. "Yes, looking at the wreckage I'd say the two ladies had a hell of a battle here."

Ignoring their comments, Stock continued to examine Francis Scott's blood-spattered body.

"Does the time of death stack up with the information we received from Lesley Saxham's husband?" Carmichael enquired.

"She's not been dead long," Stock replied, while at the same time checking the time on his wrist watch. "I'd say life was extinct at no more than an hour and a half ago, but she would have bled for a good twenty minutes before she died, so she could have been stabbed at around noon."

"That would tie in with what Mr Saxham said on the phone," interjected the PC who'd remained with Carmichael and his team.

"Was Mrs Saxham conscious when you arrived?" Carmichael enquired.

The PC nodded. "She was," he replied, "but she is badly concussed and didn't say too much, just that Francis Stock had arrived at her house unannounced and, in her words, without any warning or provocation, started to attack her."

"Did anyone go with her and her husband in the ambulance?" Carmichael asked.

The PC nodded. "Yes, WPC Berry went with them."

On hearing that WPC Berry was at the hospital, Watson smiled. "Do you want me to go over and take their statements?" he enquired.

Carmichael took a few seconds to consider Watson's offer.

"No," he eventually replied. "I'd like DC Dalton to go over to the hospital. I'll join you later," he continued, his eyes directed at the young DC. "But for god's sake, this time don't lose her."

Rachel Dalton returned a nervous, forced smile before heading away.

"So what about the three of us?" Watson asked. "What do you want us to do?"

"Well, first off," replied Carmichael, "I think I'd like to have a quick conversation with Tarquin Bishop. Then I'd like you, Marc, to take a formal statement from him while you, Paul, have a good look around here to see if you can find anything that could give us a clue as to what went on earlier today. After I've spoken to Tarquin, I'm going to get over to the hospital to talk with Lesley Saxham's husband and, if she's well enough, to interview Lesley, too."

"I take it the assignments you started to give us earlier at the briefing are now on hold," Watson enquired.

Cooper looked perplexed by his colleague's question. "Well, as we've now not only found Francis Scott, but also pretty much established that she's the murderer, I'd have thought the answer's obvious," he remarked.

Carmichael nodded. "You may well be right, Paul," he replied. "But the question I need answering is, what involvement has Hayley Bell in all this?"

* * * *

Carmichael and his two officers located Tarquin Bishop, dazed and silently sitting alone in the lounge, clutching a glass of whiskey. At first he didn't notice them enter the room, but as they got closer, he raised his head and made eye contact.

"Why?" he muttered, his eyes red with a mixture of the effects of alcohol, lack of sleep and volume of tears he'd shed in the past twenty-four hours. "Why on earth would Francis want to kill Belinda and Lesley? They were such close friends."

"Duncan, too," Watson added, much to the annoyance of Carmichael who gave his sergeant a disapproving sideways glance.

"I know it's difficult, Mr Bishop," Carmichael began, "but can you tell me what you saw when you returned here with Mr Saxham?"

Tarquin's head lowered and his eyes stared aimlessly at the officer's feet. "It was about 1.10pm when Greg and I got back from the club. He'd been trying hard to take my mind off poor Belinda's murder, but to be honest, I wasn't very comfortable being out so soon after…" Tarquin paused and wiped the tears from his eyes with his sleeve.

"Take your time," remarked Carmichael, sensitively. "We know this must be terribly distressing for you."

Tarquin cleared his throat. "When we opened the front door, Lesley was lying at the foot of the stairs, groaning and holding her head. She was barely conscious, but kept saying that she'd been attacked. At first I couldn't make out what she was talking about. Then she pointed to the kitchen and I went in and saw Francis motionless on the floor, with that knife in her."

"How long before you called the emergency services?" Carmichael enquired.

"No more than a few minutes," replied Tarquin. "Greg did that while I tried to help Lesley. She was bleeding from the head quite heavily so I stemmed the blood as best I could with a tea towel I found in the kitchen drawer."

"What about Francis?" Carmichael enquired. "Was she already dead?"

Tarquin gazed back up at the Inspector. "It was only after Lesley became a little more lucid that we realised it was Francis who had attacked Lesley. When Greg made the call, we'd assumed that an intruder had attacked both of them."

"So before you realised there was no intruder, did you or Greg check the house to see if there was anyone else inside?" Carmichael enquired.

Tarquin shook his head. "To be honest that worrying thought did cross my mind, but with Lesley in such a bad way, we were totally preoccupied with making sure she was OK."

Carmichael put on his best comforting smile. "You take it easy," he told the distraught, tired-looking man. "Sergeant Watson will take a full statement from you when you're feeling up to it."

Without another word, Carmichael nodded at his two trusted lieutenants before heading towards the front door.

Chapter 46

Carmichael's black BMW had barely left the end of the street when his mobile phone rang.

"Carmichael," he replied after pressing the hands-free receive button located on his steering wheel.

"Good afternoon, sir," came back the voice of PC Dyer, his strong Lancastrian accent instantly recognisable. "I just thought I'd better let you know that we've managed to locate a very clear image of Francis Scott's car on CCTV. It was picked up by a camera near Barclays bank in Barton Bridge, at 1.42pm on Sunday, heading towards Much Martin."

"Really," replied Carmichael excitedly. "That would be no more than fifteen minutes' drive from the Bells' house."

"More like ten minutes, sir," PC Dyer responded, "especially on a Sunday as I'd not expect there to be anything on the roads at that time."

"And can you make out Francis Scott and Hayley Bell in the car?" Carmichael enquired.

"The footage is remarkably clear," replied PC Dyer, "and there's just one person in the car and that's Francis Scott."

"Are you sure?" Carmichael asked.

"No question at all," replied PC Dyer. "The only way anyone else was in the car would be if they were lying flat on the back seat."

Carmichael took a few seconds to think. "That's great work, Dyer," he remarked.

Having left Watson to take Tarquin Bishop's formal statement, Cooper returned to the kitchen where Dr Stock was still crouched over the body of Francis Scott.

Out of the corner of his eye, Stock noticed Cooper approaching. "I see Carmichael has left you to endure the gruesome side of the investigation."

Cooper smiled. "To be truthful, the sight of another person in that state has never been a problem for me," he replied frankly. "I'm not sure the same can be said for some of my colleagues, but I've never really had a problem in witnessing this sort of thing. Mind you, if I as much as get a splinter I'm a mess. I suspect there's a medical word for that."

"There is," replied Stock, with conviction, "the word's sadist and it's an absolute prerequisite to do my job," he added with a mischievous wink and a wry smile.

As he was speaking, Stock extracted a small mobile phone from the front pocket of Francis's black trousers. He passed it to Cooper. "You might want to check her last texts and phone calls," he remarked. "It might provide you with some insight as to her motives for coming here."

Using just his thumb and one finger, Cooper carefully took the mobile from Stock's hand and carried it over to the kitchen table.

****

Carmichael's car had just come to a halt in the car park at Kirkwood Hospital, when his mobile rang once more. This time it was Cooper.

"I've been looking at the last calls on Francis Scott's mobile," Cooper announced. "I thought you'd want to know that the last call she received was from Hayley Bell at 11.45am."

"That's less than ten minutes after I'd released Hayley from custody," remarked Carmichael.

"I figured it wouldn't be much more than that," replied Cooper. "Do you want me to bring her in again?"

Carmichael puffed out his cheeks. "I've had PC Dyer on the phone this morning," he remarked. "He maintains that he's got very clear footage of Francis Scott driving towards the Bells' house on Sunday, at about the time Duncan was killed, however, according to Dyer, there's no sign of Hayley in the car."

"So do you think the murders were just Francis acting alone, or do you think Hayley's involved?" Cooper asked.

Carmichael shook his head. "To be honest, Paul, I have no idea. Hayley has lied to us almost from the word go, but for some strange reason, I'm struggling to believe that she could kill anyone."

"So what do you want me to do?" Cooper asked.

"You need to pick her up, for sure," replied Carmichael. "As soon as Watson's finished taking Tarquin Bishop's statement I want you both to bring her back to the station. I want to interview her again."

"No problem, sir," replied Cooper.

"Also," Carmichael shouted before Cooper could hang up, "get on to Dyer and see if he can find any CCTV footage of Francis Scott's car anywhere near Belinda Bishop's house at and around the time she was murdered. Given what we now know, I suspect it won't be long before we find some evidence linking Francis to her death and, maybe this time, we may see Hayley in the car, too."

"Will do, sir," replied Cooper, before he ended the call.

* * * *

"Do you know, I'm feeling much, much better," announced Aunty Audrey as Penny entered her room to bring the latest tray of tea and biscuits and collect the empty cup she'd delivered just an hour or so earlier. "I may actually get myself up and have a shower."

Penny glanced at the clock perched on the bedside cabinet, which read 3.17pm.

"That's a good idea," she replied cheerily, although inwardly Penny couldn't see why Audrey was bothering to get up now, as it would be getting dark within the hour. "I'll fetch you some clean towels."

"If you could, my dear," replied Audrey. "Maybe a couple of large fluffy bath sheets, if you have them. I find the smaller towels you have in the bathroom so difficult to get me dry."

Not for the first time in the last five days, Penny found herself having to bite her lip and hold her tongue. "Certainly, Audrey," she replied with forced cheeriness. "I'll see what I can do."

Chapter 47

It took Carmichael several minutes to find Sefton ward, which he eventually discovered, located in one of the wings on the second floor of Kirkwood Hospital. However, when he finally made it through the large, polished-pine, double doors that led to the corridor outside Lesley's room, he found the lonely figure of Rachel Dalton sitting quietly on a chair directly opposite the patient's door.

"How is she?" Carmichael enquired.

"She's now conscious and stable," Rachel replied. "The doctors reckon they may keep her in overnight for observation, but it seems like there's no major reason for concern.

"Excellent," Carmichael remarked. "Let's go in and have a word, in that case."

Without bothering to stop and talk any further, Carmichael knocked twice on the door before entering the small, spotlessly-clean private room.

"How are you feeling?" Carmichael enquired with a broad smile.

"She's doing fine," replied a tall, thin man in red and green checked trousers and a bright-yellow *pringle* jumper, beside Lesley's bed, who Carmichael took to be her husband.

"You must be Greg," Carmichael added before thrusting out his right hand in the man's direction. "I'm Inspector Carmichael."

"Pleased to meet you," replied Greg Saxham.

Carmichael wasn't a mason, but by the way Greg Saxham shook his hand, he assumed that Lesley's husband was, which immediately put Carmichael on alert, knowing that he would, in all probability, be an acquaintance of some of his superiors.

"So if you can please tell me what happened today?" Carmichael enquired of Lesley.

"It was awful," she replied. "I was in the house when, at about 12.30pm, I heard a knock on the door. When I opened it, Francis was standing there. I was very surprised because, although I've known Francis for ages through the reading group, she'd never paid me a visit at home before."

"So what happened then?" Carmichael asked.

"I let her in and invited her into the kitchen for a coffee," Lesley replied, her voice hushed and trembling. "Then, when I was filling the kettle, all of a sudden, I felt a blow to the side of my head." As she spoke Lesley moved her right hand up to a point just above her right ear. "The pain was terrible, but I managed to turn and I saw Francis holding one of my large copper pans. She had a really frightening look in her eyes."

"So what happened then?" said Rachel, her voice soft and encouraging.

"It's all a bit of a blur," Lesley replied, "but Francis aimed a few more blows at me, some which I managed to fend off with my arm, but some did hit me. It was awful."

Lesley suddenly clasped both hands to her chin and started to sob uncontrollably.

"Is it not possible to delay these questions for a while until the old girl is feeling more up to it?" demanded Greg Saxham.

"It's alright, darling," replied Lesley, who was trying hard to hold back the tears. "They need to know what happened."

"And what did happen?" Carmichael asked.

271

"Well this seemed to go on for ages, but I suppose it was just a few minutes," replied Lesley. "I was trying to get away from her, but she kept hitting me. I grabbed a pan, too, and started to fight back, I did land a few blows, I think, but she was very strong and seemed unaffected by being struck by me."

"And how did it all end?" Carmichael asked.

Lesley looked up at her husband. "She knocked me back with a really hard blow to my forehead. I felt dizzy and was sure I was going to become unconscious. I knew if I did she'd kill me, so I mustered up all of my strength and grabbed the nearest thing I could find."

"Which was the kitchen knife," Carmichael prompted.

"Yes," responded Lesley meekly. "Once I had it in my hand I knew what I had to do. I was convinced that the next blow would kill me so I pushed it hard into Francis's chest."

"It was self-defence," interrupted Greg Saxham. "Anybody would have done the same."

"Then she fell," continued Lesley. "First to her knees, then onto her side. I knew it was over."

"So what did you do then?" Rachel asked.

"I felt relieved that I was no longer in danger," Lesley replied. "But it was only then that I really started to feel the sharp pains in my head. I staggered out of the kitchen and tried to get to the phone, but I must have just blacked out, as the next thing I knew was that Greg and Tarquin were standing over me, asking me what had happened."

"It sounds like you had a very lucky escape," Rachel remarked sympathetically.

"But why?" Lesley asked. "Why would she want to kill me?"

Carmichael shrugged his shoulders. "Did Francis give you any idea at all why she'd want to attack you?"

Lesley shook her head. "No," she replied. "Once she started to assault me she never said a word, she appeared to be in a trance."

"And what time did you arrive home, Mr Saxham?" Carmichael enquired.

"It was about 1.10pm when Tarquin and I returned home," Greg announced, "and, as Lesley told you, we found her slumped and dazed on the carpet in the hallway."

Having already heard Tarquin Bishop's account, Carmichael decided to dispense with obtaining the same story again from Greg, especially as he was eager to get away and talk once more with Hayley Bell.

"I'll leave you now with DC Dalton," Carmichael advised the Saxhams with his best reassuring smile. "Rachel will take your statements when you both feel up to it, and I'll come and see you again in the morning."

"So do you think it was Francis who killed Duncan and poor Belinda?" Lesley enquired.

Again Carmichael gave a faint shrug of his shoulders. "That's certainly how it looks," he replied candidly before turning to face Rachel Dalton and continuing under his breath. "The big question is whether she acted alone or with someone else."

****

As they'd expected, Hayley Bell was at home when Cooper and Watson rapped the large brass knocker on her front door. However, to their surprise, Hayley Bell wasn't alone.

"We've been expecting you," remarked the stocky, grey-haired solicitor who answered the door. "Mrs Bell and I were just about to make our way to Kirkwood police station. Mrs Bell would like to make a formal statement to the police."

"By my reckoning," replied Watson cynically, "this will be the third statement your client has made in the last few days. I suspect Inspector Carmichael would appreciate this one being complete and truthful."

Chapter 48

It was almost 4.30pm by the time Carmichael commenced his interview with Hayley Bell at Kirkwood police station.

Given that Hayley was at the police station voluntarily, accompanied by her legal adviser, Carmichael decided to try and make the discussion as informal as he could. He'd asked Cooper to join him and instructed Watson to listen in from behind the two-way mirror, but he'd decided to dispense with any tape recording.

"I understand from my officers that you want to provide us with a new statement." he began. "Is that correct?"

"That is correct," replied Mr Tomlinson, Hayley Bell's legal adviser. "My client wishes to ensure that you are fully aware of all the facts."

Carmichael's forehead wrinkled and he took a deep intake of breath. "I want to make it clear before you say anything that I won't do any deals with your client, Mr Tomlinson. I have given Mrs Bell ample opportunity, during numerous discussions we've had, to be honest with me and, as a consequence of the misleading statements she's already given the police, we will be pressing charges relating to those serious offences. Do I make myself clear?"

Tomlinson looked sideways in Hayley's direction and, upon receiving a gentle nod, turned to face Carmichael once more.

"My client understands the situation and will co-operate fully with your investigation."

After a short pause, Carmichael looked deeply into Hayley Bell's eyes.

"As I'm sure you are now aware," he said calmly, "your friend Francis Scott was killed earlier today."

Hayley, nodded slowly. "Yes," she replied. "The incident at Lesley's house was reported on the radio and your colleagues confirmed it was Francis who'd died when we were driving down here in the car."

Carmichael again paused for a few seconds before continuing with his questioning.

"First of all I'd like to know why you and Francis concocted your elaborate plan for you to disappear after the dinner you had with the ladies from the reading group on Friday, 21st December."

Hayley Bell sat back in her chair, her face pale and her expression void of emotion. "I don't expect you to understand," she replied, "but Francis and I needed to get our hands on some cash, quite a considerable amount to be honest. I knew Duncan wouldn't give it to me so we decided to fake my kidnapping. The plan was for me to lie low and for a ransom to be demanded from Duncan for my safe return."

"What sort of sum are we talking about?" Carmichael asked.

Hayley looked uncomfortable at being asked the question.

"£500,000," she replied. "As I say, quite a significant amount."

On hearing the sum involved, Carmichael glanced over at Cooper who was clearly as shocked as he was. "What did you want the money for?"

Hayley sighed loudly and shrugged her shoulders. "To start a new life away from Duncan and to pay off some debts that Francis had built up. I'd recently found out that Francis had been gambling again, she started about six months ago and her debts had reached six figures."

"I see," replied Carmichael. "So, the plan was to fake your abduction, get Duncan to pay the ransom and then just disappear."

Hayley smiled. "That was the plan," she replied softly.

"What went wrong?" Carmichael enquired.

"Firstly, we didn't think Duncan would panic and get the police so soon," she replied. "We were genuinely shocked when it was all over the press in less than twenty-four hours. The idea was for Francis to deliver a video recording of me asking Duncan for the money in exchange for my safe return. We recorded the video, but when Francis went to deliver it on Sunday she found Duncan dead in the winter room."

"So Francis went back to the house by herself?" said Carmichael in an attempt to clarify what had happened.

"Yes," replied Hayley. "Francis phoned me when she was there, which is when I decided we needed to ensure that we weren't incriminated in Duncan's murder. So I told Francis to bring the recording back and to collect my passport, too."

"Why did you do that?" Cooper enquired.

Hayley shook her head. "Well with Duncan dead, the irony was that I'd inherit everything, so we didn't need to fake my kidnapping, however, we did need to make sure neither Francis nor I were implicated in any way. I told Francis to bring my passport as I thought we should now make it look like I was just running away and I figured you'd believe that story more if I had my passport with me."

"That was a bit of a risk, wasn't it?" remarked Carmichael. "Did you not worry that we may have already found your passport when we searched the house?"

"I'm not an expert on police procedure, Inspector," Hayley replied, "and I only had about two minutes to revise our plan, however, I thought with my passport being in one of my drawers there was a good chance you wouldn't have seen it."

"Well, you were wrong and we had," Carmichael replied with a tinge of smugness in his voice.

Hayley shrugged her shoulders again. "Well, there you go," she replied.

"So, what then?" Carmichael asked.

"Francis came back," continued Hayley, "we recorded the other message and, very early the next morning, Francis and I drove back and posted the message in the letter box at the *Observer*. You were of course, quite correct when you asked me why we did that. It was to make it seem like we had no idea that Duncan was dead. And again, as you rightly pointed out, we left the message at the *Observer* as we didn't want to risk being seen at the police station. We knew you'd see the message pretty quickly if it was left at the *Observer*."

"And then what?" Carmichael asked.

Hayley again shrugged her shoulders. "Well the rest you know," she remarked. "We drove back to Kendal and attempted to pretend we'd been in Devon."

"But what about Belinda Bishop?" Carmichael enquired. "What involvement did you or Francis have in her death?"

Hayley Bell shook her head. "None whatsoever," she replied. "I haven't seen Belinda since we parted at Kirkwood train station last Friday evening. Neither Francis nor I had anything to do with her death, just as we never had anything to do with Duncan's death."

It was now Carmichael's turn to shake his head. "I don't buy that, Hayley," he replied firmly. "We are sure Francis killed Duncan, we know she tried to kill Lesley Saxham and, if I were a betting man, I'd wager good money that very soon one of my colleagues will find CCTV evidence that places Francis and possibly you, too, close to Belinda Bishop's house at the time she was murdered. So, please, don't insult my intelligence by trying to pretend that you and Francis weren't involved in the two murders or the attempted murder of Lesley Saxham."

Clearly ruffled by Carmichael's attitude, Tomlinson sat up bolt-like. "I must protest," he remarked robustly. "My client is here of her own accord and is offering her assistance to help you identify the murderer of her husband and her friend. Mrs Bell deserves greater respect than you are giving her."

Carmichael's initial impulse was to verbally slap the pompous brief back into line, but decided he'd take a different tack. "Tell me about your husband, Mrs Bell?" he asked, not bothering to reply to Tomlinson's outburst. "If you don't mind me saying so, you've never seemed terribly upset by his death?"

"Of course I'm sad that Duncan has died," replied Hayley, "and I feel particularly sorry at the way he died. However, I'm not a hypocrite, Inspector Carmichael, the love went out of our marriage over twenty years ago, so I won't put on any crocodile tears."

In a strange way Carmichael respected what Hayley had told him and nodded his head gently as if to confirm that fact. "But what sort of man was he?" he continued.

Hayley paused for a while. "I'd say he was a complex man. At times he could be very charming, he was extremely intelligent and, when he loved you, his affection was all-encompassing."

"I sense there's a but coming," Carmichael remarked.

"There is," replied Hayley. "And the but is that he was a philanderer, a womaniser and, most of the time, a total shit!"

"And would you say he was a violent man?" Carmichael suggested.

"Actually, no," replied Hayley, "in fact, quite the opposite. As he'd often tell me when I caught him with his pants down with another young thing, he was a lover not a fighter."

Carmichael smiled as he recalled Hayley using a similar phrase to describe herself at one of their earlier interviews. "He seemed to like younger women?" Carmichael remarked.

Hayley smiled. "Oh yes," she replied ruefully. "If he got anywhere near a pretty twenty-something he was like a dog on heat, but once a woman got beyond the age of thirty he'd have nothing to do with her."

"I see," replied Carmichael, "even now?"

Hayley smiled again. "At seventy-eight, I think it's fair to say, his success rate was nowhere near what it had been in earlier times, Inspector. But I can assure you, his desire and determination was still as strong as ever. Ask Maxine Lowe if you want that verifying."

"You were aware of his attempts to seduce Maxine, were you?" remarked Carmichael.

"God yes," responded Hayley with surprise. "A miserable fail on his part, but the old devil tried his best."

"So when you first discovered that Duncan had been murdered, did you think it might have been a jealous boyfriend or husband?" Cooper interjected.

"Like Pete Thorn," replied Hayley. "Actually, yes I did, and I still do, despite what you keep saying about Francis. Why on earth would she kill him?"

Carmichael paused for a few seconds while he gathered his thoughts.

"There are just a few other questions I'd like to ask you, if I may," he said. "First of all, I'd like you to tell me what you talked to Francis about earlier today, after we released you from custody. Our information suggests that you spoke to her within ten minutes of being released and less than an hour before she attacked Lesley Saxham."

Hayley thought for a few seconds before replying. "It was a very brief call," she replied. "I just wanted to tell her how sorry I was to hear about her dad dying."

"Is that all?" Carmichael enquired, his tone suggesting he was not convinced he'd been told everything.

"We obviously talked about the murders and the

predicament we were in and what we should do, but to be honest, we came to no conclusions on that score," replied Hayley.

"I'd be very keen to know exactly what was said," continued Carmichael, "as it seems to have prompted Francis to try and kill Lesley Saxham."

Hayley looked genuinely confused. "I honestly don't know why Francis did that," she remarked. "I can't remember the exact words we exchanged, but I know for a fact that we never even mentioned Lesley."

"One final question," Carmichael remarked, his eyes now fixed on Hayley. "When you and Francis drove from the Lake District on Boxing Day, did Francis ever leave you at any stage before you arrived to be interviewed here at the station?"

Hayley shook her head. "No," she replied firmly, before stopping for a moment. "Actually, that's not true," she continued. "We stopped off at her house before we came to the station and she did pop out to get some cigarettes. She didn't smoke that much, but when she was a bit stressed she always fancied one and she'd run out."

"And how long was she away for?" Carmichael asked.

Hayley raised her palms to the ceiling as if she wasn't too sure. "I'd guess about fifteen minutes or so?"

"And how far is Francis's house from the Bishops?" Carmichael continued.

"About five minutes away," replied Hayley, her voice quiet and faltering as she realised the significance of what she was saying.

Chapter 49

Carmichael, Cooper and Watson watched through the first-floor window of the main incident room as Mr Tomlinson's expensive-looking Austin Martin glided out of the car park, carrying Hayley Bell back to her house in Much Martin.

"What do you think, sir?" Cooper enquired. "Do you think she was involved in the murders?"

"I don't know," replied Carmichael. "Unlike Francis, we can't place Hayley near her house when Duncan died. Also, based upon what Lesley told us, we can't incriminate her directly in the attack earlier today and, unless Dyer manages to find any CCTV footage showing either of them near Belinda Bishop's house yesterday, we appear to have little evidence to associate Hayley or Francis with Belinda's murder, either."

"But surely, it's obvious," interjected Watson. "She's clearly implicated in all three incidents. I can't see any jury believing she had no knowledge of what Francis was doing."

"I hear what you say, Marc," Carmichael remarked, "however, without any firm evidence, I can't see the Crown Prosecution allowing us to charge Hayley with anything more serious than wasting police time and perverting the course of justice."

"Surely not!" remarked Watson, his frustration clear in his voice.

"Perverting the course of justice is a serious crime, Marc," pointed out Cooper, albeit he also didn't sound happy about the whole situation. "It does carry the potential of a significant custodial sentence."

"And due to the fact that she has repeatedly lied," Carmichael added, "I'd imagine, if she is found guilty, there's a good chance she'll be put away."

As Carmichael turned back from the window, he noticed the tired-looking figure of Rachel Dalton entering the room.

"How's Lesley Saxham doing?" he enquired.

"She's doing really well, considering," replied Rachel. "The x-rays all show she suffered no serious damage and the doctors are really pleased with her, given what she endured today."

"Well, that's good news," remarked Carmichael with a smile.

"She must have a skull made of granite to come through that sort of attack so well," Cooper announced.

"And also the luck of the devil!" added Watson.

Rachel smiled. "That's pretty much what the specialist said, too," she remarked before plonking her weary, small frame on a chair. "They're keeping her in overnight, though, as they say sometimes there can be a delayed reaction when there's been a major trauma like she's experienced."

"Makes sense, I suppose," Watson concurred.

"What about Hayley Bell?" Rachel asked. "Is she going to be charged?"

"That's what we were just talking about when you came back," Carmichael remarked. "We will certainly be charging her, but almost certainly not for the murders and probably not even as an accessory to murder. I'm going to run it all past Hewitt in the morning, but in my opinion, we've not enough evidence to make a more serious charge stick."

"So what did Hayley say when you interviewed her?" Rachel asked.

"I'll tell you what," remarked Carmichael, before anyone had a chance to answer, "I'll leave you two to fill Rachel in on the interview with Hayley. I'm going to get myself home. It's been a long old day and I think I owe my family a few hours, given that I'm supposed to be on holiday."

Cooper smiled wryly. "No problem, sir," he replied. "Marc and I will do that. See you in the morning."

Carmichael nodded back to acknowledge Cooper's comment, before grabbing his coat and making a hasty exit.

* * * *

During his forty-minute drive home, through dinner and well into the evening, Carmichael couldn't get the case from his thoughts for more than a few minutes. There was something not right, something he felt they were missing and, as a result, he was unable to settle.

Penny could see he wasn't totally with them and guessed it would be about the case, but decided not to ask any questions until Aunty Audrey and their three children were well out of earshot.

However, getting some privacy with her husband proved more of a challenge than she'd anticipated, so, when it got to almost 11pm and there still appeared to be little sign of the others decamping to their respective rooms, Penny decided to create the opportunity.

With a subtle, but clear motion of her head towards the door, she suddenly announced, "I'm making a cup of tea, does anyone want one?"

"Not for me, thanks," replied Jemma.

"Me neither," added Robbie.

"Can I have a hot chocolate, please," Natalie asked.

"What about you, Audrey?" Penny asked, while at the same time getting up from her chair and making a movement with her head to ensure her husband was in no doubt about her instruction to him. "Would you like a drink?"

"I'll just have a mug of warm milk, please," Audrey

replied. "But can you make sure you only half-fill the mug, as I don't want to have to be up in the night for the lavvy."

Penny smiled back at Audrey. "Right you are," she replied. "Come and help me will you, Steve."

Dutifully, Carmichael rose slowly from his comfortable armchair and followed his wife down the hallway to the kitchen.

"You look bothered," Penny remarked with concern as soon as they were alone. "Is it the case?"

Carmichael nodded before embracing his wife. "It is," he replied. "In Francis Scott we appear to have our murderer, but we can't seem to be able to pin anything on Hayley Bell. It may well be that she's innocent, as she claims, but it doesn't sit well with me."

"Why doesn't it sit well?" Penny asked.

"I'm not sure," replied Carmichael. "I just have a horrible sense that we're missing something important."

"Like what?" Penny asked.

"Well, to start with, there's no obvious motive for Francis killing Belinda Bishop or for the attempted murder of Lesley Saxham," Carmichael replied. "I know Duncan was a womaniser, and Hayley has admitted they were in need of a large sum of money to pay off Francis's huge gambling debts, so I can make a case for Francis or both of them killing him, but not the others."

Penny put her head against her husband's chest. "Maybe Belinda saw one of them entering or leaving Bell's house," she surmised. "And maybe Lesley did, too!"

"That would work, I suppose," Carmichael remarked. "But, surely, if one or both of them knew it was Francis, they would have said something. Particularly Lesley, as after Belinda was killed, then you'd expect her to be worried about her own safety."

Penny nodded. "Yes, you have a point," she conceded. "And if I was Lesley and I knew Francis had killed Duncan and Belinda, I'd never let her into my house."

"Exactly," replied Carmichael. "It just doesn't make sense."

Penny moved over to the sink and started to pour water into the kettle.

"From what you've said, it's clear that Francis's need for a significant sum of money to pay off her debts is a strong motive for her killing Duncan. Maybe she did do it without Hayley knowing?"

"You may be right," replied Carmichael, "but I have a feeling it's not as clear-cut as that."

Penny turned back to face her husband. "So, what other motives are there for Duncan's death?" she enquired.

Carmichael thought for a few seconds. "Hatred, jealousy or retribution," he replied, "and most likely from an angry husband, boyfriend or father of one of Duncan's seduction targets."

"I thought you said he was in his seventies," Penny remarked, her tone sounding as though the very idea was preposterous.

"Even people of our advanced age have passions," interjected Audrey, who had suddenly appeared in the kitchen doorway. "Mary Saunders, a good friend of mine, is in her eighties and is still being pursued by a gentleman of a similar age called Tom Carter. She wants none of it, of course, but he still persists, much to the annoyance of another of my friends, Doreen Pardew. She's been holding a candle for Tom Carter for years and I'm convinced she'd rather see him dead than be with Mary."

Penny glared in the direction of the old woman in the doorway. "Audrey!" she shouted loudly. "How dare you eavesdrop on our conversation…"

Although it was crystal clear to both Audrey and Carmichael that Penny was incensed, and it was equally evident that a more prolonged and detailed rebuke was about to be delivered by the exasperated lady of the house, she was swiftly and successfully cut short by her husband who held out the palm of his hand a matter of inches from Penny's face.

"You actually may have something there," he announced, his voice buoyant as if he'd discovered something precious. "Has anyone ever told you you're a star, Audrey?"

Without bothering to elaborate, Carmichael rushed towards Audrey, planted a huge kiss on her forehead and bounced out of the kitchen and down the hallway.

Open-mouthed, speechless and frozen to the spot, Audrey and Penny remained in the kitchen as the sound of Carmichael's footsteps could be heard bounding up the stairs towards his study.

Chapter 50

Friday, 28th December

Having spent a comfortable night in hospital and having been given the all-clear to leave by the specialist, Lesley Saxham perched herself on the edge of her bed and gazed out of the window as she waited for Greg to come to take her home.

For the first time in days, the sun was now out and, although it still looked cold, most of the snow had melted away and the world beyond the thick glass pane looked much brighter and infinitely more inviting.

As she watched a group of small rabbits nibbling at the grass outside, Lesley heard the door behind her open.

"My bag's over there," she said to her husband before half-turning to greet him with a welcoming smile.

"I'm afraid it's not your husband," replied Carmichael, "it's Inspector Carmichael. I'm here with DC Dalton and we're not here to take you home."

"Do you need more information from me," replied Lesley, "I'd assumed I'd provided all the information you'd need in my statement to DC Dalton."

Carmichael shook his head gently. "I don't doubt you do," he remarked. "But we both know that what you told us yesterday wasn't true."

"Really," replied Lesley, with a look of surprise on her face. "I don't know what you mean."

"Oh, my team have been working through the night and this morning to check many things," he continued. "Your alibis for the times Duncan and Belinda were killed. And I've also had a long discussion with the specialists here about how light your injuries were, given the severe blows you took from Francis yesterday when she attacked you."

"And your conclusion is?" Lesley enquired.

"Is that it was you who was in the house when I met Duncan on Sunday," replied Carmichael. "You spied me from behind the curtains when I approached, but kept yourself hidden. I think that you probably killed Duncan fairly soon after I left."

"But, I told you, I was walking Bruno and shopping when poor Duncan was supposed to have died," Lesley reminded Carmichael.

"I know that both are true," replied Carmichael, "but we've checked the timing of each event and it's quite possible for you to have done all three, with a bit of organisation. In fact, I think you walked Bruno, went over to Duncan's house, killed him and then went shopping. Your till receipt is timed at 2.57pm, so allowing twenty minutes to drive over and a further thirty minutes to buy the shopping, you could have easily left Duncan's house as late as 2pm. Is that what happened?"

"But what about Belinda's murder? I was hosting lunch and drinks for guests at my house when she was killed," remarked Lesley.

Carmichael shook his head. "Again, we've managed to check the exact time your first lunchtime guests arrived. It was 11.50am, so by my reckoning, you had ample time to get over to Belinda's, kill her and then get yourself back to your house for the gathering. You then went back over later, when you pretended to discover Belinda's body. Isn't that also correct?"

"Again, you're forgetting that I walked Bruno prior to my guests coming over, and where we go is in the opposite direction to Belinda's house."

For a third time, Carmichael shook his head. "I'm afraid we've checked with all the usual dog walkers and not one of them can remember seeing you with Bruno that day, although they all know who you are and would recognise you and Bruno."

"They must be getting their days confused," replied Lesley.

"I don't think so," replied Carmichael with some surety. "Let's face it, we're only talking about an event you said happened two days ago. Had you been there, I'm sure one of the numerous dog walkers we've spoken to would have remembered."

"And what about yesterday, then?" Lesley continued. "Are you saying that I made up being attacked by Francis and the struggle we had? If so, how did I get these injuries?" As she spoke, Lesley lifted up her mass of wiry, grey hair to reveal a large bump on her forehead.

"According to your doctors," Carmichael replied, "you've clearly been hit, but they don't believe you were beaten as ferociously as you maintain. In fact, they believe the injuries are perfectly in-keeping with someone who has tried to make it look like they've been attacked. In their opinion, had you been hit by a copper saucepan as hard as you have said, then you would have sustained injuries far more serious, possibly life-threatening. Yours, in their words, again, are minor."

Lesley Saxham stood up, walked over to the window and gazed out.

"I'm no legal expert," remarked Lesley, "but I'd say your evidence is very sketchy. Do you think it will hold up in a court of law?"

As she finished speaking, she turned her back to the window and stared directly into Carmichael's eyes.

"I disagree," he replied. "I think we've quite a bit of evidence and so did the judge who granted us permission to search your house, which is what my officers are doing now. My guess is that they'll find evidence which will strengthen our case."

Upon hearing the news of her house being searched, Lesley's self-assured expression changed to one of resignation.

"Have you ever experienced unrequited love, Inspector?" she enquired.

Carmichael shook his head. "Not that I can recall," he replied.

"Then you're lucky," continued Lesley. "I have, for nearly forty years, a love so strong that I was willing to wait until he was able to be with me."

"You're talking about Duncan," Carmichael remarked.

"Yes," replied Lesley. "Duncan Bell was my one and only love and I thought, if I waited, one day he would be mine."

"But Duncan was married and so are you," observed Carmichael.

"Yes," replied Lesley, "Duncan and his damn wives."

"So tell me what happened?" Carmichael asked.

Lesley returned to the bed and once more sat down on the edge.

"I first met Duncan when I was twenty," Lesley announced. "He was so charming and so very clever. I fell for him straight away."

"And was there a relationship between you?" Carmichael enquired.

"Oh yes," continued Lesley. "An intense relationship and we were to be married."

"So what happened?" Carmichael enquired.

"Claudette Cotterill happened," replied Lesley through gritted teeth. "She trapped poor Duncan and he was forced to marry her."

Carmichael's forehead wrinkled. "That was Duncan's second wife, the lady who died and with whom he had two children."

"Yes, that's right," replied Lesley. "And if she hadn't got herself pregnant then he'd be married to me."

"But, because of the child, he married her," Carmichael suggested.

"Of course," replied Lesley, who looked at Carmichael, her eyes wild, yet sad.

"I see," remarked Carmichael. "And did your relationship continue after he married Claudette Cotterill?"

"No," Lesley retorted. "He told me he couldn't cheat on her as it was not fair to the child, but he promised, once he could, he'd leave her and we could be together."

"I see," replied Carmichael again, although he'd swiftly come to the conclusion that some, if not all, of what Lesley was telling him was more her distorted imagination rather than the truth.

"For nine years I waited," continued Lesley. "Then, she suddenly died and I realised that it was, at last, our chance to be together."

"But he then married Hayley," Carmichael remarked. "Why did he marry her rather than you?"

Lesley folded her arms tightly against her sparrow-like chest. "The children, again," snapped Lesley. "Those bloody children. He said they had become attached to their nanny and that it would be better for them, given their mother had died, if he married her, to care for them."

Carmichael looked sideways at Rachel, who had a look on her face that indicated she also believed Lesley to be crazy.

"So, tell us what happened on Sunday?" Rachel asked in a friendly, hushed voice.

Lesley shook her head. "I often went round to be with Duncan when he was alone and I was there on Sunday when you called, Inspector. After you'd gone, I joined him in the winter room. He was rifling through some old box of photos and documents he had, looking for something. I asked him if it turned out that Hayley wasn't coming back, would it mean we could at last be together?"

"And what did he say?" Rachel asked.

"He just laughed at me and said there was no chance of us being together, that I was too old and that the Lesley he'd loved was long dead." As she spoke, Lesley stared intently at the floor, her eyes bulging from their sockets. "He pulled out some photographs from the box and threw them at me. They were mainly old photos, but all of young women. He then held a picture of me in his hand, one he'd taken all those years ago, when we first met. He said that this was the only Lesley he'd ever love, not the wrinkled, boring hag that I'd become."

"So what happened then?" Carmichael asked.

"I was so angry with him and felt such a fool," replied Lesley through gritted teeth. "I just wanted to hurt him and grabbed the first thing I could from his desk. It was his letter opener. The next thing I knew it was in his back, he was groaning and I had blood on my hands and my clothes, Duncan's blood."

"What did you do then?" Rachel enquired.

"I took the box and all its contents, placed it in my car and drove to the supermarket," replied Lesley with an eerie lack of remorse. "The box is now located at the bottom of my wardrobe, I suspect your officers will find it pretty easily."

Carmichael and Dalton exchanged glances.

"Why did you kill Belinda?" Carmichael continued.

"She called me on Boxing Day morning," replied Lesley. "She'd found the photo of me. It was still in Duncan's hand when she discovered his body, and of course she recognised me. For some stupid reason, I'd forgotten to prise it from him in my haste to get away from the house. I'd taken all the other photos, but foolishly I'd left the one that incriminated me still in his hand."

"And what did Belinda want?" Carmichael enquired.

"She said she wanted to talk to me about it before she went to the police," Lesley replied.

"So you went round?" confirmed Carmichael.

"Yes," replied Lesley, "just as you suggested, I went round before the buffet. Within minutes, I could tell she knew I'd killed Duncan and, when she turned her back on me, I picked up the poker and, well, that was that, really."

"Then you went back to your house, entertained your guests and came back to the Bishops' house later when Tarquin was at home," continued Carmichael.

"Not before I wiped my fingerprints off the handle. I wasn't going to make any more mistakes," she replied with a malevolent smile. "But yes, I went back home. That was when Sergeant Cooper popped round, which was a bonus, I thought."

"But why go back to the Bishops' house later?" Rachel asked.

"I had to," replied Lesley. "After all, she'd called me, so I needed to be able to have some sort of story to explain away the call she'd made to me that morning."

Carmichael nodded. "Very clever," he remarked with genuine approbation. "But then along came Francis, why did you kill her?"

Lesley gave out a huge sigh. "I really wasn't expecting her, but when she arrived and started mentioning that she and Hayley had been discussing Duncan's death, I started to become concerned."

"Why?" responded Carmichael, who was keen for Lesley to explain what was said.

"Well, apparently," continued Lesley, "one of the things they both felt had a bearing on the case was the fact that whoever killed Duncan did so while he sat in his chair in the winter room. You see, the winter room was a place that Duncan would only allow people he knew really well to enter. Realising this, Francis had worked out that, as it wasn't her or Hayley who'd killed Duncan and with Belinda being dead, the only person she knew who Duncan would remotely tolerate being in his study was…"

"You," Carmichael interrupted.

"Exactly," replied Lesley.

"But why didn't she tell us," Rachel asked Carmichael. "With her and Hayley being such strong suspects, you'd have thought she'd have wanted to provide us with this information?"

"I suspect it was money," replied Carmichael. "Did Francis try to blackmail you, Lesley?"

"She wanted £100,000 to keep quiet," Lesley said, her head shaking from side to side.

"So you killed her and faked the attack," Carmichael remarked.

Lesley turned her head ninety degrees so that she could look the two officers directly in the eye. "Precisely," she replied with a calm-but-sinister expression on her face. "You can't allow people to go around blackmailing you, now can you, Inspector?"

Chapter 51

Saturday, 29ᵗʰ December

"That must go down as the longest seven days of my life," remarked Carmichael as he and Penny waved vigorously in the direction of the 10.15am to Milton Keynes Central as it started to pull away from the platform on its ninety-minute journey taking Aunty Audrey back home.

"What?" exclaimed Penny. "You only spent a few hours with Audrey. I had her day and night, without any breaks, for the whole week."

"I think that's a bit harsh," replied Carmichael with a wry smile. "After all, I've also had her to contend with and three murders to solve, hardly the peaceful, relaxing Christmas I had in mind."

Penny shook her head disparagingly. "You're priceless," she remarked before grabbing his arm and starting to walk slowly down the platform. "Anyway, the other day you told Audrey she was a star, so I take it that had it not been for her, you'd never have cracked the case?"

Carmichael considered the statement for a few seconds. "I'd not go that far," he replied, "however, her little anecdote about Mary Saunders, Tom Carter and Doreen what's-her-name…"

"Pardew, if I remember correctly," interjected Penny.

"Well yes," continued Carmichael, "that story did get me to look at the case from a slightly different perspective."

"Namely that the murder of Duncan was a crime of passion rather than a hate crime," Penny remarked.

"Exactly," replied Carmichael, who was, as always, impressed by how quickly his wife picked up his thinking and the gist of his cases. "And, once I had that in my head, to be honest the only possible contenders were either Francis Scott or Lesley Saxham. We'd already spent a good deal of time investigating Francis Scott, but we hadn't delved too deeply into Lesley Saxham's alibis for the first two murders. So, I asked the team to focus on her and, based upon what they uncovered, it was pretty easy to work out that Lesley murdered Duncan and Belinda…"

"And confirm that the so-called attack," interrupted Penny, "actually never happened. It was just Lesley trying to cover up the murder of Francis."

"You've got it!" responded Carmichael, once more impressed by how his wife was able to grasp the key points so quickly.

"Fancy her waiting forty years for Duncan to be with her," remarked Penny. "That's real devotion."

"Wouldn't you wait that long for me?" Carmichael enquired.

Penny stopped and looked up into his face. "Forty minutes tops," she replied before raising herself up on her tip-toes and planting a large kiss on his lips, "and not a minute more."

Epilogue

Saturday, 26th January

"£215!" Carmichael exclaimed as he read his bank statement for the umpteenth time. "Are you telling me that the old…"

"Steve!" interjected Penny, who had no desire to let Natalie hear whatever noun he was about to select to describe Aunty Audrey. "I'm sure she had no idea that when she bought credits on Candy Crush the money she was spending was real money and the game was linked to your debit card," Penny suggested, trying her hardest to defend Audrey's actions.

"Oh, that's OK then!" replied Carmichael as he angrily stomped out of the room. "As long as she didn't know, she's forgiven," he moaned as he disappeared into the hallway, the offending statement clenched tightly in his hand.

"Do you want me to pay some of it?" Natalie asked rather sheepishly, her face ashen with worry and guilt with it being her who had introduced Aunty Audrey to Candy Crush.

Penny smiled and shook her head. "No," she whispered. "It wasn't your fault and he'll calm down, eventually."

The sound of Carmichael's angry footsteps resonated through the house as he climbed the stairs towards his attic study. Natalie looked up into her mother's eyes and shook her head gently. "I think this particular 'eventually' may take quite a long time," she replied astutely.

Penny smiled again and put her arm around her daughter's shoulders. "You could well be right," she conceded. "But as soon as he has another case to occupy him, he'll forget all about it."

"It's almost worth murdering someone," announced Natalie, her words spoken in jest, but delivered without any sign of a smile.